TAngels

Book One of A:R Heaven

Tricia Owens

Sin City series
Dom of Las Vegas
Limited Liability
Acceptable Sacrifices
High Roller
Most Wanted
Lessons in Obedience
Death Defying Acts
The Doms Club
Easy Money

A Pirate's Life for Me series
Book One: Captain & First Mate
Book Two: Island Paradise
Book Three: Pirate Triumvirate
Mr. Anteros

Juxtapose City series
Fearless Leader
In the Blink of an Eye
The Battle for Black
The Ultimate Team
My Lover, My Enemy
The Sound of Truth
Shattered Alliance
Exchange of Power

Realm of Juxtan series
The Sorcerer's Betrayal
The Gathering
Beneath the Greying Cliffs

The Forgotten One

A:R Earth series
Angel: Reversed
Angel: Redeemed
Angel: Released

A:R Heaven series
Territory of Angels
Spoils of War

Standalone Novels
Favorite Flavors Short Story Collection
Hunter and Hunted
Master of No One

Author's Note

The A:R Heaven and A:R Earth storylines are meant to run simultaneously. So while Finn is on Earth, we see though the Heaven series what's happening in his absence. Either series can be read first and won't diminish your enjoyment of the whole.

Find the A:R Earth books and more on Amazon and at
http://www.triciaowensbooks.com

Join the mailing list for the latest updates and promotions
http://www.triciaowensbooks.com/list

With many thanks to Grace Hudson for her encouragement when I needed it most, and to Samantha Ashpaugh, who never fails to come through for me.

Territory of Angels

1

When Ryan had been alive, he'd been the assistant manager of a women's retail shoe store. Sure, it had been Hell on Earth, but he'd done his job competently. He'd never flipped out on a customer and he'd never received any complaints about his service. Maybe that was why once he'd died he'd ended up in Heaven. Because it certainly hadn't been because he was good at respecting other people's privacy.

"This is so bad," he muttered to himself for at least the fourth time. But just like the previous three times, the admonition did nothing to change his behavior.

He was crouched behind a knoll overlooking a small pool of water fed by a bubbling spring at its center. The grass around it, like all the grass in the Middle Tier, was lush and green. The water was a pure Caribbean blue, and of course the sky was beautiful, with a light that came not from a single source but from everywhere, so that a shadow never fell in Heaven.

Certainly none were cast by the two Angels that Ryan spied on. The shorter one was his friend Finnian. With bright red hair and mischievous turquoise eyes, Finnian was beauty incarnate. Short, sweet, slender, and playful, he was the very definition of adorable not only in Ryan's eyes but in the eyes of every denizen of Heaven. That was because Finnian was an Angel who had been designed by the Creator—whoever or whatever that was— to be lovable. Mostly, he was made to be loved by one Angel: Anifiel.

"The Big Guy," Ryan said beneath his breath. Also known as the Commander of Heaven's Army.

It was a badass title and Anifiel himself was a badass Angel. Physically, he was a combination of every gorgeous man Ryan had ever seen on Earth. Golden-haired, green eyed, with a body to make you faint and a deep, masculine voice that reached into your underwear, Anifiel was a walking wet dream.

Much to Ryan's chagrin, he'd had several dreams about the golden Angel. Naughty dreams. Dreams that had no place in Heaven. Dreams in which Anifiel pinned him against trees and pressed Ryan to the grass. Dreams in which Anifiel grabbed his jaw and forced a kiss on him that blew Ryan's mind. And then there were sexier dreams, in which Ryan learned what hid beneath Anifiel's tunic…

Unfortunately, Anifiel was not very nice to

humans, so all those dreams were pipe dreams at best. Anifiel considered humans to be no better than bugs, and therefore Ryan was a bug, too. Ryan straight up didn't like Anifiel as a boyfriend for Finnian. Ryan's vibrant friend deserved someone more like him. Someone fun and spontaneous. Someone who could tell Finnian jokes and suggest games or adventures for them to take.

Anifiel was not that Angel. Anifiel was as fun and exciting as a bag of bricks.

The most gorgeous bricks in existence but that's beside the point. Anifiel didn't deserve Finnian.

"Beloved," he heard Finnian say as he embraced Anifiel.

Ryan watched from his vantage point as the two Angels pressed their mouths together. Though it was a non-sexual kiss like that of friends, Ryan smothered a gasp at the intense feelings that swelled between the two Angels. The emotions radiated outward from them like heat from a suddenly stoked furnace. Ryan was flooded with a love so pure it made his heart ache. He felt his eyes well with tears and he had to rapidly blink them back. Just as quickly, a wave of pleasure swamped him. It was like receiving the best backrub of his life while eating chocolate and having sex. The endorphin rush left him panting.

When the kiss ended, so did the wash of feelings and Ryan nearly sobbed at the loss. He ached. He yearned for the union these two Angels shared. Was this what awaited him in the Upper Tier? Or was this something only Finnian and

Anifiel shared because their love came by design?

"You steal my breath," Anifiel said, gently rubbing their cheeks together. "You fulfill my every passion. You meet my every need. No being will ever be loved as I love you, my Finnian."

Ryan told himself he should gag at the flowery speech. Instead, his eyes welled with tears.

He watched with yearning as Finnian touched Anifiel's mouth, tracing its sensual slopes. "Would you like to make love the way the humans do?" he asked softly but hopefully. "Ryan has told me of the physical pleasures they enjoy. I would like to try it with you."

Ryan jerked upright. Holy hell! He jammed a thumb between his teeth and gnawed anxiously on the nail. Finnian shouldn't mention him around Anifiel, ever! And especially not in regards to sex!

"Ryan," Anifiel echoed. His handsome face twisted with irritation. "You spend too much time with the human. He will only corrupt you, as he has clearly already begun to do."

Screw you, buddy!

Even though he was kind of right.

Finnian laughed. "He is no threat to you. In fact, his influence may bring us pleasure if you are willing to try?"

Aw, jeez, Finn, thanks. Paint me as the bad influence, why don't you?

Anifiel smiled down at him. "Curious consort. But we are Angels, are we not? Not humans. Leave them to their play. It is not our way."

Anifiel hugged him again and Finnian was left gasping.

Beginning to feel uncomfortable at spying on such an intimate moment between the Angels, Ryan ducked down behind the knoll and slid onto his back. He shouldn't have spied, but he felt protective of Finnian. Though the cute Angel had been created to be loved by all, Ryan thought the Creator had gone a bit overboard. *No one* could resist the red-haired blue-eyed Angel. Finnian was adorable and beautiful and the most cheerful being Ryan had ever known. He'd turn a visit to the DMV into the highlight of your year.

Ryan feared someone would take advantage of that loveable nature. No, not just someone. Anifiel. The Commander took it for granted that Finnian was his. Though technically this was true, it didn't seem fair to Ryan that Anifiel got to be with him.

In fact, Ryan would gladly sacrifice himself to deflect Anifiel's attention away from Finnian. He pictured himself throwing himself at the Commander, giving Finnian time to fly away. He'd have to distract Anifiel somehow…A shiver rushed through Ryan. Would any human survive intimacy with Anifiel? Or would the Commander literally tear them apart?

I'm so sick I almost want to find out.

Definitely not the most Angelic of thoughts, Ryan reflected. And it wouldn't help him to achieve his goal here which was to find enlightenment. To have an epiphany. Or as he liked to put it, "To make everything click." Once that occurred—and no one could predict when it would—an Angel from the Upper Tier would come down to escort Ryan to wherever it was that humans went when they became Angels.

Sometimes he thought that moment might be right around the corner. Sometimes, like today, it felt like it would never come.

Maybe I should stop being such a horndog.

~~~~~

"When you were on Earth, did you have many lovers?" Finnian asked Ryan.

After leaving Anifiel, Finnian had sought out his human friend, only to discover him jogging several hundred yards from where the two Angels had kissed.

"Oh, hey, just out for a run," Ryan had said with a wave. "What are you doing out here?"

Finnian had only smiled. He was aware that Ryan kept tabs on him. He thought it was sweet.

Now, they were reclining in the grass, watching the clouds drift overhead. The grasses were soft against Finnian's bare legs and he huffed, wishing he wasn't one of the few Angels in Heaven forced to wear a tunic to cover up the rest of him. He wasn't ashamed of his body. Was there a reason he should be? Typically only humans chose to wear the garments, such as Ryan, who was still self-conscious.

"Did you have someone as I have Anifiel?" he asked Ryan.

He could sense the human's unease with the question.

"I, well, I didn't have much luck in that

department," he heard Ryan mumble. "I was kinda shy and...stuff."

Finnian quirked an eyebrow as he glanced askance at his friend. "Stuff?"

A blush broke over Ryan's face, which Finnian found adorable. The brown-haired human was very attractive. Cute, as he'd heard the humans say. Ryan's brown hair fell in soft ringlets around his face and his eyes were a pretty blue that turned violet in certain lighting. His face was intriguingly animated and expressive. Finnian liked the truth in Ryan's face.

"I had a lot of trouble dealing with my sexuality," Ryan admitted, his face brighter than ever. "My parents were pretty old-fashioned and they didn't like— " he took a deep breath, "—they didn't like homosexuals. Especially having their only son be one."

Finnian studied him curiously. "Your desire for other men created conflict?"

Ryan looked miserable. "It wasn't something I wanted, believe me. I dated girls through high school and college, hoping if I found the right one that I'd be saved from myself." He chuckled, but not happily. "What a waste. All it took was one glance at a guy in the shower next to me and months of dating girls went down the toilet."

The humans' beliefs about love pairings had always struck Finnian as odd. So much angst and misery over something that should have been wonderful.

"Did you take on a male lover?" he pressed,

hiding a smile as Ryan blushed anew.

"I did a few things." When Finnian continued to watch him expectantly, Ryan mumbled, "You know. Hand jobs. Blowjobs. More..."

Finnian cocked his head. "Hand jobs? Blowjobs?"

Ryan looked around anxiously. "Maybe I shouldn't be telling you this stuff, Finn. I don't think Anifiel wants you to know about or talk about any of this. It's kinda, well, it's not what Angels should think about."

But the comment concerning what Anifiel would want only irritated Finnian. "If I want to know about hand jobs then I want to know them," he declared. "Anifiel is not my keeper."

Ryan nodded in support, but Finnian had to look away in dismay. They both knew that Finnian ultimately answered to Anifiel no matter what Finnian might pretend to the contrary. For a fleeting second, Finnian imagined what it might be like if he were human...

Finnian sighed. There were, he decided, a lot of disadvantages to being the consort of the Commander of Heaven's Army. Finnian was at Anifiel's constant beck and call. While Finnian loved the Commander with every ounce of his being, the unnatural tie between them was beginning to chafe. While the humans and most Angels considered Finnian to be enviable—he was, after all, the Angel created as a gift for the Creator's most beloved Angel—Finn considered the honor to be a dubious one.

Actually, he considered it to be a major pain in

the neck. Finn grinned. He'd borrowed that phrase from the humans.

Speaking of which...

"Are we going down to the Lower Tier?" he asked, blithely changing the subject.

Ryan eyed him suspiciously. "You know you're not supposed to go down there. If Anifiel finds out you leave the Middle Tier, he might go so far as to paddle you in public."

Finnian yawned. "He would not dare. He cannot stand the thought of anyone seeing my bare bottom but him."

Ryan choked. "I didn't say he'd do it on your bare—your bare—" Ryan turned away, blushing madly.

"No, but you thought it," Finnian teased with a wink.

"You are definitely not a model Angel."

Finnian grinned. "I do not need to be model, just lovable. I am not supposed to be anything else, remember?"

Ryan looked sad. "Finn..."

Finnian sat up and wrapped one of his wings around the human's shoulders. "Come on, Ryan. You know you want to. We haven't been down to the Lower Tier in ages."

"I thought you're an Angel? You're beginning to sound very much like a Demon. Temptation is supposed to be bad, remember?"

Finnian smirked. "This is Angelic temptation. I believe it is very different. Come on. Anifiel will never miss us."

~~~~~

Ryan sat cross-legged on a cloud. He was sitting. On. A cloud. He always got a kick out of that.

"What is that they are doing there?" Finnian asked. The red-haired Angel was lying on his stomach beside Ryan, feet kicking back and forth as he peered over the edge of the cloud to Earth below.

Ryan followed the direction of Finnian's pointing finger. He breathed a sigh of relief that the Angel hadn't caught someone doing something unsavory that Ryan would have to explain. Humans could be pretty deviant.

Pot calling kettle...

"Ah, that guy in the chair is getting a tattoo. See that big guy with the gun-like thing in his hand?" Ryan had described guns to Finnian and knew that the Angel understood the reference. "That gun-thing has a bunch of needles in it. He dips the needles in ink and then those needles stab beneath the skin and plant the ink there."

"Decoration for the skin," Finnian murmured in awe. "Why does the guy in the chair have that expression? Does it hurt?"

Ryan smiled, amused by how his Angel friend fell into human lingo whenever they descended to the Lower Tier. "Yeah, it hurts. But I've never gotten one myself so I can't tell you how bad it is."

"What are those silver things on his chest?"

Ryan squinted. They were probably millions or trillions of miles from Earth—who knew?—but the distance seemed like only a few hundred feet. Another mystery.

"Those are, er, nipple rings."

Turquoise eyes fixed on Ryan's face. "What are they for?"

"Just more decoration. They make some people look sexy, I guess." Damn. He could feel his face heating up again.

Finnian had a sly smile on his face. "Do you have a nipple ring?"

Ryan sighed. He couldn't really lie to an Angel. "Yes, I have one. It was mostly a silent protest against my parents," he tried to justify. When Finnian continued to grin, Ryan gave in. "Okay, yeah, and I thought it might look sexy on me."

Finnian scrambled upright, completely oblivious of what his tunic did or did not conceal. "Let me see it, Ryan. I want to see what you humans think is sexy."

"Well, it kinda involves the person..." Ryan mumbled, looking wistfully at the Middle Tier. "Maybe we should go back now."

"Not until I see your nipple ring." Finnian leaned forward, pale hands reaching for the opening of Ryan's tunic.

Embarrassed, Ryan quickly batted his hands away. "I'll do it." Feeling extremely self-conscious, Ryan pulled down the shoulders of his tunic, revealing his bare chest and the silver ring that pierced his right nipple.

Finnian's eyes went round, his lips pursing into an 'o'. "So pretty," he murmured, reaching forward before Ryan could stop him. Finnian flicked his finger against the ring, looking up startled when Ryan sucked in his breath. "Does that hurt?"

Ryan laughed ruefully. "Try the opposite. That's another reason humans get pierced—it makes you hypersensitive."

"Really?" A pale finger flicked the ring again and Ryan had to bite his lip as the sensation went straight to his groin.

"Finn, don't."

"It makes you feel good, doesn't it?" Finnian asked coyly.

Ryan's face was on fire. "Yes and no. Right now, it's mostly no."

Finnian sat back on his heels, eyes latched onto the ring.

Ryan decided he did not like the calculating look on Finnian's face. "Look, Finn—"

"I want one of those."

Ryan blinked. "You can't. You'd have to go to Earth. And well, besides the fact that you're Finnian, only Guardian Angels can walk the Earth, right?"

"I think it's time I went down to Earth," Finnian announced, standing up. "I've been watching the humans forever. I want to taste their ice cream. I want to listen to their techno music. I want to slide down a slide and get a raspberry burn on my bottom!"

Ryan, who'd stood up to avoid the temptation of looking up Finnian's tunic, broke into laughter. "Finn, you just can't do that. You have to stay here. Besides, nothing's better than Heaven. Trust me on that. There are a lot of bad things on Earth. Bad people. It can be pretty rough and I wouldn't want you to experience any of that."

The red-haired Angel turned to him with the first annoyance Ryan had ever seen on those beautiful features. "Are you my keeper now, too?"

Ryan had never felt more terrible. Finnian was his best friend. "Of course not, Finn. I'm sorry. I'm only looking out for you. I don't want you to get hurt for something silly like ice cream."

Finnian studied him for several moments, his face unreadable. At last he sighed. "I'm sorry, Ryan. I did not mean to be cross with you. I have everything I need in Heaven. I don't know why I am so curious about Earth."

"It's natural, Finn. You're one of the True Angels. You were never a human, so you don't know what Earth is like." Ryan hesitantly laid a hand on the Angel's foot, suppressing a shiver of pleasure at the feel of that petal-soft skin. "But an Angel like you should stay up here, where it's safe and good. I wouldn't want you to be tainted."

"Such a good friend," Finnian said with a smile. "I'm lucky to have you."

Ryan beamed.

It was on that high that Ryan found himself once again deposited in the pleasure lands of the Middle Tier. Finnian had flown off to do whatever it was that consorts did. Ryan lay on his back with the eternal sun beating warmly upon his face. The grasses waved gently in the breeze, tickling his ankles.

He fell asleep, dreaming of Finnian dressed as a Goth boy and dancing in one of Ryan's favorite clubs. He awoke to the blaze of horns and the bellow of a voice he knew well.

"FINNIAN!!!"

Gasping, Ryan shot upright. The wind swirled around him and it took his sleep-fogged brain a moment to realize it wasn't a natural wind. Anifiel hovered above him, the handsome Angel's face contorted into such distress that Ryan scampered backward on hands and feet to get away from him.

"Where is Finnian?" Anifiel demanded, his great wings pounding the air above Ryan. "Where is my consort?"

Ryan moaned at the great voice that rattled his bones and set his blood screaming through his veins. Anifiel terrified him. Anifiel transfixed him.

"I-I don't know where he is!" Ryan cried out. "Honestly!"

But the moment he said the words, Ryan knew.

"Finnian is no longer in Heaven," Anifiel told him. The great Angel's voice shook with emotion. "He is gone!"

Ryan shook his head, fearing the next words, knowing what they'd be.

"My beloved has gone to Earth." Anifiel pointed an accusing finger at the human. "Because *you* tempted him with it!"

Ryan closed his eyes and huddled against the grass, not bothering to deny anything while that great rage and loss roiled in Anifiel's green eyes. He whimpered when strong arms plucked him off the ground as though he weighed nothing.

"Are you going to drop me to the Beneath?" Ryan asked in a small voice as they rushed through the air more quickly than Finnian had ever flown him. The Angels and humans below them looked up at their swift passage in confusion and worry. Ryan knew if he fell right now he might not die again but he would experience extraordinary pain.

Anifiel's deep voice rumbled right beside Ryan's ear. "You are going to help me get my beloved back, or you will indeed be dropped with the Demons." A band of iron tightened around Ryan's chest as Anifiel crushed him. "You have corrupted Finnian, and now you will set things right."

With Anifiel's threat echoing in his mind and the Middle Tier rushing madly beneath them, Ryan closed his eyes and did what any self-respecting human would do in his position. He fainted.

2

Ryan woke up.

He lay on his back on a softly padded bed, staring up at a tangled canopy of vines and white flowers. He recognized the flora as honeysuckle. The soft, sweet scent helped soothe his nerves. As he gradually began to relax, he picked out the sound of gurgling water, though it didn't come from a specific direction; it seemed to float on the air. He lay in what looked like an open-sided gazebo. A gentle breeze blew through the structure, playing with his hair.

Where am—

"Oh, my god," he blurted as he recalled why he'd fainted.

"Your human religion means nothing here," said a cold, hard voice.

Ryan yelped and sat upright. A wave of dizziness swept through him, but he fought back the inkiness to stare dumbly at the tall figure standing grimly beside the bed.

In all his dreams of Anifiel, never had Ryan had one in which he woke up in the Angel's bed and feared for his life.

"Did you enjoy your repose?"

By Anifiel's fierce scowl, the question seemed to be a rhetorical one, but Ryan decided to respond as if the concern were genuine.

"I-I'm fine. I think I fainted. I'm sorry." His ears burned. He wondered yet again if Angels could read minds. Or dreams. *Please no!*

Anifiel watched him steadily, which didn't help the nervous blushing at all. "Humans are weak," the Angel finally stated after a long, assessing pause.

Ryan just nodded. He wasn't about to argue with Heaven's greatest Angel. He'd happily be meek if it kept him out of trouble.

"You are also deceitful."

Ryan stopped nodding. "What do you mean? I haven't lied to you, Anifiel." When the Angel's eyes narrowed, Ryan quickly added, "Err...sir. Anifiel, sir." He winced. "I haven't done anything to Finn. I told him not to go—" He broke off and mentally slapped himself.

Anifiel took a menacing step forward. "So you knew he intended to descend to the Earth!" Ryan hastily scooted backwards on the bed, his back coming up against a wooden, vine-covered post. "You knew he meant to leave and yet you did not warn me of his intentions?"

"Finn always talked about one day visiting the

Earth," Ryan protested, waving one hand helplessly. "I didn't know that this time he really meant it. I had no idea! Please believe me. I don't want him down there any more than you do."

"You do not wish him to be further *corrupted*, you mean." Anifiel's look was disdainful. "The humans of Earth will seek to turn him. You cannot help yourselves. Temptation and sin is the easier path for you, so you take it."

Ryan knew to keep his mouth shut. He watched with wide eyes as the blond drew nearer. The great Angel stood next to the bed now, his bare knees pressed against the pad. The hem of his ivory tunic brushed the golden hairs of his powerful thighs.

Ryan had never thought much about why Anifiel wore a tunic, but he questioned it now. Unlike Finnian, Anifiel had no need to present the enticement that came from a selectively-clothed body. He was a warrior. His body was an instrument of war, not of pleasure. He wore shining silver armor to battle, but there was no need for modesty during times of peace.

But as Ryan's eyes fell helplessly to the strongly corded thighs of the Angel, and as he took in the wide, broad hands that promised a strong, sure grip, he thought he might know why Anifiel was clothed in this land where nudity was considered freeing: Anifiel might be too good-looking for the humans to handle. His naked body just might start a riot.

The conclusion made a nervous giggle slip from Ryan's lips, which in turn hardened Anifiel's face. Ryan's amusement shriveled.

"You find the loss of my consort amusing?"

Ryan gulped and shook his head. "Of course not. That's not why I laughed. I want him back, too. He's my friend."

Anifiel's eyes narrowed. "So you say."

Ryan sucked in his breath as one broad knee slid onto the bed pad beside his hip. Anifiel reached above Ryan's head and braced himself against the wooden pole, bringing his face mere inches from Ryan's. The pleasant scent of green apples filled Ryan's nostrils. Anifiel's natural scent?

So many of my dreams begin this way, but something tells me the ending will be different this time.

This close, Ryan could see that Anifiel was more than just handsome—he was the ideal man. Unlike Finnian's cute, softly seductive features, Anifiel's were bold and almost haughty in their declaration of his maleness. Two sharp grooves—Ryan was afraid to call them dimples—slashed either side of the Angel's wide mouth. His jaw looked hard and square enough to hammer a nail. He had blond lashes that were very pale. They were the only hints of vulnerability on an otherwise intensely masculine face. A face that made one's heart stutter with fear and desire. With respect.

Ryan was awed by this Angel, but he was also scared enough of Anifiel to wet himself, which dampened (figuratively) his interest. Anifiel was too imposing, too dominant, too...much. Ryan longed for Finnian's simple, soothing presence. It was no wonder Finnian had requested to be made Anifiel's equal in gender. As a woman, Finnian would be overwhelmed. Even as the Angel that Finnian was, the scales did not equal out.

"My consort is more than a friend to you," Anifiel stated. No question. No speculation. His eyes were diamond hard with accusation. "You desire him."

"No, he's just my friend," Ryan argued weakly. He was afraid to move. Anifiel was so close their noses might bump. The Angel surrounded him in a cage of muscle and bone, ready to crush him. "I know Finn belongs to you. I'm very, very aware of that."

An odd, speculative gleam came into the Angel's eyes. "Yes, you are very aware, aren't you?"

The change in Anifiel's voice threw Ryan off. "What are you talking about?" he whispered.

Green eyes flicked over his lap dismissively. "Your human body betrays you. I can smell you." Anifiel raised his eyes to Ryan's mortified face. "You smell hot, little human. You smell like lightning. Like the clouds before war. Your body craves physical satisfaction. You crave it by my hand."

It would have been dirty talk from anyone else, and Ryan would have been instantly hard. But this was Anifiel, who hated humans, and...Ryan shivered, unable to stop the reaction when Anifiel stared at him so menacingly. Ryan had spent most of his life feeling ashamed of his sexual inclinations. He'd fallen for people he shouldn't have and lusted after men who wanted no business with him. He didn't like discovering that not much had changed in Heaven. Frustration bubbled inside him, begging to be released in a yell or a punch. He knew he deserved better than Anifiel's scorn.

"I may be human, but that doesn't mean I want to have sex with you," he said, his voice trembling yet defiant. "I'm not a rutting animal. I have my standards."

"You are trying to inflict your human lust on me, just as you have attempted to do with my consort." Anifiel's voice was sharp. "You will not succeed with either of us."

Ryan felt like he was being treated like a teenager with an obsessive crush. He wanted to crawl under a rock. "I'm doing no such thing!"

Anifiel came as close as an Angel could to sneering. "I am not interested in human passions. Finnian is a curious Angel, but even he respects that Angels should not succumb to your failings."

"Love and sex aren't failings," Ryan argued.

But Anifiel was already moving away, treating his response as an unnecessary footnote to a foregone conclusion.

With his back to Ryan, his immense wings mysteriously absorbed into his body with some kind of Angel power, he said, "You will tell me where Finnian went."

Ryan's shoulders slumped, hating the dismissal but knowing he couldn't do anything about it. This was Anifiel, and Ryan was just a lowly human.

"He could be anywhere," he sighed. But then he remembered Finnian's interest in his nipple piercing. "Wait! I think I know where he might have gone first." Excited, he asked, "If we find him you can bring him back, right?"

Anifiel turned to face him again. Ryan was surprised to see that the Angel didn't appear to share in his optimism. "That is yet to be determined. It is not by my will." Anifiel walked to the grass. "You have had enough of lying about. Come with me."

Ryan cautiously slid his legs off the bed. "Where are we going?"

"To speak with the Creator."

Ryan froze, heart thumping. "The C-Creator?"

Anifiel's smile was smug. "You had better behave yourself, human. Do not give in to your human weakness if you can help it. It will be amusing to see you try."

Ryan bit back the retort balanced on his tongue. Why did Anifiel have to goad him like this? Considering his next destination, though, Ryan was willing to let it slide. If he was about to meet the Creator…he needed all the good karma he could buy.

~~~~~

The flight to the Forest of Contemplation was as harrowing as the first experience in Anifiel's arms had been. Flying with Finnian was joyous. It was as if Ryan himself had wings. When flying with Anifiel, Ryan was very conscious of being a passenger or, more accurately, unwanted baggage. The blond Angel's wings beat furiously with his urgency to reach their destination and dump Ryan. His heart pounded like a fist against Ryan's back.

When Ryan tried to adjust himself more comfortably in the Commander's grip, the iron bar of a forearm squeezed his chest, practically crushing his ribs. Ryan heeded the warning and kept still.

Ryan had never been to the Forest of Contemplation, though he had of course heard of it. All the humans knew of it. It was their goal while in the Middle Tier. The Forest was the final step to enlightenment.

Ryan pictured the clichéd stairway to the Upper Tier. Or maybe it was an escalator? He brimmed with curiosity over what he would see.

The pools and streams of the Middle Tier gave way to solid fields of grass and flowers. He and Anifiel flew over fewer and fewer humans and Angels, until Ryan rarely saw another being at all. After several minutes, when it became clear that they had flown to the outer reaches of Heaven—wherever *that* was—Ryan began to relax. The stress of being carried by Anifiel had given way to a sensation of peace. It was like they were the only two beings in Heaven. It would have been nice if it were Finn and me, Ryan thought wistfully.

A sudden drop in altitude left Ryan crying out and clutching frantically at a muscular forearm.

"My apologies," Anifiel murmured, sounding anything but sorry.

Ryan turned his head and eyed the Angel suspiciously. He thought the Angel might have been trying to suppress a smirk.

After a few minutes, the grassy lands gave way to a thick copse of large willow trees. Their drooping limbs swayed gently in the breeze, giving them the appearance of hunchbacked old women with long gray hair, shifting from foot to foot. Anifiel slowed, his wings flattening to send them into an easy bank. Ryan looked around with interest, but all he saw were the trees, no stairs.

He was privately glad not to see an escalator.

He tensed as they neared the lush grass, but Anifiel's sandaled feet hit the ground and cushioned their landing so skillfully that Ryan was released to the grass as though Anifiel had simply been holding him in his arms, not flying him. Ryan smiled up at the Angel, grateful for his care. Anifiel expression's revealed how little he cared about impressing a human.

"You will wait here," he ordered, pointing to an area before the nearest willow tree.

Ryan looked, and where before there had been only grass, there now sat a cream-colored stone bench, facing the tree.

"How did that—"

"I will return once I have spoken with the Creator."

Ryan was surprised. And both relieved and disappointed. "I'm not going with you?"

Anifiel smirked. "Have you found enlightenment already? We've only just entered the Forest of Contemplation. I find myself speechless at your progress."

I wish you could be speechless, Ryan thought, throwing the Angel a dirty look. "Why are you so mean to me?" he blurted. "I thought Angels were supposed to be kind and encouraging. I thought you were supposed to be perfect so we would have an example to follow."

Anifiel's smirk slid away. His look for Ryan was close to, but not quite, contemptuous. "If aspiring to be like an Angel was truly your mission, then your failure would be most pitiful to watch. Be grateful your goals need not be so lofty." He shook his head as Ryan flushed. "Remain here. I will return once I have resolved this catastrophe which you have caused."

Ryan bit his tongue. Arguing about who was to blame for Finnian's defection was useless with Anifiel. The Angel had a skull thicker than brick. He was nothing more than a handsome Neanderthal.

Ignoring the Angel as he took to the air once more, Ryan flopped down onto the bench, facing the tree. The bench was surprisingly comfortable for being made of stone. It was probably some magical working of Heaven, like being able to sit on clouds.

Ryan rested his hands in his lap and stared at the tree. It was an old one, and nearly as wide as a grain silo. Its leaves were a silvery green and rustled musically. Ryan's anger with Anifiel began to fade away as he watched the sloping branches dance to their own music.

Okay, so if he was in the Forest of Contemplation it would probably be a good idea to contemplate something. But what?

Finnian came instantly to mind. Now that the stress-inducing Anifiel was gone, Ryan was able to finally face his feelings about his friend's actions. Ryan was scared for Finnian. The red-haired Angel was the best friend Ryan had ever had. They were drastically different in the obvious ways, and yet somehow they enjoyed each other's company tremendously. Ryan was rarely as happy as he was when he was with Finnian. He felt the absence of the sweet Angel like a hole in the heart.

He was desperately worried, alright. He knew Finnian all too well. Finnian's curiosity had the potential to get him into a lot of trouble. And if the Angel went to the neighborhood of that tattoo parlor, he'd headed directly into a seedy part of the Earth. Someone as beautiful and innocent as Finnian would draw the worst kind of attention there.

Finnian was a powerful Angel in Heaven, but how did that translate on Earth? Could he protect himself there?

And what about the fact that Finnian had left in the first place? Somehow, Finnian had managed to talk the Head Guardian Angel into helping him to leave Heaven. Ryan wouldn't be surprised if Finnian had done it without bothering to ask how— or if—he could return to Heaven. The Angel was impetuous and reckless—traits Ryan often loved about Finnian—but Finnian didn't know enough about danger to appreciate that it was, well, *dangerous*. Finnian was completely unprepared for everything on Earth. He'd get robbed by a Girl Scout. Not to mention Anifiel's fear for Finnian made Ryan scared because it suggested that the Commander might know something Ryan didn't. Did Anifiel fear Finnian could never return?

"Oh, Finn, you beautiful idiot," Ryan moaned,

burying his face into his hands. "If you get hurt—"

The soft, familiar sound of wings displacing the air made Ryan reluctantly lift his head. He wiped hurriedly at his eyes, expecting to see Anifiel. His nerves drew taut in anticipation of bad news.

But what he saw wasn't what he expected at all.

Next to the willow tree to Ryan's left, another stone bench had magically appeared. Sitting upon it was another human. Maybe Ryan had been too absorbed in his woes to notice her earlier. But he doubted it.

As Ryan watched, the human stood up to greet an Angel who had just descended from the air. The Angel said something indistinguishable to the woman before embracing her in arms and wings. When the Angel pulled back, Ryan could see that the human woman was silently crying in joy.

Ryan covered his mouth to hold back a gasp as he watched the Angel gently take the human in his arms once more and fly them both up into the clouds.

He had just seen a human reach enlightenment and make the transition to the Upper Tier.

Ryan blinked, realizing he could suddenly see other benches that weren't there before. There were hundreds of them. Maybe thousands, all occupied by humans contemplating their own willow tree. As Ryan watched in awe, every few seconds an Angel would quietly descend from the Upper Tier and greet a sitting human who had just found enlightenment. The exchange was the same: a few soft words, an embrace, and then the joyous ascent.

The scene was so magical and emotional that Ryan felt like a trespasser for being here. He had not earned the right to sit in the Forest of Contemplation. He had no idea how to find enlightenment. He barely knew himself. Feeling heartsick, he turned back to his own tree and gazed at it in despair.

He felt lost in Heaven. On Earth, he hadn't been religious, but he'd believed that everything would be better in Heaven. He'd had to believe that because life on Earth had been awful for him: the discovery of being gay, which had not been a happy one; his misery-inducing attempts to become the straight son his parents wanted; their subsequent rejection of him when he failed...

Bitterness made him frown as he stared at the swaying leaves. Few things had made him happy while he was alive, but the afterlife was not proving to be much better. It wasn't fair. His best friend was in danger because of him. His friend's lover thought him little better than a bug. And most disappointingly of all, Ryan did not see an end to what had plagued him on Earth—his ever-present loneliness. He thought for sure he would find someone here. *His* someone. But in Heaven, as on Earth, Ryan was doomed to be alone.

"Contemplation should not cause you distress," spoke a gentle, masculine voice to Ryan's right.

Startled, he looked up to find a handsome, black-haired Angel standing beside him, arms clasped behind his back.

"It should open your heart and your eyes to accept what is, and what is not. And to accept them without pain."

Ryan stood up, panicked. "You're not here to take me to the Upper Tier, are you? Because I'm not really supposed to be here. I haven't found enlightenment. I'm just waiting for someone. I shouldn't be here—"

"Hush," said the Angel with an amused smile. "I am not here for your journey. I, too, am waiting for someone. We both await Anifiel, yes?"

Ryan nodded, releasing a breath in relief. He didn't want to add duplicity to his list of offenses in Heaven. "Yes. He told me to wait here while he speaks with the Creator."

The Angel frowned slightly and tilted his head back, as if he could see through the clouds to the Upper Tier. "He seeks a way to return Finnian to Heaven, is that so?"

"That's right."

Ryan hesitated, unfamiliar with this Angel, but seriously doubting he needed to distrust him. This was an Angel, after all. "Do you—do you think Finn will be able to come back? It shouldn't be difficult, right? I mean, this is the Creator. The One who controls everything."

The Angel smiled at him again. "Is that what you believe? Is that what the teachings of your religion tell you?"

Ryan flushed. "I'm not religious, actually. I mean, I believe in Heaven and Hell. Err, the Beneath. And I now know there's a god—the Creator."

"The Creator is not a god," the Angel replied,

still smiling.

"Then who—"

"Your enlightenment is not my duty," the black-haired Angel said, but his tone was polite and Ryan understood he wasn't being chastised. "Your knowledge will come in time, but not by my words. You are Ryan. Finnian's friend. I am Vithius. I am Anifiel's battle companion."

The term piqued Ryan's interest. "Battle companion? You're a warrior in Heaven's Army?"

"I mean I am Anifiel's battle companion. Each warrior is paired with another during battles of the Eternity War to guard the other's back. Anifiel and I fight together to prevent the other from falling."

The information made Ryan study the other Angel closely. Vithius was not as solidly built as Anifiel, but he was clearly very fit. His skin was the color of tea-stained silk. His limbs were firm, though not as heavily muscled as Anifiel's. He looked like he would be fast. Agile. He was probably a good foil for Anifiel's strength.

Vithius' hair was the color of black coffee, cut just below the ears and slicked back in a way that on Earth Ryan would have assumed was an effect of hair gel or pomade. He doubted Vithius used either. The Angel was very attractive with straight, dense eyebrows and deep-set brooding black eyes. His nose was wider than Anifiel's. It was balanced by the curve of his generous, thick lips. Ryan stared at Vithius' handsome, smiling face because it was easy to do so. It was also easier than staring at the Angel's attractive and very naked body.

"You must be a great warrior to be Anifiel's

companion," Ryan said, automatically trying to picture this Angel as he fought back to back with Anifiel, an Angel who was as bright as Vithius was dark. They would make a striking pair in battle. Ryan idly wondered if Finnian was jealous of Vithius. He remembered Finnian's complaint about being forbidden from going to war alongside the other Angels.

"Anifiel has not been turned, and that is the mark of my success," Vithius replied modestly. "What I lack in skill, I make up for in loyalty to my Commander. I would willingly turn to the Beneath if it meant saving him from such a fate."

"Wow," Ryan breathed, unable to help himself. "You really mean that, don't you? You'd do anything for him."

Vithius arched a thick eyebrow. "Why the surprise, young human?"

Ryan shrugged and glanced away, suddenly uncomfortable. "No reason. Just surprised."

"You lie to an Angel in the Forest of Contemplation?"

Ryan looked up in a panic, but Vithius was smiling indulgently at him. Ryan smiled back weakly. "I'm sorry. You're right. I shouldn't lie like that. The truth is, well, the truth is that I was surprised to hear that you feel so strongly about Anifiel. He hasn't been—" he flushed, "—he hasn't been very nice to me, that's all. He must act differently around Angels than he does around humans."

Vithius approached the willow tree and idly ran

his hand down its bark. Ryan thought he heard a faint musical tremor come from the tree, but he knew he must be mistaken.

"Anifiel is not fond of humans, this is true. He prefers his own kind."

Ryan nodded glumly. "I just don't get it. Why would the greatest Angel in Heaven be made that way? Why wouldn't the Creator want Anifiel to love everyone? Why make him a jerk?" His eyes bulged when he realized what he'd said, but Vithius only laughed.

"I suppose to you he may seem that way." The dark-haired Angel leaned his back against the tree, his hands clasped behind his hips. Ryan wished Vithius would cover up his groin. The Angel's sex was distracting him. "But I think you misunderstand a basic truth about Angels. We are created, yes, but our development is left mostly up to us. Anifiel is the exception in that he was given much guidance by the Creator initially. Heaven needed a great Commander, and that could not be left to chance. But in the end, Anifiel, too, was left free to become the Angel he is now...or can be."

"I asked Anifiel this before: why not make all of you perfect? Why not make the Angels something to aspire to?" A wry smile crossed Ryan's lips, possible only because he felt increasingly comfortable with Vithius. "I hate to say it, but, I don't want to be anything like Anifiel."

"Ah, but Anifiel is glorious for a reason. Perhaps it is not obvious to you as of yet, but in time it will be."

"I doubt it," Ryan muttered.

Vithius acted as though he hadn't heard him. "We Angels are imperfect because the Creator discovered that when humans are faced with perfection, they lose hope and motivation. Why put forth the effort when you believe you can never live up to the examples given to you? By allowing Angels to have 'faults' humans can relate to us." Vithius' black eyes danced. "Do not worry, young Ryan. There is enough perfection in Angels to give you much to emulate."

"I-I know that," Ryan stammered hastily. "I didn't mean to imply that I don't think all of you are incredible. You are. I think I understand how it is: each Angel is superior in some way, but not in all ways. Is that it?"

"Very good, Ryan."

Vithius' voice became deeper as it grew quieter. It sent pleasant warmth over Ryan's face. He prayed it wasn't a blush. He coughed nervously and sat on the edge of the bench, trying to keep his eyes above Vithius' neck.

"Does my nudity make you uncomfortable?"

The inquiry was spoken mildly, curiously, as if Vithius was genuinely intrigued by the concept.

"Not uncomfortable, I guess." Ryan's eyes darted helplessly to Vithius' penis. It was not overly large, but Ryan hadn't seen that many guys' cocks up close like this and the experience gave him a minor, embarrassing thrill. "Just not used to it. I guess I prefer it when you cover up. It's less distracting."

"So Anifiel must please you."

Ryan's mouth fell open.

"In that he is clothed," Vithius clarified, though Ryan saw the amusement on the Angel's face at Ryan's floundering.

"He's—he's good-looking. There's no way I can lie and say he's not the hottest guy I've ever seen. But his personality—" Ryan broke off with a scowl. "That's a huge turn-off."

"As I said, in time you will come to realize what the majority of Heaven knows: Anifiel is the glory of Heaven." Vithius pushed off the tree and flexed his wings with a contented groan. Ryan watched in awe as the feathers extended and separated. It probably felt like cracking your fingers. "You will love him as I love him," Vithius added with a wink.

Ryan gaped. "You mean you—"

"Finnian is Anifiel's consort," Vithius cut him off smoothly. "And that is all that matters to both of us."

Ryan was dying to pursue this further, but like all pleasant situations, Anifiel showed up to end it. The blond Angel descended with a heavy rush of air, hitting the grass with a loud thud.

Ryan took a frightened step backward when he saw Anifiel's expression. The Angel's face was red and his lips were pursed to a tight white line. His fists, clenched at his sides, looked like mallets, eager to pound someone's head in. Ryan was pretty sure he was the target.

"Anifiel," Vithius greeted in a calm, soothing voice. "I take it the audience did not go well?"

"I cannot bring Finnian back!" Anifiel's deep

bass rattled the trees. "The Creator will not allow me to interfere. Finnian must find a way to return on his own. It is preposterous! The Creator is punishing us! Why, Vithius? What have we done?"

"You are so quick to assume it is punishment," Vithius pointed out. The dark-haired Angel spoke easily, and was unfazed by Anifiel's anger, as if he were used to it. "Perhaps it is not punishment, but a test."

"Or a lesson," Anifiel seethed, eyes shooting accusingly to Ryan.

Ryan cringed and took a step closer to Vithius.

"The human has done nothing but give in to your consort's desires," Vithius pointed out as Anifiel took a step toward them. "We both know that Finnian can be persuasive when he wants something."

That brought a sudden tightening to Anifiel's face, and pulled his attention from Ryan. "What are you saying? That Finnian was the seducer?"

Vithius didn't so much as flinch at the outrage on the Commander's face. Ryan's respect for the black-haired Angel bloomed. Standing up to Anifiel when he was like this was like holding up a hand against a tidal wave.

"You know that is not what I meant." There was an edge to Vithius' voice that had not been there before. "Your emotion is clouding your judgment."

"I know you well," Anifiel countered. "This situation does not leave you in poorer straits."

Vithius gasped.

Looking between the two powerful Angels, Ryan realized that the tension between them hadn't solely been spurred by Finnian's disappearance; it had existed for a long time. Studying Vithius' tensed features, Ryan guessed that it was something not openly spoken of, either.

"Say nothing more," Vithius warned. Ryan heard the first touch of anger hit the Angel's voice. "We must concentrate on bringing Finnian back, not on placing blame for his disappearance."

"Oh, there is a place for this blame to fall." The green eyes zeroed in on Ryan again. It literally felt like being electrocuted. The intensity of Anifiel's attention left Ryan faint.

"I'm sorry," he insisted desperately. "Whatever I did or didn't do, I'm sorry! I'd give anything to take his place. Anything!"

"I will keep that in mind," was Anifiel's grim reply. He spared a dismissive glance for Vithius. "We are leaving. I have business with his human."

Vithius placed a protective hand on Ryan's shoulder. The Angel's touch, combined with the turmoil of the situation, nearly sent Ryan to his knees. As if aware of this, Vithius moved the hand to beneath Ryan's elbow to steady him. "Do not harm this human in your frustration, Anifiel."

Anifiel's face was stony. "Do not tell me what to do. Your claim on me extends only to the edges of the battlefields, Vithius. Never forget that."

Vithius paled, his dark skin turning ashen. "I cannot, even if I wanted to."

"See that you don't."

Ryan gasped as he finally recognized the

undercurrent running beneath the Angels' conversation. Did Finnian know of this?

He was left with no time to think of it because Anifiel grabbed him by the upper arm and literally yanked him out of Vithius' grasp. "We are leaving." Who the words were directed at didn't make a difference as Anifiel didn't wait for a reply before launching himself into the air.

Ryan groaned in fright and clutched at Anifiel's arms. He could feel the Angel's fury vibrating through his golden skin. Anifiel couldn't kill him, but he could definitely hurt him.

The land rushed past them so quickly it was a green and blue blur. Ryan had to close his eyes or risk throwing up.

"Please, please, please," he mumbled desperately, like a prayer.

"Quiet," Anifiel ordered.

Ryan bit his lips together.

They flew for what seemed hours; torture always felt that way. When Anifiel finally slowed, Ryan was exhausted from fright. He opened his eyes slowly. When he discovered where Anifiel had flown them, his heart sank completely.

"So you're actually going to do it," he said in a dazed voice. "I thought it was like the bogeyman— just a threat to scare people with. I didn't think it actually happened."

"I do not know what you refer to, nor do I care," Anifiel declared, landing upon the narrow puff of white cloud. He released Ryan immediately, only to push him so that he fell backward onto his butt.

Ryan looked up in confusion. "You aren't—you aren't going to push me over the side?"

Anifiel looked gigantic as he towered over Ryan. The ever-present light made his entire body glow.

"As meddling as you have been so far, I will nonetheless attempt to pull some usefulness from you. Tell me where Finnian went. You said you know."

Ryan thought back frantically. "I might know," he hedged, worried about pretending to be more helpful to Anifiel than he was. He didn't want to give the Angel false hope. Or another reason to be angry with him. "We were looking at something. A place. And he seemed interested in it. But I could be mistaken!" he hastily added. "It was just a funny thing. He could have been joking and not been serious at all."

Anifiel watched him steadily. "What was this joke?"

Ryan swallowed hard. "We were looking at a tattoo parlor. He saw someone with a piercing. A nipple piercing. When I showed him mine, he acted like he wanted one, too."

Golden brows stabbed together. "What is a nipple piercing?"

Ryan stopped breathing for a second. Oh, no. "It's—it's when you put jewelry through your, um, nipple." He could feel himself blushing furiously at the thought of Anifiel imagining what his nipple looked like.

"You say you have this? Show me."

Ryan shook his head and wrapped an arm around his chest. "No."

He yelped when Anifiel dropped on him without warning, pinning him on his back to the cloud.

"Get off me!" Ryan gasped as he tried to buck the Angel off.

Heavy limbs effectively brought his thrashing to an end. Panting, Ryan found himself trapped with his wrists above his head in one of Anifiel's hands. The Angel's other hand, to his horror, tugged at the neck of Ryan's tunic.

"What are you doing?" Ryan asked, incredulous.

Anifiel ignored him, frowning as he seemed to realize he could not lower Ryan's tunic while his arms were held above his head. "My apologies," he muttered with that same lack of sincerity as earlier. Ryan twitched as Anifiel grabbed hold of the neck of his tunic and simply ripped through it.

Ryan stared up at Anifiel, wide-eyed at what he'd done. This was his fantasy, and yet the reality scared him down to his toes. To be this vulnerable to the Commander was both the hottest experience of Ryan's life (and death) and the most terrifying.

The Angel's green eyes rounded for a split second as they latched onto the silver hoop adorning Ryan's chest.

"This is what Finnian desired?" Anifiel looked dumbfounded. "Why would he want this?"

In a voice laced with nerves, Ryan told him. "He thought it was pretty. And when I told him that it feels good, he was curious about that, too."

Green eyes flicked up to him. "It feels good? In what way?" Without waiting for an answer, Anifiel flicked the ring with his index finger.

Ryan gasped loudly and pushed his hips up. He'd never reacted this intensely to someone touching the ring, but something about the fact that it was Anifiel—the fear of being hurt by him, maybe—made Ryan's cock surge to a full erection.

"Get off!" he all but yelled, panicking. "Get off me!"

"Human lusts," Anifiel said coldly, eyes narrowing to slits. "Always it is about your corruption. Is this how you seduced my consort? By offering him pleasure of this sort? Did you give him an example of how it would be?"

Ryan shook his head vehemently. He needed Anifiel to get off him. The Angel's pelvis was pressed against his own and it was all Ryan could do not to pump against him and find relief for his throbbing cock. It was bad enough that Anifiel had aroused him and could feel it. But now Ryan had to fight his own body's demand for more than that.

"Get off," he pleaded. "Please, Anifiel."

Something thick and drugging moved through Ryan's veins. His inhibitions began to dissolve like mist, replaced by a growing desire. He felt strange, and yet not bad, as if he'd just taken a hit of Ecstasy. In fact, it began to feel incredible…He rolled his hips up into Anifiel's and groaned at the beautiful friction against his cock. *Oh, yes.*

"What are you doing down there?" Anifiel asked. "Why do you rub against me so?"

Ryan was in no state of mind to be giving lessons. "Because it…feels good," he moaned.

"This is what Finnian asked me for," Anifiel murmured. Even through the lusty fog enveloping his brain, Ryan heard the wonder and resentment vying for dominance within Anifiel. "He wanted to make love as you humans do. He was dissatisfied with me because of you!"

The Angel gripped Ryan by the hair. "Show me your filthy human lust."

It didn't matter that Anifiel's demand wasn't made out of sexual interest. The husky command made Ryan moan because it sounded exactly as it did in his fantasies.

"Show me how you tempted my precious consort," Anifiel ordered, his green eyes narrowed.

Ryan strained against the grip on his wrists, not to get away, but so he could grab hold of the Angel. He needed every inch of the muscled Angel against him, because only then would this dizzying, mind-blowing desire be satisfied. His cock throbbed like a pulsing sun. His heart pumped an aphrodisiac that weakened and excited him at the same time.

When Anifiel snarled menacingly, "Human—" Ryan climaxed so hard he thought he might have died a second time.

He spilled all over his thighs and tunic. Each jerk and twitch of his cock made him shudder. When his cock lay spent, the reality of what had happened drained the last of Ryan's energy. He slumped into the cloud, exhausted, bewildered, and tingling all over.

Anifiel did not get off him immediately. Most likely he was trying to figure out why he was so sticky. Ryan bit out a harsh laugh. As amazing as that orgasm had been, in the aftermath he only felt regret.

"Get off," he forced through gritted teeth. "Get your damn hands off me. You proved your point. Now get off."

The weight lifted. Ryan could breathe again. He didn't expect to feel so cold, though. He wrapped his arms around himself and drew his knees up. After a long moment of silence, he opened his eyes and looked up. Anifiel stood above him, studying Ryan as if he were a new species.

"You have proven that you are at fault for Finnian's corruption," Anifiel stated, the lines of his dimples looking like angry exclamation points for his words. "You are a slave to your weakness, and you have tried to lessen your misery by dragging my consort to your level."

Ryan had not known many strong emotions since he had come to Heaven, but he felt one now. He felt one emotion so intensely that it shook his limbs as he struggled to sit upright. He clutched the remains of his torn tunic to his chest and glared up at the Commander of Heaven's Army, letting his feeling pour free, damn the consequences.

"I hate you!" he cried. "I don't care if you are an Angel. I still hate you! You don't deserve Finn. You don't deserve to be in Heaven. You should rule the Beneath! You're a horrible Angel!"

A muscle in Anifiel's cheek twitched. Ryan didn't believe for a second that it was a guilty flinch.

The Angel looked down his nose at Ryan, his face a cold, hard mask.

"Enjoy the Middle Tier, little human. For I will see to it that you will never become a full Angel while I am here."

3

Ryan climbed to his feet and backed away from the Angel.

"Take me back to the Middle Tier," Ryan demanded. "Do what you want to me. I don't care. My life can't get any worse."

"You no longer live," Anifiel reminded him sternly.

Ryan flinched. *Oh, yeah.* He'd forgotten that minor detail. Minor, and yet the most important in the world. He hated himself for it, but the stress of everything piled onto the fact that—hey, he was dead—suddenly brought tears to his eyes.

He murmured unhappily as strong fingers caught his chin and forced his head up. He tried to pull free, but Anifiel wouldn't release him. Ryan glared through watery eyes as Anifiel studied him with scorn.

"Feeling sorry for yourself? Your play for pity

is in itself pitiful. There are humans who fare far worse than you. They left behind friends and family members—humans who had relied upon them for survival. Do not make a mockery of their trials." Anifiel's eyes narrowed. "What *was* the method of your Earthly passing?"

Ryan's face went cold. He knew he'd gone pale. "That's none of your business."

Anifiel released his chin as though disgusted by the touch. "I will make it my business. Know thy enemy." Anifiel pointed a finger at Ryan, making him cringe at the slim possibility that fire might burst from the end of the digit. "I will know *you*, human."

Ryan watched Anifiel's great wings unfurl and wondered for a second if the Angel was going to beat him with the powerful appendages. Anifiel's feet lifted from the cloud and as he launched himself away, the Angel warned, "Pray that the Head of our Guardian Angels has better news than *you* have provided for me."

"I'll pray alright," Ryan mumbled. "Pray that you fly into a rain cloud."

He flopped back onto the cloud and considered rolling over the edge and ending it all. He wondered if anyone had ever done that, just thrown themselves out of Heaven. He seriously doubted it. Plus, he was pretty sure that he wouldn't be allowed to fall all the way to the Beneath. Some Angel would swoop to his rescue. Unless, that is, Anifiel had left instructions to allow Ryan to fall his merry way. It was highly possible.

Ryan flung an arm across his eyes. "How can anyone be so awful?" *And why can't I hate him?*

"In truth, I had not considered myself to be so."

Ryan quickly sat up to find an amused Vithius standing before him.

Embarrassed by his state, Ryan clutched the torn fabric of his tunic across his chest. "I-I didn't hear you fly up."

Vithius' smile widened. "I glided down. You seemed deep in contemplation."

Ryan looked away. "Not the sort I should be doing." He returned his attention to the dark-aired Angel. "Are you here to, um, give me a ride back to the Middle Tier? Anifiel sort of left me. I guess he sent you back to pick me up?"

"He did not," Vithius answered, ruining Ryan's attempt to give Anifiel some credit for being decent. Obviously a mistake. "I know Anifiel, however, and I guessed something of this might have occurred." Black eyes fell to Ryan's tunic. Vithius frowned. "I am curious about the condition of your garment. How did this happen?"

The last thing Ryan wanted to do was share his humiliation with the one Angel who treated him with some respect. "It was an accident. I-I fell while we were flying and Anifiel tried to catch me and, uh, grabbed my tunic and it ripped." His cheeks burned. He was such a terrible liar.

Vithius said nothing, but his frown remained. "You are dishonest with me a second time."

The comment wasn't meant as an accusation, more like an observation, but Ryan still felt terrible.

But not terrible enough to reveal the truth.

Admitting Anifiel had forced him to have an orgasm was something Ryan would *never* tell.

When Ryan remained silent, Vithius sighed. "For every step forward you take, young Ryan, deceit pushes you back two. Anifiel will help you to see this."

"Yeah. I'm sure he's thrilled to help me."

Vithius arched a brow at his tone. Ryan flushed. "I'm sorry. I meant no disrespect. Anifiel just—" He sighed, jamming his fingers into the brown curls on his head. "He makes me behave in very un-Angelic ways. It's hard to be a good person while he's around."

Vithius regarded him steadily until Ryan began to squirm. "Remember what I told you in the Forest of Contemplation, Ryan. Anifiel is the glory of Heaven. There is much about him that will inspire you to your own greatness."

Ryan caught back the retort he longed to speak. Vithius' feelings for his battle companion were clearly blinded by personal reasons. The Angel didn't know Anifiel very well if he thought the blond Angel could inspire humans to like him, much less learn from him.

But Ryan needed an ally now that Finnian was gone, so he nodded. "I hope you're right. I don't want to dislike him."

Which was true. Anifiel was just making it very, very difficult to feel anything else for him.

Vithius broke out with a handsome, blinding smile which left Ryan a little dazed. "Excellent, Ryan. You are progressing already. You will find yourself in the Upper Tier far sooner than you think."

Ryan smiled weakly.

"Come." The Angel held out his hand. "I shall return you to the Middle Tier and we shall talk. I admit I don't partake of the company of humans as often as I should. I would like to rectify that omission with you, if you are willing."

"That would be great." Ryan shook his head, flattered beyond belief. "Thank you."

It wasn't a request for friendship, but it was attention that Ryan's bruised ego could use. And it certainly wouldn't hurt to make an ally of a powerful Angel with the strength to stand up to Anifiel.

"You are comfortable with flight?" Vithius' hands felt warm and comfortable on Ryan's shoulders. They were nearly the same height, giving Ryan a small sense of equality with the Angel that he didn't share with the taller Anifiel.

"I'm fine. I usually like it. Just depends on who's doing the flying..."

Vithius smirked as Ryan trailed off, but the Angel didn't prod for details. "Then let us return you to your home."

Vithius flew him calmly, the way Finnian did. Ryan was immensely grateful. He didn't want to develop a fear of flying because of Anifiel.

"Would you care to walk with me on the Path to Inspiration?"

Ryan paused before answering, confused by the question. "Well, I would like to learn everything from you that I can," he hedged uncertainly.

Vithius chuckled. "The Path is a place, Ryan, not a figure of speech."

"Oh." Fortunately with Vithius, Ryan didn't feel dumb for his ignorance. "Okay, I've never been there. I'd like to see it. Is it near the Forest of Contemplation?"

"We are nearly there."

They entered a bright green clearing that was bisected by a wide white line. It reminded Ryan of a soccer field. But the white line wasn't paint or chalk; it was a stone path wide enough for two people to share. Vithius set them down upon the white pebbles that were as smooth and pretty as polished marble. Ryan looked around them curiously. The rest of the clearing was empty. But along one side of the path was a row of gleaming bronze statues stretching into the distance for as long as the path continued.

"The Path to Inspiration," Vithius declared.

Ryan eyed the long white path. "Am I supposed to find inspiration at the end of it?" His stomach danced uneasily. He didn't respond well under pressure. With his luck, he'd fail somehow just like he had in the Forest of Contemplation.

"The Path is not a test," Vithius reassured him while laying a friendly hand on his shoulder and urging him to walk. "Here, you will find the statues of the greatest Angels of Heaven. Often, humans find inspiration in studying them. But if you do not, you will not be punished nor frowned upon. This place is meant only to provide hope to those who need it."

"I guess that's me," Ryan muttered.

He paused before the first statue. It was life-sized, standing upon a broad pedestal. It looked like it weighed several tons. And the detail on it—Ryan let out a soft murmur of admiration. It was as if this Angel had been magically turned to bronze less than a minute ago. It was so real Ryan was sure that if he touched the metal it would feel as warm as flesh.

"Ambriel," Vithius said reverently from over Ryan's shoulder. "He built the gates of Heaven with his bare hands."

Ryan blinked. "There are gates?"

"They appear when the Eternity War rages. Otherwise they are invisible to the human eye." Vithius studied the statue. "Ambriel resides in the Upper Tier. When you meet him, you will enjoy his company. He is a very clever Angel."

"He looks like a nice guy," Ryan said without thinking.

Vithius laughed quietly. "Indeed, he is a 'nice guy'."

Ryan flushed, but Vithius was guiding him down the line of statues, naming Angels Ryan had mostly never heard of. He did recognize a few of them as friends of Finnian. He wished he'd known when he met them that they were so great. He would have made a better effort to show his respect.

At last they stopped before two statues which were placed closer together than the others were. One glance at the smaller of the two, and Ryan broke out in a smile. "Finn."

The beautiful Angel was on his knees, hands resting primly in his lap. Not very Finn-like, Ryan thought as he grinned. But he did notice that the statue had a little mischievous smirk on its lips. And if a statue's eyes could dance with merriment, this one's did.

Ryan immediately stepped up to the statue of his friend and cupped a smooth, cold cheek. "Hey, Finn," he whispered, his smile tinged with loneliness. "Why did you go and leave us all like that?" He hesitated and dropped his voice even further. "I miss you. It's not the same without you."

The statue was so life-like Ryan half-expected it to wink at him and whisper reassurances. It didn't, of course, and he was forced to drop his hand guiltily as Vithius stepped up beside him.

"He makes the heart flutter," Vithius observed. "A more beautiful, beloved Angel was never created."

Ryan studied the dark-haired Angel in confusion. "You're attracted to Finn?"

Vithius regarded him with surprise. "Finnian is irresistible to human and Angel alike. The Creator ensured this."

"I know that, but I thought..." Ryan trailed off as his eyes slid to the statue that had been placed close to Finnian's.

The bold, magnificent form of Anifiel towered over them, somehow managing to look like a giant. The Angel was depicted in his role as the Commander of the Army—the Spear of Righteousness held aloft in one hand and what looked like an olive branch held in his other. The look on his face was one of determination and pride.

At least as a statue, Anifiel truly was as glorious as Vithius claimed him to be.

Vithius followed Ryan's gaze to his commander's statue and a knowing smile curved his lips. "Anifiel and Finnian are together, Ryan. The Creator meant for that to be. But that does not mean that we are not permitted to find them, separately and together, pleasing to the eye and heart."

"You're saying you love them both?"

Vithius just smiled, and continued walking down the path.

Ryan shook his head as he stared after the Angel. This was Heaven. Why were love and relationships confusing even here?

He looked up at Anifiel again. The light reflected off the surface of the statue, making it appear to glow. It must be his imagination, but it seemed like Anifiel's statue was brighter than the others. Or maybe it wasn't a trick of the light; Anifiel was the Creator's favorite, after all.

But why? Why favor the equivalent of the schoolyard bully?

Ryan hesitated, and then lightly rested his hand upon Anifiel's solid thigh. The Angel's leg was thrust forward as though he were taking the first step to face a hoard of Demons. It was a magnificent statue. Anifiel probably looked this way in war and Ryan admitted he was awed by that. If Anifiel had even a shred of kindness in him, Ryan would be head-over-heels in love with the golden-haired Angel.

But those haughty carven features remained the same whether molded in metal or flesh. They gave up nothing of kindness, and they allowed nothing resembling human understanding to penetrate. Ryan didn't need a challenge like Anifiel. His entire life had been a challenge. Right now, he wanted easy.

His eyes slipped from the statue of Anifiel and landed on Vithius, who was admiring another unnamed Angel. The dark-haired Angel's profile was sensual and sleek compared to Anifiel's. Vithius' body against Ryan's while in flight had stirred him; he couldn't deny it. As Ryan stared, the black-haired Angel turned back to him and smiled as if aware of the attention.

Ryan smiled back.

"First my consort, now my battle companion. Your corruption knows no bounds."

Ryan stumbled backward against Finn's statue as he looked up at Anifiel hovering high above him.

"Stop accusing me of things I'm not doing," Ryan shot back, but his cheeks burned guiltily.

"You covet what I possess, little human. It is no wonder you remain in the Middle Tier."

Ryan frowned. "You're the reason I'm still here, remember?"

Anifiel simply smirked and flew away, calling out, "Do not covet my statue, human."

Ryan snorted. "You wish."

Anifiel's wings dipped in mocking salute.

~~~~~

Vithius brought Ryan back to the pavilion where he had first woken up. Anifiel was not there, allowing Ryan to heave a huge sigh of relief. If the golden Angel never returned, it would still be too soon.

"This is where Anifiel and Finn live, isn't it?" Ryan walked the perimeter of the vine- and flower-covered structure. Besides the simple bed he had lain upon, nothing else suggested habitation. It was absent of other furniture. No closets or shelving existed since there weren't any walls. Because of that, there also weren't any pictures or personal knick knacks that usually cluttered up the surfaces of human living space.

"Angels have no need for sleep," Vithius explained. "Nor even a place of shelter, for the weather is never inclement in Heaven." The Angel motioned to the overhead lattice which was draped with honeysuckle. "But Finnian wished for an enclosure, and so Anifiel built one for him."

The answer caught Ryan by surprise. He studied the pavilion, noticing how carefully built it was. Not only was it beautiful—the wood was artfully turned at the edges to resemble leaves sprouting from a tree limb—it looked sturdy enough to withstand a tornado. "Anifiel built this for Finn?"

Vithius smiled in amusement. "Anifiel loves his consort. There is nothing he would not do for Finnian."

Ryan looked away, saying nothing. There were lavender hills in the distance and he kept his gaze on them as he felt Vithius studying him. Ryan wondered if the Angel had felt the pinch of jealousy the same as he had. What would it be like to have a relationship as loving and secure as Anifiel and

Finn's? A relationship carved in stone, as it were?

"How do you feel about the fact that they have no choice in who they love?" Ryan asked quietly, still tracing the hills. "The Creator took away their free will. Finn was created for the sole purpose of being a gift. Anifiel had no choice but to accept him. What if they could have loved other people or other Angels?"

Vithius leaned against a post and crossed his hands behind his head as he stood in contemplation. "The Creator has a reason for everything. Anifiel and Finnian's bond serves a purpose, whether it is evident to us or not. There is a lesson in everything in Heaven."

"Then you meant what you told Anifiel: Finn's going to Earth is a test of some kind? Maybe a test for Anifiel?"

"Perhaps."

Ryan finally turned from the hills to face the dark-haired Angel. "But you still didn't answer my question: do you think Finn and Anifiel could have loved other people if they weren't bound to each other?"

What he was really asking Vithius was, *do you think either of the Angels could have loved you back?*

Vithius' smile was enigmatic. "We shall never know, shall we?"

"If Finn never comes back—"

"We shall see," Vithius cut in smoothly. "In the meantime, it is best that we do not covet that which does not belong to us."

The comment brought Ryan's mind back to Anifiel's words on the Path to Inspiration. "How long does it normally take a human to ascend to the Upper Tier, Vithius? Is there an average?"

"Time has no true measurement in Heaven," the Angel pointed out. He dropped his arms to his sides again. "It is not a competition to see how quickly you ascend, Ryan. Every human must find enlightenment when he or she is prepared for it."

The answer, like many of Vithius', was frustrating to Ryan. Angels must have gone to school to learn how to give cryptic answers, he decided.

"Well, let's use an example." Ryan wasn't about to give up so easily. "Do you know my human friends Eric and Samantha? They sometimes hung out with Finn and me. They're brother and sister."

"I know them. They lost their human lives through the accidental actions of another."

Ryan winced. "Yeah, they were washing a car and an old lady lost control of her car and struck them. At least they died quick." He shook off the sad image. "So, um, how long do you think it'll take them to ascend?" He didn't know if Vithius had that sort of knowledge, but it didn't hurt to ask.

Vithius crossed his arms over his chest, relaxed. "It is my understanding that they have taken great leaps in their enlightenment. No one may predict when understanding will come upon a human, but I would not be altogether surprised if your friends joined the Upper Tier in the equivalent of your Earthly month."

"Wow." Ryan was genuinely amazed. "That's

quicker than I thought." To him, the twins didn't seem very, well, deep. He'd already been in Heaven a short while by the time they'd shown up, but he hadn't noticed much of a difference in them now compared to that first meeting. They still struck him as being carefree, simple, and a little slutty. "They haven't been here that long, either."

Vithius' dark eyes were piercing. "No, they have not. In your measurement of time, they have been here just over five months."

"Wow!" Ryan blurted again. "Five months? It seems like it's been about a week since I first met them." He turned over the information in his head. "Five months. That's not a very long time to take to reach enlightenment. I've heard that Tibetan monks take their whole lives to achieve that." A hopeful thought occurred to him. "I haven't been here much longer than Sam and Eric. That means I'm probably pretty close, too, right?"

"You have been in the Middle Tier nearly three years," Vithius said, watching Ryan's face.

Ryan's smile faded. "Three—three years?"

Vithius pushed off the post, one hand extended. "Every human must progress at their own pace. It is not an indication of how good your soul is, Ryan. Every human is different."

"Three years?" Ryan repeated quietly, automatically backing away from Vithius' touch.

The Angel looked troubled. "Ryan, you dwell on that which is inconsequential—"

"Eric and Sam have a combined I.Q. of 110. Sam washes cars in a bikini. Eric used to wear the same pair of socks four days in a row." Ryan heard his voice rising. "But I've been here seven times as long as they have. Why am I still stuck here? What am I doing wrong?" His voice caught. "What's wrong with *me*?"

"Ryan—"

He tried to dodge the arms that reached for him, but Vithius was quick. The Angel firmly embraced him, tucking Ryan's head beneath the Angel's chin. Ryan hid his face against the Angel's throat. Vithius smelled of pine forests and dark, wet moss. His scent was the essence of cool mountains. The essence of an Angel, which Ryan might never become.

"Why am I failing?" Ryan whispered, heartbroken. "I'm trying so hard, Vithius. I want to be good at something. I want to finally be good enough. Just—good enough..."

Warm hands rubbed soothing circles on his back. "You will be, Ryan. You will be more than good enough. You will be great. You have merely been caught in stasis. Eventually, you will encounter something which will be your ultimate inspiration. And then you will see the light of the Upper Tier. You will feel it in your soul. Until then—until then you are suspended."

"Like Sleeping Beauty?" Ryan sniffed. "She needed a kiss in order to wake up."

He could sense Vithius smiling. "Yes, Ryan. In your way, you are waiting for that kiss."

"I hope it comes soon," Ryan whispered, wiping at his eyes. "Because I'm tired of not being good enough."

~~~~~

Vithius eventually left Ryan on his own in the pavilion. Though Ryan enjoyed the dark-haired Angel's company, he needed time to think about what he was doing in Heaven. He needed time to consider his feelings and what he might need to change about himself in order to ascend.

He spent the time meditating, or lying on his back watching birds and insects fly overhead. He cried a couple of times when he recalled his life on Earth. And when he became exhausted by all the emotions, he let his mind go blank and concentrated on the image of Finn. He thought of how beloved the red-haired Angel was and tried to find aspects of his friend that he could emulate. But it was difficult, because Finn was Finn. He could never be ugly or say something to offend, hurt or anger. Finn inspired only love, and Ryan was well aware that he didn't inspire much of anything in anyone besides apathy or at his worst, disgust or pity.

And feeling that way about myself isn't going to help my case any.

Catching himself in the act of putting himself down made him aware of how often he did it. Pretty much all the time, really. *Well, step one is putting a stop to that, obviously.*

Without a setting sun or moon to mark the passage of time, he had no idea how long he remained alone. Occasionally, Angels would fly by, waving as they passed overhead. Some of them landed to speak with him, intrigued why a human was left alone in the Commander's pavilion.

Every thump of wings made Ryan's heart leap in dread. But Anifiel did not return. Wherever the golden Angel was—probably beating up those responsible for Finn's disappearance—Ryan hoped he stayed there.

Ryan still slept in cycles on the bed that had been supplied for his use. He'd long ago discovered that he didn't actually need to sleep. But he did so anyway, because he enjoyed dreaming. In this way, he was able to measure "days".

Eight such days had passed before he saw Vithius again. The black-haired Angel grinned widely as he landed outside the pavilion. Having not seen him for so long, Ryan was struck again by how handsome Vithius was. He pictured the dark-haired Angel gazing at him from across a candlelit table for two, while sensuous dance music played in the background. Vithius would be dressed, of course. Most of that tea-colored skin would be hidden beneath a black silk shirt with the throat open and the sleeves rolled up. Or maybe a white dinner jacket to set off his complexion.

Or maybe it would be better if he remained naked.

"You look well," Vithius commented, embracing Ryan easily.

And you look hot, Ryan thought to himself. He inhaled deeply as the Angel hugged him, filling his lungs with the scent of the mountains. He tentatively curled his arms around Vithius' naked sides. One brush of his palms over the hard flesh of

Vithius' buttocks, though, made Ryan quickly drop his arms again. He didn't want to embarrass himself.

"I am well." He stepped back and smiled at the Angel. "I worked some things out. I'm feeling positive. My time will come."

Vithius' pleasure with the answer made Ryan's chest swell with pride.

"You will make a glorious Angel," Vithius assured him, briefly stroking one of Ryan's curls. "I look forward to that moment."

Ryan blushed. "Thanks."

Vithius looked around the empty pavilion. "Anifiel has not returned to you?"

"I haven't seen him since we left the Path to Inspiration."

Vithius did not look pleased at that bit of information. The Angel's brows drew together and something of his battle ferocity appeared briefly on his face. Ryan nearly shivered, though not in fear.

"He must be continuing to hound the Guardians for a way to bring Finnian back. He refuses to accept the Creator's decision." Vithius' displeasure gave way to grudging fondness. "Anifiel has ever been the most determined and courageous of us all. I suppose it should not surprise me that he refuses to give up his consort without a mighty fight."

"I guess that is a good thing," Ryan mused. If Anifiel were his lover, he'd want the Angel fighting nail and tooth for him, too. So in that regard, Ryan was happy for Finn. Anifiel cherished him.

But in every other way, Ryan was happy he wasn't stuck with the cranky blond. Finnian could have him.

"Would you care to join me for a swim, Ryan?"

Swimming meant getting naked, because Ryan hadn't figured out yet where he could get his hands on a pair of swimming trunks. His smile was sheepish. "How about I just watch you?"

Vithius laughed. "Fair enough."

~~~~~~

Ryan lay on his side, his head propped on one hand as he watched Vithius glide lazily through the lake. He was used to watching Finnian bathe, who tended to splash around a lot, so it was a relaxing change to watch Vithius cut smoothly and quietly through the azure waters. The Angel's movements were slow and hypnotizing. Ryan fell happily beneath the other male's spell.

It was the first time Ryan found himself at ease with an Angel's nudity. Vithius continued to show no inclination toward covering himself any time soon and, left with no other choice, Ryan had stared at the Angel's genitals—while Vithius wasn't looking, of course—until he could look at the flesh without blushing. Ryan was rather proud of his efforts at de-sensitizing himself.

That all changed the moment Vithius strode from the water holding his cock by the base and stating, "You shared affection of a sexual nature with Finnian, did you not?"

The sensual spell snapped with an audible click.

"What?" Ryan scrambled upright and stared up

anxiously at the dripping Angel. Thankfully, Vithius didn't appear aroused in the slightest, but Ryan wished the Angel would stop holding his cock like that. It was...distracting.

"We didn't do anything," Ryan quickly assured him. "Finn is Anifiel's consort."

Vithius tilted his head before running a hand through the dark locks of his hair. He had beautiful ebony hair that looked extremely soft.

"But Finnian requested human intercourse from Anifiel."

Ryan groaned, remembering Anifiel's accusation while he had pinned Ryan down in the Lower Tier. "I guess he did. But it wasn't my idea," he added hastily.

"It comes to reason that Finnian would have experimented with you. Or else learned of such passions from you. You are his closest human friend." Vithius waited patiently.

Ryan bit his lip, trying to figure out where Vithius was going with this. He couldn't imagine any good destination. "We didn't fool around, Vithius."

Cool water sprinkled Ryan's lap as Vithius approached and dropped to his knees. The Angel regarded him curiously and still—*oh, man*—held his cock as if deciding what to do with it. Ryan had some ideas but...no.

"Would you be willing to experiment with me?" Vithius asked softly.

Ryan's eyes went round. He glanced around once, just in case this was some sort of trick that the

Angel was performing in cahoots with Anifiel.

"I-I can't," he gulped. "I mean, I-I shouldn't. Angels shouldn't get involved with things like that."

That stirred Vithius' interest. "Why? Is it wrong? Does it degrade the participants?"

Ryan thought of Anifiel's treatment of him on the cloud. "That depends on who you ask. But I'm pretty sure there's a good reason why Angels don't have sex. Anifiel probably knows all the reasons, actually." He laughed uncomfortably. "Go ask him."

Vithius frowned and thankfully dropped his hand from his cock. Ryan couldn't help stealing a quick glance at it. It was impressive, even while soft. A part of him was disappointed that Vithius hadn't gotten aroused while proposing sex with him.

"If you will not experiment with me, will you share the tales of your human experience?"

That didn't sound much better. "Kiss and tell?" When the Angel looked back in confusion, Ryan waved off the comment. "Never mind. There's nothing to tell, Vithius. Sorry to disappoint you, but my sexual escapades on Earth weren't much to write home about."

"You did not engage in sex?" Vithius looked doubtful. "You are an attractive male. I find it difficult to believe you would not attract a lover."

Ryan simply stared at Vithius. He wondered if he looked like he worshiped the Angel which, at this moment, he kind of did. To receive a compliment like that from this Angel was—wow.

"Thank you," Ryan said, eyes round. "I-I can't believe you think that."

Vithius smiled and briefly caressed Ryan's

cheek. "An Angel does not lie, Ryan. I do indeed find you pleasant to look upon."

Ryan found himself short of breath from the contact. Every time he had any kind of close—even innocent—contact with an Angel he nearly embarrassed himself. What would it be like if he actually had sex with one of them?

It would probably kill him a second time.

"I know you have had lovers," Vithius murmured. "Please tell me?" With his dark eyes trained so intently on him, Ryan would have made up something simply to keep Vithius happy.

Fortunately, he didn't have to lie. "I fooled around with a couple of guys," he admitted hesitantly. "I only had sex once, though." He felt himself blushing hotly at the not-so-pleasant memory.

"It was pleasurable?"

"For him, yes," Ryan answered honestly. "It was the first time for both of us. And he, um, went too fast and didn't use enough lube—lubrication. It burned a lot. He was nice to me afterwards—he didn't mean to hurt me—but it still wasn't the best way to lose my virginity."

Lost in the memory, Ryan was alarmed to find that Vithius was very close to him. He leaned back, but the Angel followed him.

"Tell me what it feels like when another male is inside your body," Vithius whispered.

Ryan gasped. His face blazed even hotter, but not from embarrassment. He quickly slid a hand over his groin to hide the sudden bulge beneath his tunic.

"Vithius—I made a mistake with Anifiel." Ryan looked up with pleading eyes. "Please don't make me do the same with you. I want you to like me."

Vithius' eyebrows lifted. "I will not cease to like you for telling me of your experiences. An Angel does not judge, Ryan."

Ryan gave a weak laugh. "But this is something different."

To his relief, Vithius sat back, giving Ryan room to breathe again. The Angel studied Ryan's flushed face, which only made him blush more. Vithius then nodded.

"It will help you if you do not have to look me in the eye," Vithius declared.

Ryan's brain was still frazzled. "What do you mean?"

"While you relate your experiences to me." Vithius nodded, making up his mind. "Yes. I see you are a shy human. It is very appealing."

"That doesn't help," Ryan muttered, immediately imagining the dark-haired Angel boldly overcoming his shyness. His cock pulsed hotly between his legs. He had more than a few fantasies of being overwhelmed by another man. He wished it weren't an Angel reminding him of those dreams, though.

"Roll onto your side," Vithius instructed.

"We're not going to have sex, are we?" Ryan hoped he sounded offended, rather than as excited as he actually was.

Vithius chuckled. "You said I should not

participate in such an act. Therefore, you will only tell me about it. Roll over, please."

Bemused, not completely trusting the Angel even though he was an Angel, Ryan cautiously rolled onto his side. He watched nervously from over his shoulder as Vithius smiled his approval and lay down on the grass behind Ryan. Unable to see the other male clearly, Ryan turned his head and stared straight ahead.

He could feel Vithius hot against his back. The Angel wasn't touching him, but Angels must radiate tremendous amounts of heat because Ryan was burning up. He was especially aware of the nape of his neck—always a sensitive spot for him—and the pull of his tunic across his hips.

Was Vithius looking at his butt?

In my dreams.

"Now tell me," Vithius whispered, his breath rushing over Ryan's ear. "Tell me how you made love with another male."

Ryan swallowed a moan and clutched the grass to keep himself from rolling back against Vithius. He couldn't believe how much the sound and feel of Vithius' voice turned him on. What was it about Angels? For non-sexual beings, they inspired the most outrageous urges in him.

"What did—" Ryan cleared his throat,"—what did you want to know?"

A puff of breath tickled the curls around his ear. Ryan shut his eyes. "What did your human lover look like? Was he beautiful like Finnian?"

Ryan shook his head.

"Was he dark like I am?"

This is so not good, Ryan thought anxiously. He shook his head.

A weighted pause. "Do you think of him when you see our great Commander? Does your body leap at the sight of Anifiel because he reminds you of human sex?"

The turn of phrase made Ryan groan. "They don't look alike, honestly. Anifiel is taller and-and more muscular, and his hair's more gold—"

"And yet he reminds you of this male who pleasured your body," Vithius prodded, his voice slow and warm.

Ryan's heartbeat thundered in his ear as he felt Vithius draw closer to him. He waited for a touch, his nerves straining, but the Angel didn't make contact.

"If Anifiel were capable of this human love, what would it be like?" Something soft and wet touched the top of Ryan's ear and his cock literally jumped beneath his tunic. "How would he pleasure you? What would he do with his body? I wish to know."

"Anifiel would probably beat me to a pulp," Ryan joked, but it fell flat. He and Vithius both knew he wasn't imagining Anifiel hurting him. Ryan gulped. "Please don't make me do this," he whispered.

Vithius asked lightly, "Anifiel is pleasurable to look upon, is he not?"

"If-if you ignored his personality," Ryan agreed carefully.

Vithius chuckled. "And if you did, you could

see him as he is..."

"Gorgeous," Ryan whispered.

"What kind of lover would he be to you?" Vithius wondered, aloud. Something brushed lightly over Ryan's buttocks. He sucked in his breath harshly, his fantasies spinning out of control. "Tell me what he would do with you, Ryan."

This can't be wrong. He's an Angel. We're in Heaven. This can't be wrong. Ryan latched onto the reasoning because he knew he couldn't hold out against Vithius' seductive questioning any longer.

"When males become aroused," he began hesitantly, eyes clenched tight, "their sexual organs lengthen and...become very hard."

"Like yours is now?" Vithius made a sound deep in his throat. "You are hot and you writhe like a serpent in the grass. Your organ must be firm."

Ryan shivered at the husky question. "Yes."

He longed to touch himself and measure just how hard he was. But that would be pushing this too far. At this point all they were doing was talking. If he masturbated, it would become something more. Something Ryan wasn't sure he wanted to share with Vithius. At least not yet.

"If Anifiel were aroused and his organ grew, it would be magnificent," Vithius commented in a deepening voice. "He has a powerful staff."

Ryan found himself nodding in agreement. He wondered if Vithius had ever considered Anifiel sexually. Ryan was pretty sure the Angel had. Finnian couldn't be the only curious Angel in Heaven...

A wet touch to the back of his neck made Ryan moan softly in surprise and lust. "Vithius—"

"What would you wish Anifiel to do to you as a lover?" Vithius' tongue traced a circle against the nape of Ryan's neck. Round and round until Ryan couldn't help but imagine that circle being drawn between his legs. Around the head of his erection...

"Tell me how he would pleasure you," Vithius coaxed.

"He'd kiss me hard," Ryan whispered. The fantasy grew in his mind, potent because he knew it would never happen; Anifiel was too much of a jerk. But the illusion of the golden Angel made for a highly charged fantasy. Anifiel was the perfect inspiration for lustful thoughts. "He'd hold my head still so he could kiss me as hard as he wanted." Ryan remembered the scent of Anifiel in the pavilion. "He'd taste of apples."

"Apples." Vithius' voice was hushed.

Ryan nodded and licked his lips. "After he stopped kissing me, he'd be desperate for me. He wouldn't be able to control himself." Ryan moaned and squeezed his legs together. He really liked the idea of high and mighty Anifiel wild with lust for him. It made Ryan hot. "He'd roll me onto my stomach and flip up my tunic so he could grab my butt with both hands."

Ryan imagined that firm grip massaging his cheeks and he twisted against the grass anxiously. "He would squeeze me and tell me how much he liked touching me."

"What would he do with his organ?" Vithius asked eagerly. "How does he use it?"

Ryan stabbed his fingers into the grass, gripping the stalks when all he wanted to do was grab his throbbing erection. "He'd put it between my legs and push...push it up inside my body." Ryan finally fell backwards against Vithius' chest, groaning as his own words made his insides quiver. "Anifiel would open me up on his cock. Make me take the whole length of him in one hard thrust. It'd be so intense that I'd open my mouth to tell him to stop. But I wouldn't be able to say anything because he'd know and he'd start pounding into me, making me cry out. Making me moan and beg him even though I know I shouldn't."

He couldn't believe the words coming out of his mouth. He was turning himself on and, judging by Vithius' panting breaths, was doing a good job on the Angel, too. Ryan's legs began to spread of their own volition. He knew his tunic must be tented by the fierce arousal that jutted from between his legs.

Strong hands gripped Ryan's shoulders. He opened his eyes blearily to find Vithius looking down at him with passion-filled eyes.

"So he would be inside you?" The Angel sounded as breathless as he. "His organ would penetrate you?"

"Penetrate me," Ryan moaned, the words making his hips rotate. "As far as he could go." He shuddered at the crudeness of the words. "He'd make me spread my legs—make me take his entire length. And it'd be good, Vithius. It'd feel incredible to have him inside of me. A part of me."

"Intimate," Vithius breathed, eyes shining. "As

one."

The tone of the Angel's voice finally pierced Ryan's senses. He blinked twice, clearing the glaze from his eyes. Vithius above him was as flushed as he'd ever seen an Angel become.

"You do want him," Ryan gasped.

Vithius' eyes widened. He shot to his feet, practically dumping Ryan onto the grass.

Ryan propped himself up on his elbows, doing his best to ignore his aching groin. He studied the tense muscles of the Angel's back. "You don't only love him as a fellow Angel or warrior. You want him as a lover."

Vithius shook his head vehemently. "Anifiel belongs with Finnian. The Creator has made this so."

Ryan waved away the familiar defense. "That's what everyone keeps telling me. But what about you? And what about the other Angels? Aren't you allowed lovers, too?"

"Yes. But..."

Ryan sat up completely. "But, what?"

Vithius turned around again and for the first time, Ryan saw an Angel's body aroused. He whimpered as his eyes drank in the sight of Vithius' firm, swollen cock curling up from the dark hair between the Angel's legs. Ryan had to fight every urge in his body that demanded that he crawl to Vithius' feet and take that beautiful cock between his lips.

"Ryan—" The Angel looked almost panicked as he looked down at his weeping sex. "I have never experienced this feeling before."

Ryan rubbed his backside against the grass as his inner muscles clenched. "You're aroused. It's alright. It happens to me all the time." *Let's do something about it.*

Vithius' expression was tortured as he lifted his head. "But I feel this way for Anifiel. It should not be so."

The whispered confession combined with Vithius' obvious misery dampened Ryan's lust. He forced himself to take a series of deep breaths, willing down the ache in his body.

"He's incredible looking," Ryan shared reluctantly. "It's normal that you'd be attracted to him, Vithius. I can't stand him, but I'd have sex with him in a second."

"You would?"

"Yeah, but, don't tell him that, okay? I meant it when I said I can't stand him."

That made Vithius smile, and with it the Angel's lean body visibly relaxed. His cock still stood at rigid attention and Ryan still battled the inner demons that demanded he launch himself at Vithius, but the Angel no longer looked as stressed.

"Anifiel will never be mine. He is my battle companion and nothing more," Vithius said sadly. "The Creator wishes for him to be with Finnian. I respect that."

"But—" and here Ryan wondered where the betraying words were coming from, "—what if the Creator has decided it's time for Anifiel and Finn to separate? What if that's what this whole thing is about?"

Ryan loved Finn. He truly did. So although his words were technically stabbing the red-head in the back, Ryan didn't think of them that way. He thought of this as saving Finn from someone who didn't deserve him. Anifiel wasn't good enough for Finn. He probably wasn't good enough for Vithius, either, but at least Vithius would be thrilled to have the golden Angel. Finn hadn't always appeared to be completely happy to be locked in his unique situation with the Commander.

Ryan could salvage this for everyone.

"Think about it, Vithius. The Creator is giving all of you a chance to find new partners."

"Or the Creator is testing our loyalties," Vithius pointed out darkly.

Ryan flushed. "Well, yeah, there's that, too."

He was beginning to feel more than a bit bad about himself, sitting here with a hard-on while trying to coax an Angel to seduce the lover of his only real friend. "Look, maybe—"

"Would you help me to test Anifiel's feelings?" Vithius said slowly.

Ryan nodded eagerly. "Of course. I'd love to help you. I think—I think you two would be good together."

Vithius' expression remained doubtful. "But Finnian?"

"Knowing Finn, he's already roped some poor human into falling madly in love with him," Ryan joked. But he hoped it was true.

Vithius' doubt began to give way to hope. "And you?"

Ryan gaped. "What about me? I don't want

Anifiel!"

Vithius laughed. "Why did you shout that?"

"Just wanted to make sure there wasn't any doubt in your mind," Ryan mumbled. Because there shouldn't be. There was no way in Hell—the Beneath—that Ryan wanted Anifiel. *No way, Jose.* "He's all yours, Vithius. You can have him."

Vithius beamed. "Then you and I shall test Anifiel's interest in me."

Ryan grinned. "Better than that. I'll help you win him over."

It sounded like a great idea.

Operation Seduce Anifiel had just gone into effect.

4

Seduce Anifiel.

Yes, such a good idea. But weren't most good ideas doomed to failure? This wasn't something as harmless as playing around with Finnian. This was Anifiel. Heads would literally roll if things went wrong. And Ryan's would be the first to drop. He was the bad influence, after all.

But surprisingly enough, it was Vithius who assured Ryan that their plan held merit.

"I know Anifiel as few others do save Finnian," the Angel had stated confidently. "If there is a way to win his heart, we shall find it."

So Ryan forged ahead with his scheming, even though guilt still lingered in the back of his mind. He felt like he should be turning over rocks looking for Finnian, or at least sitting around fretting over his friend's disappearance.

But Vithius assured him there wasn't anything

either of them could do to bring the redhead back. Anifiel was wasting his time trying, but neither Vithius nor Ryan were about to tell him that. So they let the furious Angel tromp around Heaven, intimidating the Angels and humans he came in contact with.

"We shall do him a service by distracting him from his pain," Vithius told Ryan, a smirk on his lips.

Angels could scheme, too, apparently.

By Ryan's questionable time keeping, a week and a half had passed since they'd last seen Anifiel. He and Vithius were in the pavilion, waiting for Anifiel to return. Ryan wondered how many blubbering victims now cowered in the golden Angel's wake.

"What is on your mind, my human friend?"

Ryan tapped his chin with a forefinger. He'd been thinking long and hard about their strategy to seduce Anifiel. He had a vested interest in seeing the plan succeed.

"As much as I get off on the idea of seeing you jump him, I think we need to take a different approach with him. He's one of those macho control freaks. We need to trick him into thinking he's the one dictating this entire seduction."

"I do not want to trick Anifiel. If he does not truly desire me, I will respect his decision."

"That's not what I meant. Anifiel needs to see you differently," Ryan declared. "That's the key to this whole thing."

"See me differently?" Vithius was lounging on

his back on the grass, his wings tucked beneath him. His long, dark legs were spread casually, framing his soft sex. Ryan was trying hard not to look anywhere but at his friend's face. "How does he see me now?" the Angel asked curiously.

Not the way he should, Ryan thought, his brain still burning from the sight of Vithius aroused.

He was glad he was lying on his stomach beside the striking Angel. His earlier effort at de-sensitizing himself had completely bombed. Erections seemed to be par for the course whenever he was in Vithius' company and it was very embarrassing even though the Angel didn't seem to mind, nor ever let on that he noticed Ryan's reaction. But Ryan knew and that was bad enough.

"He sees you as his battle companion," Ryan elaborated. "You're asexual to him. Well, more so than usual. Finn's the only person he's ever thought of in a romantic way." He paused, crinkling his brow. "And that's only because of the bond. I think Anifiel feels compelled to want Finn by his side, but there isn't any sexual urge there."

"There is not," Vithius confirmed, chewing on a stalk of grass. His dark eyes watched the clouds move. "There is only boundless love and affection."

When Vithius started to frown, Ryan quickly sat up. "But it's an unnatural bond, remember? Anifiel and Finn have never been given a choice. This is our chance to test whether that attraction is genuine or not. I'm betting that it's not."

"Anifiel loves Finnian very much," Vithius said softly, wistfulness sweeping over his handsome features. "I have yet to experience such feelings for another."

Ryan laid his hand upon a muscled shoulder, resisting the urge to caress the taut skin. "But you have experienced those kinds of feelings. You feel them for Anifiel. In fact, you feel more for Anifiel than he's ever felt for Finn. You lust after him."

"Lust," Vithius breathed, tasting the unfamiliar word. "It is a new feeling. It is very...powerful."

Ryan's cheeks heated. "Yeah, it's pretty potent stuff. You've got to be careful. It can make you do some pretty dumb things." *And I've done them twice now.*

"Lust is dangerous?"

Ryan carefully avoided the black eyes that searched his face. "It can be. But usually only if the feeling isn't mutual. Unrequited lust can be bad news. It makes you act without thinking of the consequences. But if we learn that Anifiel can be aroused by you—" oh, god, "—then everything will be okay."

He forced a hopeful smile, trying with all his might not to imagine Anifiel actually being aroused. Ever since seeing Vithius with a hard-on, Ryan's dreams had been tortuous. What was it about an Angel's sexuality that was so much more intense than a human's? Vithius' cock wasn't any larger than ones Ryan had seen in magazines. The Angel's body was worth drooling over, but it wasn't completely amazing. Anifiel might possibly lay claim to that, though Ryan needed to see him naked, first.

Regardless, there was something about Anifiel and Vithius that reduced Ryan to a puddle of goo.

Any kind of contact—or even nearness, he'd noticed with humiliation—filled him with the overwhelming urge to do anything for them. To worship them. To love them with every inch of his body and allow them to do the same to him.

I am in so much trouble here.

So it was probably a really, really good idea to set the two Angels up with each other. It would keep Ryan from making a further fool out of himself if they were too involved with each other to notice him. *I wonder if they'd let me watch, though?*

"So!" he said loudly, jumping out of his thoughts. "Once Anifiel admits he wants you, then everything will be good. The bond will be broken and you and Anifiel will be happy."

He smiled brightly, falsely. It hung unspoken between them that Finnian's fate would be left uncertain. Ryan prayed his friend was doing alright. Finn's super-human powers of seduction had to work the same on Earth, right? Ryan fervently hoped so. It was better to believe that Finn was on Earth being loved. Ryan couldn't stand to think of the alternative.

"Do you prefer that we not do this?" Vithius' tone was gentle. His posture, even while reclining, reeked of noble self-sacrifice. "I have long lived in the shadow of their love. If I must continue to reside there, I shall survive."

The resignation in the dark-haired Angel's bearing tore at Ryan's heart. What they planned to do might be wrong, but Ryan didn't care. Finnian deserved someone better. Vithius deserved to be happy. And Anifiel—Ryan didn't care what that bully wanted. He would be lucky to receive Vithius.

"We'll do this," Ryan said, squaring his shoulders. "The least we can do is try. If Anifiel isn't interested, he's a fool. And if he is, then he's a lucky Angel."

Vithius reached up and ran the backs of his fingers down Ryan's throat, prompting him to swallow nervously. "I cannot wait until you are an Angel," Vithius whispered.

Ryan's voice came out like a squeak. "Why?"

Vithius just smiled and didn't answer him.

~~~~~

At the rate they were going, Ryan would be in the Middle Tier another three years before Anifiel returned.

"We've got to find him," he insisted, looking imploringly at Vithius. "He probably knows I'm here waiting for him so he doesn't want to come back."

Vithius shook his head. "Anifiel does not run from anything, much less an uncomfortable confrontation. His courage is boundless."

"Yeah, well, he's not coming, Vithius." Ryan looked to the skies he had been scouring day in and day out. The sky was blue and perfect but it didn't hold their wayward Angel. "We have to go to him. We have to bring this to him."

Vithius rubbed his chin thoughtfully. "Pursue him."

"No, just...find him." Ryan shifted

uncomfortably beneath Vithius' suddenly piercing gaze.

"The idea of pursuit disturbs you," Vithius noted. "Tell me why this is?"

Ryan sighed, turning away from the Angel. "I don't want to get into it. I just—it's complicated."

In truth, it was laughably simple. When he was alive, Ryan had chased the men he'd been attracted to. He'd been pathetic. A loser. A needy little gay boy. It shamed him to think of how he'd acted. And it was worse to dwell on how he'd been rejected time and time again by straight and gay men alike.

Vithius thought that Ryan was a human worth knowing. He believed Ryan would one day make a glorious Angel. Ryan wanted to keep that illusion intact.

He turned back around, his chin raised. "But you're right: we need to find him. So we should go."

Unfortunately, brains and beauty did go together. Ryan stepped back as the Angel approached him, shaking his head in disapproval.

"Why do you attempt to deceive me again?"

Vithius was up against him, surrounding Ryan in the cool scent of pine trees. The solid wall of his chest seemed to bounce Ryan's hormones right back at him. "I thought I am your friend, Ryan?"

He forced himself to hold the Angel's dark gaze. "You are my friend," he whispered. "You're my only friend now that Finn is gone."

"Then why—"

"I want you to stay my friend," Ryan insisted. There was no hiding the bitterness in his voice. He looked away, ashamed. "Right now you like me, so let's keep it that way. Please, Vithius."

He shivered and shut his eyes as Vithius' lips brushed his ear. "We shall always be friends, Ryan. Forever and always. You cannot drive me away from you."

Ryan clutched the Angel's hard biceps to keep himself upright. Vithius' nearness was dizzying. "Vithius, please—" he moaned softly.

Vithius stroked his hair soothingly. "Come, my friend. Be at ease. Let us find the Commander."

Dumbly, Ryan allowed himself to be turned. Those strong arms wrapped around him, pulling him back against the Angel's chest. Ryan kept his eyes closed until they were in flight. The brisk wind cooled his heated cheeks.

"I hope this works," he said, watching the landscape whiz past them. "I hope he gives you what you want, Vithius. You're a good Angel. I want you to be happy."

Vithius chuckled gently and squeezed him. "I am already happy, young Ryan. Having Anifiel's love will merely make me more so." His words sighed out, "It will make me complete."

"What is it?" Ryan finally asked. "What is it about him that you love?"

Because he couldn't understand the interest in Anifiel. Was it a purely physical attraction? No, it couldn't be, he quickly reminded himself. Angels didn't think that way. What, then, did Vithius see in the domineering Angel that Ryan couldn't?

"You see him differently," Vithius commented.

Ryan snorted. "You could say that. He's been

nothing but rude and mean to me."

"He defends Heaven. He defends me." Vithius' wings beat steadily, each down stroke sending them faster through the air. "He would face a horde of Demons with his bare hands to protect me and those he loved. I cannot help but admire his courage." Shyly he added, "I cannot help but be thrilled by his noble heart."

Ryan was embarrassed that he'd asked. He felt like an intruder on Vithius' feelings, which had next to nothing to do with carnal desires and everything to do with goodness and greatness.

"I also desire his firm buttocks," Vithius added.

Ryan choked on his own spit as the dark-haired Angel chuckled.

"That wasn't funny," Ryan muttered, wiping his mouth with the back of his hand.

"Indeed," Vithius murmured, sounding suspiciously smug.

Ryan watched the landscape pass beneath them and realized he knew where they were heading. "The Path to Inspiration?"

"I know my battle companion well," was Vithius' suddenly solemn reply.

Vithius kept them high in the air as they flew over the clearing with its row of gleaming statues. But it wasn't so high that Ryan couldn't clearly make out the figure of Anifiel kneeling upon the white pebble path at the foot of Finnian's statue.

"What is he doing?" Ryan whispered, staring at the bent golden head.

"Ah, Ryan." Vithius' voice held sadness. "Do you not recognize loneliness when you see it in another?"

Ryan's eyes widened as they swept over Anifiel's downcast head and slumped shoulders. He couldn't see the Angel's expression from their vantage point. He wasn't sure that he wanted to. An odd ache squeezed his chest.

"He really misses Finn," he whispered.

"Anifiel loves him," Vithius replied in a tight voice.

They circled the Path twice before Vithius beat his wings to take them away. Anifiel never once raised his head, and Ryan was glad of it.

~~~~~~

Ryan needed to get away from Angels. They were stressing him out. As soon as Vithius returned him to the pavilion and flew away, Ryan sought out his only human friends.

It wasn't the reunion he was hoping for.

"Gah! You're both naked!" he cried out in dismay as the twins ran down a hill to join him. Bobbing breasts and a bouncing cock were the last things Ryan wanted to see while his libido was strained to its limits.

"So what?" Sam challenged, jiggling her breasts with her hands. "There's no reason to be ashamed, Ryan. We're in Heaven."

"Yeah, buddy!" Eric echoed his twin. He had a hold of his limp cock and wagged it at Ryan as if it were speaking to him. "Just be free!"

"We're in Heaven, not Woodstock!"

The twins laughed at his exasperation. "You're too uptight, man." Eric grinned widely and slapped Ryan on the shoulder. "Something got you worked up?" He winked and wiggled his hips, making his cock dance like a worm on a hook. "Or is it just me?"

Ryan groaned and slapped a hand over his face. "No, it is not you. Will you quit shaking that thing at me?"

"Aw, Ryan, with Finn gone, we have no one else to play with," Sam teased. To Ryan's relief, her expression grew more serious. "Have you heard anything about him? You've been spending time with the Commander, right? Does he think Finn will be back?"

Ryan sighed and dropped to sit cross-legged on the grass. The twins sat across from him. "Anifiel's trying, but I don't think he can do anything about it."

Eric's green eyes went round. "So Finn's stuck?"

"Maybe. I don't know. Look, I'd actually rather not talk about it. It makes me depressed." Ryan forced a smile. "So how have you guys been? I haven't seen you in a while." He waved vaguely in the direction of their nude bodies, trying not to make eye contact with any genitals. "This is new."

Samantha giggled. "Isn't it weird? One day we asked ourselves, why are we embarrassed by our bodies? There's nothing to be ashamed of. We're in Heaven!"

"So we ditched the tunics and we've never been happier," Eric finished for his sister. "You should try it, Ryan. It's liberating."

Sam nodded. "Once the clothes came off, it was like we got rid of a bunch of baggage." She shrugged, making her breasts jiggle. "It was weird. But in a good way, you know?"

"Uh huh." Ryan smiled weakly at them. "I'm happy for you guys. That's great. I don't think I can do that just yet. In fact I know I can't."

Eric patted his knee. "That's okay. It's probably not a good idea to be naked while you're hanging around the Commander anyway, am I right?" He wagged an eyebrow. "He's the best-looking Angel in Heaven. You probably throw wood every time you're around him."

"Oh, geez," Ryan muttered. "I do not." He could feel himself blushing.

"Ha! I knew it!" Sam crowed, pointing at him. "You're perving on Finn's boyfriend! I always suspected that about you."

"What?" Ryan scowled. He hated when people acted like they knew what he was thinking when even he had no idea. "I'm not interested in him. He's a total jerk."

Sam rolled her eyes as she fell backwards to recline on her elbows. It put her in a suggestive pose that left Ryan glad he was gay otherwise he would indeed be throwing wood.

"Please," she scoffed. "Every time Anifiel showed up while we were hanging out with Finn you'd start stammering and getting all nervous. It was sooo cute."

"And obvious," Eric added helpfully. "We all knew you were hot for the Commander."

Ryan wanted to slap them both silly. "Are you nuts? The guy is a megalomaniac. You'd stammer too if you thought you were going to be beaten to a pulp by his wings. He doesn't want anyone hanging around his consort. Especially not humans."

"Whoa, dude, you're really upset by this." Eric held up his hands defensively. "Looks like someone's in denial."

"I am not in denial!" Ryan wanted to tear his hair out. These two were ascending to the Upper Tier before *he* was?

"I am not. Interested. In Anifiel," he ground out. "End of story."

Sam shrugged again. "Not for nothing, Ryan, but it's going to be hard getting into the Upper Tier if you continue to deny how you feel."

That shut Ryan up like a slap to the face. He looked at his two human friends and realized she was right. They were right and he was wrong. And yet he had no idea how to change that.

"I'm not happy here," he blurted. He looked expectantly from brother to sister. Sam and Eric appeared shocked by his admission. It made Ryan feel even more alienated.

"But, Ryan," Eric began, "how can you not be happy in Heaven? It doesn't get better than this!"

"That's right," Samantha echoed, wide-eyed. "If you're not happy here, well—there's nowhere else left!"

"I know," Ryan said, choking on the words. He heard the fear in his voice. "So what do I do?"

He was met with two pairs of blank green eyes.

And that was the problem. It wasn't until he'd seen his friends again that he realized it was *his* problem. No one could help him to solve it because no one else understood it. Sam and Eric were ascending to the Upper Tier not because of some fluke, but because they deserved to. They'd come to an understanding about themselves. Ryan could make fun of them all he wanted, but in the end it was he who would be stuck in the Middle Tier for the rest of eternity, not them.

"It was—it was great seeing you guys," he mumbled, standing up, "but I gotta go." He looked away from the pity on their faces. "I'll keep you informed if I learn anything about Finn."

"Ryan, wait—"

He turned his back on them and ran across the hills as fast as he could.

~~~~~

Vithius was waiting for him at the pavilion. One look at Ryan's face and the Angel strode up to him and wrapped Ryan in his arms. "You are upset."

"I'm confused," Ryan clarified. "Which makes me upset, which leads to a big circle I can't figure out." He forced himself to step out of the comforting embrace. He was tired of being perceived as weak. Maybe he was, but he didn't want it to be anyone else's problem but his own. "Don't worry about me. Our biggest challenge right now is you."

Vithius was one of those rare males who could show vulnerability as easily as he could show his determination and strength. The ebony eyes he turned upon Ryan were soft and open with understanding.

"I would hope that you would come to me if you need to discuss something that is bothering you," he murmured, briefly cupping Ryan's cheek. "Though you are my first and only human friend, I find myself dedicated to achieving your happiness."

And just like that, it didn't matter to Ryan that Eric and Samantha thought he was in denial, or that Ryan couldn't figure out what his true purpose was in Heaven. He had one good friend who would be there for him. Ryan vowed he would do the same in return.

"What would make me happy is to see you and Finn happy. That's what matters most to me at this point. And the way that's going to happen is if Anifiel ends up loving the Angel he's supposed to: you."

A light flush came to Vithius' cheeks. Was the Angel blushing? Ryan was enthralled.

"That remains to be seen," the black-haired Angel demurred.

Ryan smiled at his friend's reaction. For a moment he felt a pinch in his heart. Anifiel didn't deserve Vithius. But that really wasn't for him to decide.

Hypocrite! I decided that for Finn!

No, this was different.

"I think it's time we got serious, Vithius. We

need to find him and put Plan A into effect immediately."

Vithius arched an elegant eyebrow. "Plan A? I was unaware we had such a plan."

Ryan tapped his forehead. "It's up here, and it's a good one. But it won't work if we don't have Anifiel. Do you have an idea where he might be?" He hoped it wasn't the Path to Inspiration again. Seeing Anifiel kneeling at the foot of Finnian's statue had left Ryan feeling too guilty for comfort.

Vithius' eyes panned the mountains in the distance as he considered the question. "I know of a place he goes when he wishes to be alone. He goes there often after battles. When his heart is heavy." He flashed a warning look at Ryan. "But as I said, he goes there to be alone. He will not take kindly to our presence."

"That's just too bad. The whole idea behind this plan, Vithius, is to ruffle Anifiel's feathers. He's too used to being the big man on campus. We've got to shake him up."

Vithius looked uneasy with the idea. "Anifiel does not take well to being shaken."

Ryan's smile was more confident than he felt. "He doesn't have a choice in the matter, does he?"

~~~~~

Anifiel's private spot was not too far from the Forest of Contemplation. It lay in the meadows where few, if any Angels ever tread.

Ryan held his breath as he and Vithius coasted

down to the clearing where Anifiel sat upon a small knoll. Vithius set them down beside a stream that wound its way past the foot of the hill where Anifiel sat. They were a good fifty or so yards away from the golden Angel, but Ryan knew Anifiel had seen them come in.

Anifiel remained where he sat, one arm propped on a bent knee while the other leg lay extended before him. His expression was unreadable as he looked at the interlopers. He might have been curious as to why his peace had been broken, but Ryan doubted it. The mighty Angel was probably trying to figure out how best to beat them black and blue for the invasion of his privacy.

"So far so good," Ryan muttered, leading Vithius to stand within the cool stream. The water barely reached mid-shin. "Are you sure you want to do this? We can fly away now and forget we ever considered this."

Vithius looked steadily at Anifiel, who for his part returned the attention impassively. "He is glorious to me," Vithius said so softly Ryan had to strain to hear him. "It is worth every risk to have him desire me in return."

Ryan cleared his throat, uncomfortable at witnessing his friend's infatuation. He felt like a voyeur to Vithius' passion. "He will," he assured his friend. "He has to."

Vithius broke the eye lock with the other Angel and smiled down at Ryan. "You are so certain. It gives me hope."

"Anifiel just needs to see how attractive and sexy you are," Ryan told him.

"You think I am attractive and sexy?"

Ryan blushed beneath the interested look Vithius gave him. "It's pretty obvious," he muttered, moving around behind the Angel. "I doubt you need me to say it."

"No one has ever said as much to me."

That gave Ryan pause. Of course Vithius would never have been complimented like that. Who would tell an Angel that besides him?

"Well, you are," he said more firmly. "And it's time we made your Commander aware of it, too." He hesitated as he stared at the dark-haired Angel's smooth, muscled back, which only moments before had sported luxurious wings. "I'm going to kind of—massage you," he mumbled, glad Vithius couldn't see his red cheeks. "I think if Anifiel sees me touching you he'll begin to look at you differently."

Vithius' face turned in profile. "How will massaging me make me appear differently?"

"Just trust me." Ryan had a trick up his sleeve that he wasn't about to reveal just yet. "Glance over there and tell me if he's looking this way."

Vithius' head turned away. "He has not stopped looking since we entered the water."

Ryan smirked. "Good. This may be easier than I first thought."

Before beginning their flight, he had requested a bottle of oil from Vithius. He removed the stopper from that bottle, pouring a small amount of oil into his palm. The luscious scent of oranges wafted from the bottle's throat. Soap would have been more practical, but this wasn't about washing Vithius. It was about touching him. Oh, was Ryan going to enjoy this.

"Whatever I do," he began after he tossed the bottle onto the grass beside the stream, "don't turn around, okay? This is for Anifiel. I know it's going to work."

"I trust you, Ryan."

I wish I could trust myself, Ryan thought with an inward laugh.

"Alright, here goes."

He rubbed the fragrant oil between his hands and then slowly placed his hands on Vithius' strong shoulders. His palms glided over the smooth swells of muscles as he mapped the Angel's shoulders and upper back. Vithius' skin glistened where the oil touched it, giving it the illusion of being coated with a thin sheen of sweat. It was how Ryan imagined Vithius would look after a long bout of sex. Ryan's cock, already half-full, swelled completely.

He breathed deeply, trying not to hyperventilate as he massaged his way down the long lines of muscle bracketing the Angel's spine. Vithius had the beautiful body of a swimmer—sleek, yet powerful. His upper body tapered into the perfect V. Ryan's fingers dug into the firm bundles of muscle while his palms pressed in, easing out knots and kinks. Vithius released a quiet moan.

The sound made Ryan freeze, his eyes shooting to the back of Vithius' dark head. The Angel didn't turn around, so after a moment, Ryan continued his careful massage. He rubbed the heels of his palms in circles across the other male's concave lower back. This was one of Ryan's favorite parts of a man's body, so he spent a few minutes stroking and caressing the smooth indentation. Vithius moaned again, a little louder this time.

"Is he still watching?" Ryan whispered as his fingers drifted lightly across the upper swell of Vithius' buttocks.

The Angel took a suspiciously long time in answering. "He is...looking in our direction."

Ryan nodded to himself and let his hands slide down either side of Vithius' hips. He couldn't help letting his palms slip into the dimples of the Angel's powerful buttocks. Vithius was so defined that the dimples resembled hand holds. Ryan shuddered and tried not to think too hard about that.

He kneeled in the stream, his tunic greedily soaking up the water, and massaged his way down the Angel's strong thighs. Vithius had dark hair here, but it wasn't too thick. It was a tactile contrast to his skin and Ryan took a moment to push his fingertips through the dark hair to stroke the skin beneath. Then down he went, squeezing calf muscles that would make a bodybuilder envious until he came to Vithius' ankle. Then he slowly made his way back up to repeat the process with the Angel's other leg.

Vithius groaned appreciatively. "You are very skilled with your hands," the Angel murmured above him. "This is pleasurable."

"Thanks. I've always wanted to do this for a sexy guy," Ryan mumbled. He flushed red when Vithius laughed.

"I am grateful I am worthy of your attentions, then."

If you saw the front of my tunic you'd know who should really be thanking who, Ryan thought wryly. He was aching something fierce and he was pretty sure the wetness on his tunic wasn't entirely from water.

He cleared his throat and instructed, "Spread your feet a bit."

Vithius obeyed without hesitation and from his kneeling position behind the Angel, Ryan was faced with an unobstructed view of his tightly drawn sac. He could tell Vithius was hard, which was the point of this whole thing. But Ryan needed to up the ante and make Vithius irresistible to Anifiel.

"Whatever I do," he told his friend, "just relax. Trust me."

"I do."

Ryan stood and did what he'd wanted to do since pouring the oil into his hands—he cupped Vithius' buttocks. He tentatively squeezed the tight globes and heard himself give a groan of longing.

"Vithius, if Anifiel doesn't desire you, he's an idiot," Ryan gasped, sliding his palms up and down the curve of the Angel's buttocks. "You're perfect."

Vithius' reply was an indistinguishable murmur. His shoulders rose and fell as if he were breathing more heavily as Ryan caressed him. Ryan tried to picture what Vithius looked like to Anifiel with his body aroused and trembling. The thought nearly sent Ryan to his knees.

But this wasn't done yet. Ryan still had to apply the icing to the cake. Willing down his own impending orgasm, he slid his fingers into the cleft of Vithius' buttocks. The Angel jerked, startled, but when Ryan merely rested his fingers in the crack, Vithius relaxed again.

"This is going to feel a little weird," Ryan warned softly. When Vithius remained silent, Ryan carefully pushed one cheek to the side, revealing the Angel's virgin pucker. Listening intently for his friend's reaction, Ryan slid the fingers of his other hand down the cleft, letting the tips brush lightly across the other male's opening. Vithius' reaction was every bit as intense as Ryan had hoped.

"Ryan!"

Vithius arched his back and clamped his buttocks together, squeezing Ryan's fingertips between them. For a second, Ryan feared his fingers might end up broken. "Vithius—"

The powerful muscles relaxed, allowing him to withdraw his fingers. Vithius spun around in the water, nearly gutting Ryan with his fiercely aroused cock.

"What did you do?" Vithius demanded.

Ryan swallowed and felt his knees tremble. Vithius' normally smooth, sleek hair now fell in tousled waves around his temples. His cheekbones were highlighted faintly with color and his black eyes looked like pitch. His magnificent chest heaved.

"You're gorgeous," Ryan whispered with awe. When he realized what he'd said, his eyes widened, but Vithius appeared not to have heard him.

"The fashion in which you touched me..." The

Angel trailed off, looking both perplexed and helplessly aroused.

"I-I'm sorry," Ryan stammered. "I thought if Anifiel saw you turned-on he'd be unable to help himself."

Vithius turned his head, seeking Anifiel. The golden Angel still sat upon the hill, watching them. "But he remains where he sits."

The disappointment in Vithius' voice broke through Ryan's erotic stupor. "I can try something else—"

"No!" Vithius' head whipped around. A touch of shyness softened his expression. "I need time to absorb this new sensation. I think it is time we employed a new tactic. One of...jealousy."

Uh oh.

Ryan took a step back, acutely aware of the way his cock tented the front of his tunic. "That's not such a good idea, Vithius. I really shouldn't get involved in this. Anifiel hates me, remember? He might hate you for liking me."

A smirk slid over Vithius' face, the look so sexy Ryan bit the inside of his cheek to keep from swooning like a girl.

"No, you are wrong. He has been aware of my feelings for him for a long time. I believe he takes it for granted. If he were to see that I may show interest in another, he may react the way we wish him to."

"W-what about another Angel?" Ryan looked around frantically, but of course there was no one else here. It was why Anifiel had chosen this spot. "I mean it, Vithius, this isn't the best idea. You should do this with another Angel. Someone Anifiel would believe you're interested in."

Vithius closed the distance between them. "He would believe I am interested in you."

The husky words sent shivers down Ryan's spine. He could feel that weird Angel fugue that he'd experienced with Anifiel coming over him again. In another minute he was going to be flat on his back with his legs in the air. "Vithius, please..."

"I am going to remove your tunic," the Angel whispered, holding Ryan's gaze and refusing to allow him to look away. "You will trust me, because I will not hurt you. I would never hurt my friend."

"Vithius—"

The world spun and suddenly Ryan found himself facing the hill where Anifiel sat. A touch to his shoulder let him know that Vithius was now behind him.

"I am going to remove your tunic. Do not be afraid."

Easier said than done. Ryan never removed his tunic except when he bathed, and even then he made sure he was alone. But his mind flashed back to his conversation with Eric and Samantha. They were moving on to the Upper Tier. If he wanted to join them it would probably be a good idea to start changing the way he felt about things like modesty.

"Go ahead," he said on a loud exhalation of breath. He fisted his hands. "Do it."

The fabric whipped over his head, leaving him standing shivering in the stream. The water wasn't cold and neither was the air. His body was burning up actually, but he couldn't stop himself from shaking. He was afraid to look to the hill to see Anifiel's expression. If the Commander was laughing at him, Ryan would be crushed.

"You are beautiful," came a whisper against his ear.

Ryan laughed nervously. "Sure. Whatever. Just get on with it, okay? I'm not exactly thrilled with this."

"But you are doing this for me, and for that I am grateful." The warm hand squeezing his naked shoulder was surprisingly relaxing. It reminded Ryan that however humiliating this might be for him, this was ultimately for Vithius' benefit. Vithius, his only friend now that Finn was gone.

Ryan relaxed slightly. He took a deep breath, which made him feel better. "Go ahead, Vithius. It's alright."

He heard the Angel open the glass bottle. Ryan's skin broke out in goose bumps as he anticipated the touch of slippery hands against his bare skin.

The first touch nearly made his knees buckle. He closed his eyes and tried not to moan as strong hands kneaded the tight muscles in his neck and shoulders. Vithius wasn't a massage therapist but he made up for his lack of knowledge with firm, confident strokes that soon had Ryan melting where he stood.

Strong fingers worked in ever-widening circles down his back, finding tight knots and working them out until Ryan's head fell back in sheer pleasure.

"Wow," he breathed, "you're good at this."

Vithius said against his ear, "I enjoy touching your body. I have never touched anyone this way. It is inspiring."

Inspiring. Ryan smiled. Yes, that was a good word for it. He was inspired to have about ten hours of non-stop sex right about now.

"Is Anifiel watching?"

Ryan's head jerked up. Crap. He'd forgotten about the reason for this little love fest. Reluctantly he glanced toward the hill. Green eyes were pinned to Ryan's face. The heat in those emerald orbs stole Ryan's breath.

"He—he's watching." Ryan gulped. "He might look upset. I can't tell for sure."

"Excellent. He is becoming jealous." Vithius' hands boldly grabbed Ryan's butt. Ryan would have jumped a foot in the air were it not for the firm grip the Angel had on him. "Let us inspire him to movement."

"What do you—"

A slippery finger slid down his crack. Ryan gasped and began to twist away, but he was too late. The blunt end of Vithius' finger caressed his hole.

"V-Vithius!"

"Let him see how much pleasure I bring you," Vithius urged, his voice nothing less than warm honey. "Let him wish it were he in your place."

Vithius' finger stroked back and forth across his opening, each pass sending a shudder down the length of Ryan's body. How long had it been since he'd been touched back there? At least three years, wasn't it? Three long, long years. He was practically a virgin again. He was definitely responding like one.

"Mmm, Vithius...oh...yes."

"This brings much pleasure, does it not? It feels nice to be caressed this intimately by one who wishes to see you undone."

When had Vithius become Heaven's version of a sex phone operator?

"You touched me only briefly," the Angel continued in a lust roughened voice, "but it brought me exquisite pleasure. You are feeling it, yes?"

"Are you joking? Of course I—nnh!" Ryan squeezed his eyes shut as the finger at his opening pressed in experimentally. "Oh, please, Vithius...d-don't do that."

"Why?"

The hot rush of air against his ear made Ryan give up and let go the way he'd been yearning to.

"B-because it feels—too good," he moaned.

Teeth nibbled on the nape of his neck. "This is where Anifiel would mate with us, is it not?"

An image filled Ryan's head of he and Vithius laid out on the grass, legs spread while Anifiel switched back and forth between them, drilling his cock into each of them until they both reached incredible orgasms.

"Don't say that!" he gasped, his eyes shooting open.

He looked to the hill and it was the wrong thing to do. Anifiel was striding towards them, his face a thunderous mask.

"Vithius!" Ryan cried out in warning.

Right at that moment, the dark-haired Angel pushed a single finger into Ryan's body. The last thing Ryan saw before he shut his eyes and came in a jetting arc of pearl was a scowling Anifiel storming straight toward him.

5

What are you doing?" Anifiel demanded in a booming voice as he splashed through the water toward them. "What are you doing to my battle companion? Answer me!"

Ryan stared up fearfully at the golden Angel, his knees on the verge of buckling. "I-I—"

"He is teaching me the ways of human pleasure," Vithius replied, gently removing his finger, which made Ryan bite back a moan. He felt empty inside as the Angel placed a supportive hand on his shoulder. "It is something I was curious about and asked him to show me."

"He is corrupting you!" Anifiel exclaimed, scowling at his fellow Angel, and then down at Ryan. "He is turning you in his own devious, human way." He frowned deeper. "And what is this?"

Ryan followed the path of the Angel's hand as Anifiel reached down and scraped something off of

Ryan's abdomen. The touch of the Angel's fingers against his bare stomach made Ryan's legs shake, but what made him nearly pass out was when he realized what Anifiel had just scooped up.

"Oh, that's—that's, uh, that's nothing," he stammered in mortification as Anifiel inspected the dollop of cum on his finger. "Human stuff. Just—er, just ignore it." *Please*.

"Human 'stuff'?" Anifiel's brows lowered even further. He brought his finger to his nose and sniffed.

Oh, my god, Ryan thought, staring at the Angel's mouth. *Please don't...please don't*...If Anifiel tasted him, he'd faint right on the spot.

Fortunately—or was it?—Anifiel didn't do anything more than smell the fluid before he bent and swished his hand through the stream to clean his skin. Watching the magnificent Angel wash him off like that, as if the release of his body was something dirty, made Ryan deflate.

But what did he expect, after all? The day a glorious Angel like Anifiel wanted to taste him was the day Heaven and the Beneath switched places. There was a clear class system in Heaven and Ryan was in the lowest one.

"Disgusting," Anifiel declared. "Everything about humans is disgusting."

"It's natural," Ryan mumbled, hanging his head.

"What did you say?"

Anger lifted Ryan's head. "I said it's not disgusting. It's natural. And—and it's more than natural. It's beautiful." He pointed a finger at the taller male. "Stop trying to make me feel bad about myself. Just stop it. I'm sick of it!"

Anifiel's eyes narrowed. "I do nothing to shame you. That is your own doing." He pointed at Ryan's softening cock. "You taint Heaven with the device of your sin. You defiled my battle companion's body by urging it to mimic your responses. You have much to be ashamed of."

The words infuriated Ryan. The edges of his vision went red and he lost it. "No, I don't! Stop making me out to be some pervert! I turned Vithius on because he liked what we were doing. But you wouldn't know anything about pleasure like that because you're as sexual as a rock. I pity Finn for being stuck with someone as boring as you! He was probably going crazy with sexual frustration!"

Anifiel's face turned a dull red. His mouth pulled so tight his lips nearly vanished.

Vithius' hand on his shoulder tightened warningly. "Ryan, please calm yourself."

"No!" Ryan shook off his friend, backing away from both Angels until he stood on the grass. "I'm done being the helpless, dirty human who gets all the blame. Anifiel's a jerk." Ryan glared up at the golden Angel, who returned the look just as fiercely. "He's worse than that but we're in Heaven and I'm actually trying to be good, believe it or not. Forget about him, Vithius. I know I'm not an Angel but I can make you happy the way he can't. I can treat you with respect and—and love."

He didn't know where the words came from— he wasn't even sure he meant them—but what Ryan did know was that he didn't want good, kind Vithius falling into an abusive relationship with Anifiel. Forget about Operation Seduce Anifiel. Ryan would rather protect his friend. He hadn't been able to help Finn but now that he knew the score, he could certainly help Vithius.

He held out his hand to the dark-haired Angel, who looked confused and concerned as he watched Ryan back away. The Angel's erection had wilted, but his body was still turned toward Anifiel, to Ryan's dismay.

"Please, Vithius," Ryan tried to reason with the lovesick Angel. "You don't want him. Anyone else just—not him. I'm not letting two of my friends become chained to someone like him."

"Someone like him," Anifiel repeated, taking a step out of the stream toward Ryan. Ryan wished he possessed wings so he could race out of there. "What does that mean, *someone like him?*"

Anifiel growled as he advanced on Ryan who, for his part, backpedaled as fast as he could. Why do I have to be naked during this? Ryan thought wildly as his limp sex flopped between his legs.

"You know what I mean," he shot back, stumbling as his heel caught in the grass. He quickly righted himself, but Anifiel had gained ground and was an arm's length away, reaching for him. "Get away from me!" Ryan cried.

He gave up dignity and turned to run. He got no further than a yard before a large hand shoved him between the shoulder blades, sending him sprawling across the grass.

He grunted as his chin hit the ground, then

grunted even louder when a sandal-covered foot pressed down on his spine, pinning him.

"Get off, you big bully!" He tried to push upright but it was like doing a push-up with an elephant sitting on his back. He collapsed into the grass, red-faced. "I hate you," he gasped, stalks of grass rippling violently in front of his mouth. "I swear I've never hated anyone as much as I hate you, Anifiel."

"You say this as though I should be bothered by it," was the droll reply. "What do I care if a measly human dislikes me? I have no need of your regard or your affection. I have no need of you at all, nor does Heaven."

The words crushed Ryan. He'd heard them before in different combinations:

"Sorry, guy, but you love a little too hard, you know?"

"No offense, Ry, but you're a little clingy. I need a break."

"We didn't raise you to be gay...it's better if you don't come home for a while."

He closed his eyes to hide the tears and dropped his forehead to the dirt.

"Heaven may not need him but I do," announced the calm, clear voice of Vithius. "Ryan is my friend."

"And you forget where your loyalties lie," Anifiel retorted sharply.

Vithius sighed. "Or perhaps I am not afraid to expand them."

Ryan listened to them with only half an ear. He lay still, emotionally exhausted. He breathed in the sweet aroma of the grass and tried to pretend that he was alive again and that he was in a park and there were years ahead of him in which he could turn his life around. Years in which he could make his life his own and be happy with it. He'd read and heard the stories about young gay men who were not afraid to be who they were. He'd always thought one day he would be one of them, living proudly with a boyfriend, living freely...

But Anifiel's foot shifted, the leather sole grinding into Ryan's skin, and Ryan couldn't hold onto the illusion however hard he tried.

Another place, another existence, and you still can't be anything other than what you are, he thought, bitterly. *Once a loser, always a loser. The truth will always find you.*

"Just let me go and I promise you will never see me again," he said dully. He opened his eyes and stared at the hills rolling out before him. He doubted it could be difficult to disappear in Heaven. The place was huge and no one would miss him. No one would come looking for him. "Let me go and I promise I will stay out of your way."

But instead of sounding pleased, Anifiel scoffed above him. "Let you go? And what of my consort? Do you believe I will allow you to slink away unpunished for his defection? You are responsible for his disappearance. Therefore it is you who will find a way to bring him back to me."

Ryan pounded the ground with his fists. "I don't know how! Why won't you listen to me?"

"Anifiel, stop this at once!"

The foot slid off his back. Ryan rolled over in time to see Vithius push his fellow Angel backward. Anifiel's handsome face went slack with surprise.

"Leave Ryan alone," Vithius demanded, facing up to his battle companion.

Ryan was ashamed that he grew aroused watching the two magnificent Angels square off against each other. *I'm so hard up, it's pathetic.*

Vithius stood toe to toe with a shocked but angry Anifiel as he stated, "This human is no more responsible for Finnian's actions than you are. We all know that curiosity has ever been Finnian's weakness. This time it overcame him. If your consort's disappearance may be blamed on anyone—" Vithius hesitated, "it should be blamed on Finnian himself."

Anifiel paled. "Dare you speak ill of my consort?"

"You know that I hold tremendous affection for him," Vithius soothed. "I point out his curious streak only as a possible explanation for Finnian's actions." He looked down at Ryan, the Angel's expression instantly softening. "Do not blame this human. He is my friend and he is a friend of Finnian's. He would not willing hurt either of us. Nor would he hurt you, though you have been no friend to him."

Anifiel's wings suddenly burst free, fluttering anxiously from his shoulder blades. Ryan stared, bewildered by the act. Nothing on the golden Angel's face reflected anything but pure fury.

"I lost my consort because of him. I will not lose my battle companion, also!" Anifiel grabbed hold of Vithius' arm, the golden skin of his hand a bright contrast to the other Angel's dark bicep. Anifiel pulled Vithius closer and Ryan held his breath, wondering if the great Commander was going to kiss his friend right in front of Ryan. "I refuse to let this human turn you," Anifiel said urgently. "You are my strength, Vithius. I rely on no other in my hour of need. Do not forsake me."

He's begging, Ryan thought, his jaw falling open. Anifiel is begging. Was the glorious Angel softer than he appeared?

"If you allow yourself to be corrupted by him I will turn my back on you and banish your name from my memory!" Anifiel bellowed.

Ryan winced. Okay, maybe begging was jumping to conclusions.

Vithius pulled his arm free with great reluctance. Ryan could see his friend's inner turmoil even if Anifiel could not.

"You are the greatest Angel of Heaven," Vithius murmured, staring deeply into the other Angel's eyes. "You are courageous and mighty and you possess a heart that humbles me. I will be there for you always. But understand too that Ryan is more than my friend. He inspires me to new feelings." Vithius' cheeks darkened as he glanced away shyly. "I do not believe these feelings are sinful for they bring me much joy."

Ryan's heart melted. Vithius was a dream come true, a dream Ryan had never dared to have. He ached to embrace the gorgeous Angel and show him what little he did know of sex and love.

"You are falling to temptation as Finnian fell," Anifiel accused in a hushed voice. Betrayal and hurt flashed across his features so quickly Ryan was half certain he'd imagined them. He must have, for the Commander's face immediately became harder than stone without any trace of vulnerability. Anifiel was granite. "All because of this human," he muttered angrily.

Ryan cringed when Anifiel's green eyes swung his way. Anifiel had a gaze that pinned you in place and peeled open your soul. For the barest of moments, Ryan imagined that intense look turned upon him for different reasons. In the bedroom. He gasped when he realized it would be the most incredible, intimate moment of his life. *No! I don't want him that way!*

"I will not allow you to be stolen from me," Anifiel insisted, his gaze locked with Ryan's. With another Angel, Ryan might have hoped Anifiel was speaking of him, but in this case it was clear who Anifiel wanted. "He may not have you. You are my companion, Vithius. You are mine."

Ryan dropped his eyes when he saw Vithius take a deep breath of excitement. Here was what Vithius had wanted: Anifiel staking a claim. Ryan had wanted it for his friend, too. Now, he wasn't so sure. He imagined Anifiel's possessive gaze upon him in the dark, and he felt again Vithius' supportive hand on his shoulder, and Ryan wasn't so sure what he wanted anymore.

"You cannot have your consort as well as me," Vithius said softly, his voice laced with a nervous flutter. "You must choose."

Ryan looked up at his friend's boldness. Anifiel was studying the other Angel with a closed expression. Ryan realized too late that he and Vithius had been playing Anifiel for a fool. The Commander was no fool.

"You are wrong. I may have you both because you hold separate places in my heart," Anifiel stated simply and firmly. "And that is how it will be."

Ryan read the slump of Vithius' shoulders and his heart ached in shared disappointment. It wasn't fair. Someone gorgeous and kind like Vithius, one of the most attractive males Ryan had ever known in this life or his previous one, had been rejected. What hope did that leave for *him*? Ryan quickly scrambled to his feet.

"If you come with me, Vithius, you will be the only one in my heart," he declared, feeling a little foolish at the formality of his speech, but suspecting Anifiel would respond better to it. He held out his hand to the dark-haired Angel. "I will give you all the love and affection that Anifiel won't. Forget about him. Be with me and I will make you happy."

Vithius turned to him, his eyes wide. "Ryan—"

"Enough of your meddling!" Anifiel pushed past Vithius and grabbed Ryan by the elbow. "You covet everything in my possession, is that it?" he hissed. "You seek to take everything from me."

"It has nothing to do with you!" Ryan protested, but he flinched back when Anifiel leaned toward him.

The golden Angel stilled, a dark gleam coming into his eyes. His voice was a low burr as he said,

"Indeed, as I suspected it has everything to do with me."

Oh, crap.

Green eyes swept his body and there was no way for Anifiel to avoid seeing Ryan's half-hard, swiftly rising cock.

"It's because I'm angry," Ryan tried lamely to explain. "Sometimes stimulus will do that."

"I understand too well," Anifiel murmured, and Ryan's lungs were filled with the crisp, dizzying aroma of green apples. As the Angel continued to stare at him, Ryan felt his face flush with heat. Anifiel locked gazes with him and he very slowly smirked.

"I smell you again, little human," he whispered.

Ryan swayed in the Angel's grip. "Leave me alone," he panted, drowning in waves of lust.

From over the commander's shoulder, Ryan saw Vithius approaching them. "Anifiel, leave him—"

"You will not see this human again," Anifiel announced in his deep voice. He abruptly launched himself into the air with Ryan dangling precariously from his grip. "Say your farewells, Vithius."

Ryan's screams drowned out whatever Vithius called out in response. The last Ryan saw of the dark-haired Angel before he closed his eyes in terror was Vithius hugging himself in concern.

~~~~~

Ryan kept his eyes closed until he landed. His wish that this was all a bad dream shattered when

Anifiel dropped him lightly onto the grass outside of the pavilion. He opened his eyes as Anifiel herded him into the enclosure and once there, yanked him around to face the Angel.

"I am wise to your deception with Vithius," Anifiel told him, eyes narrowed. "I abhor your tactics of seduction. You taint my battle companion with your deviousness. He would never have attempted such a thing on his own."

"He loves you," Ryan gasped, feeling only slightly guilty over spilling his friend's secret. He had a feeling Anifiel already knew, anyway. "How can you turn him away when he's willing to do anything for you? He's ten times a better Angel than you. You should be on your knees, begging for his attention."

Anifiel's lips curled humorlessly, the slashes on either side of his mouth digging in stubbornly. "And you know this how, pray tell? From your experience in Heaven? Yes, that must be it, for you are a veteran of the Middle Tier, are you not? Three years is it?"

Ryan trembled with emotion. He wanted to slap Anifiel. He only refrained because he was afraid if he started, he wouldn't stop.

"Why do you hate me?" he asked in a strained voice. "From the moment you saw me with Finn, you've hated me. Why? Are you that insecure? Is the great Commander of Heaven's Army afraid of a little competition? Maybe you're lacking in some department that the rest of us don't know about."

He knew he was inviting the worst sort of

retribution but he was beyond caring. Anifiel drove him past all restraint and reason. Plain and simple, Anifiel drove him crazy.

"So conceited to think that it was you I cared about." Anifiel laughed harshly. "Did the Earth revolve around you while you lived, little human?" His eyes raked Ryan briefly. "Something tells me that was not the case."

Something in Ryan finally snapped. He yelled and dove for the taller male, trying to tackle him to the ground.

Except the problem with trying to tackle an Angel like Anifiel was that you couldn't do it. Ryan jumped up, wrapping arms and legs around Anifiel's torso, but the Angel didn't topple over; he just stood there. Ryan felt like an idiot and tried to rectify it by grabbing fistfuls of golden hair. That spurred the Angel into action.

"Enough of your foolishness!"

Ryan cried out as iron manacles—also known as Anifiel's fingers—wrapped around his wrists and pried his hands away from the Angel's head.

"You wish to act like a beast," Anifiel panted, striding towards the bed with Ryan now flailing and trying to escape, "then you will be bound like one."

Ryan's heart leapt into his throat at the words, but there was no escaping the powerful Angel's intentions. Though he thrashed wildly with every ounce of his strength, he couldn't prevent Anifiel from pinning his limbs to the bed. As Ryan bucked against the arms and legs holding him, he heard the leather cords on the Angel's lace-up sandals snapping and then felt the thin cords wrapped around both wrists.

Ryan looked up, gasping for breath, as Anifiel leaned over him, crushing his bound wrists between them.

"Do you wish me to bind your feet, or will you behave?"

Ryan's cheeks burned with humiliation. He wanted to shout an obscenity at the infuriating Angel, but at the last moment better sense ruled. He shook his head vehemently.

"Very good," Anifiel murmured with a patronizing smile. He leaned back slowly, leaving Ryan panting on the bed with his wrists bound before him. The Angel's eyes skimmed over his nudity, pausing on Ryan's cock which, to his consternation, was fully erect. Anifiel raised an eyebrow at this. "Your body enjoys my company far too much I think."

"Don't flatter yourself," Ryan shot back, though he couldn't deny that his body hummed from the contact with the handsome Angel.

"Flatter myself..." Anifiel considered the words as his eyes continued to linger on Ryan's groin. "If this reaction is not because of me, then what reason is there? You last hardened this way when my battle companion was touching you." Anifiel's voice sharpened, though his expression remained carefully neutral. "You play with Vithius to your peril, little human. There are worse ways to end up in the Beneath than by being pushed out of Heaven for seducing Angels."

Anifiel opened his hand, revealing a feather.

One of his own. Ryan held his breath as Anifiel touched the brilliant white tip to Ryan's inner thigh and slowly dragged it upwards. Ryan tried to roll away, but a large, hot hand landed on his knee, stilling him. Ryan swallowed hard as the delicate feather drifted up to his scrotum and gently touched it. He closed his eyes and released a shuddery breath.

"Human bodies are quick to rouse," Anifiel commented softly, using the feather to circle and trace the circumference of first one tight ball and then the other. "It may be considered a weakness."

"Only...you—would say that," Ryan gasped, rolling his head on the pillow as the feather moved, this time teasing his perineum. He didn't want to— he tried to resist, he really did—but he couldn't prevent his thighs from parting and baring more of himself for Anifiel's explorations. He bit his lips as the tip of the feather tickled between his buttocks. "Stop—" he gasped, opening his eyes and trying to sit up. "Stop teasing me."

"Spoken by one who sought to do the very thing to me, did you not?"

Ryan gulped as he locked gazes with Anifiel. Shame filled him that the Angel had caught on to his and Vithius' plan.

Ryan shook his head. "It's different. What we did didn't bother you because you said yourself that you don't want him."

Anifiel lifted the feather and brought the tip that had touched Ryan to the bottom of his own lip. "Different you say? Why? Because this time you play with me?" Anifiel dragged the feather across his mouth, teasing Ryan with the possibility that he could taste Ryan. "Or different because unlike with Vithius, you do desire me?"

When Ryan remained silent, Anifiel dropped the feather, letting it float to the ground. "My consort is Finnian," he announced, all teasing gone. "My battle companion is Vithius. These roles will not change no matter how you interfere." Ryan cried out when Anifiel grabbed a handful of his curls and dragged him off the bed to fall to the ground. Ryan balanced on his knees as the Angel stood above him, one hand still tight in his hair. "And what role is yours in this, little human?"

"As the defender of everyone you come in contact with!" Ryan retorted angrily.

He didn't know where this passion came from. He was amazed by it. On Earth he had been quiet. Reserved. Go with the flow, was his motto. Yet here in Heaven he had become some sort of crazy crusader whose focus was the greatest Angel in Heaven—the one Angel he was least likely to sway. What kind of a masochist am I? he wondered. He didn't have an answer for that but he really didn't need one.

Since the moment Ryan had learned that Finn's companion was Anifiel, Ryan had been hyper aware of the Commander in a way he never noticed anyone else. But was that a good thing? Or would it bring his destruction?

"You don't deserve Finn or Vithius," he told Anifiel, fisting his hands in front of him. "They're too good for you."

But Anifiel didn't grow angry as Ryan expected. The Angel studied him for long minutes, his expression unreadable.

"If I do not deserve them," he began calmly, "whom do I deserve? Tell me."

The mellowness of Anifiel's voice, such a stark contrast to his usual over-the-top bellowing, made Ryan shiver. He licked his lips nervously as Anifiel continued to watch him. Again, Ryan was struck by how intensely Anifiel looked at a person. It was as if you were the focus of his world and he would stave off any who tried to come between you.

He bit his wet lip when Anifiel shifted his grip from Ryan's hair to the back of his neck. "Tell me," the Angel urged softly. "Whom do I deserve?"

The Angel fugue was coming over him. Ryan tried to fight it, but it was like fighting someone offering to give you a blowjob—who was crazy enough to say no? He sank down beneath the gentle but steady pressure on the back of his neck until his forehead hovered inches from the ground. He braced himself there with his bound hands. Anifiel's foot, bare of the laces, slid forward and a voice in the back of Ryan's head shouted in outrage. But the voice was quickly muffled.

"Do you deserve me, Ryan?" Ryan barely noticed the alteration of the question as he stared at Anifiel's bare foot mere inches from his face. Warm fingers kneaded the back of his neck. Ryan shuddered in pleasure.

"Yes," he whispered, licking his lips again. Anifiel's foot was strong just like the rest of his body. Golden hairs curled around his ankles and a few stray curls dusted the tops of his square toes. The arch of his foot was magnificent. It reminded Ryan of ancient Roman archways—beautiful and elegant, yet built to withstand the weight of a hundred passing armies. "I deserve you," Ryan went on. "I do."

The weight on his neck increased and Ryan gave in to it, moaning as his lips touched the top of Anifiel's foot. He parted his lips and touched his tongue to the Angel's skin. Anifiel tasted salty, not dirty. Ryan imagined this to be the taste of Anifiel's skin elsewhere on his body and the thought made him hump the air in excitement.

Ryan closed his eyes and kissed down the top of Anifiel's foot to the base of the Angel's toes. He'd never done something like this before. A minute ago he would have said this was the lowest of the low, especially when it concerned Anifiel.

But as Ryan dipped his tongue between each strong toe, listening to Anifiel's breath change tenor, Ryan accepted that he had rarely been as turned on as he was now. He pictured himself on his knees before the most glorious Angel of Heaven, kissing and licking his feet and Ryan couldn't help moaning in rapture. He wanted to worship. He wanted to adore. He wanted to be Anifiel's slave for the rest of eternity.

"Yes, you are an obedient human, aren't you?" Anifiel said in his deep, sensuous bass. His fingers caressed the nape of Ryan's neck, making him whimper in uncontrollable lust. "You find pleasure in knowing your place." Ryan licked him more passionately, trying to suck a toe between his lips. Anifiel chuckled with pleasure. "Yes...rest easy, little human, for now that I know, I will not let either of us forget."

Ryan moaned helplessly, his cock so hard he considered humping the dirt floor to find relief. Yet he immediately rejected it because the denial of his pleasure was part of the turn-on. Anifiel wasn't giving back anything except the offer of himself, and Ryan loved it.

"What is going on?"

Vithius' shocked voice brought Ryan crashing to his senses.

"Oh, my god!" he cried out in horror, wrenching himself out of Anifiel's grasp and falling backwards onto his ass. He pointed shaking fingers at the golden Angel. "What did you do to me? You—you put me under some spell, you sick bastard! You made me k-kiss your feet...oh, my god!"

Anifiel smirked at Ryan's blustering. "You enjoyed it and you will do it again, so spare us the dramatics, human."

"Anifiel, I do not approve of this," Vithius said, upset, as he strode up to the other Angel. He extended a hand down to Ryan, but Ryan stumbled awkwardly to his feet on his own.

Vithius studied Ryan's shakiness with disapproval before turning to glare at Anifiel. "You know as well as I that humans respond strongly to us. It is unfair and dishonorable of you to take advantage of him this way, Anifiel. I do not approve."

"And you are not my keeper, Vithius." Anifiel pointed smugly at Ryan's fierce erection. "I did not force interest where it did not already exist, as you may see. I sought to show the human his place so he would cease trying to usurp others'." He smiled at Ryan. "He now knows where he stands—or should I say, kneels."

Ryan thought he was going to throw up. "You're sick, you know that? The only good thing about you was that you had Finn. Vithius keeps telling me that I'll come to see how wonderful and great you are, but I doubt that will ever happen. Finn was the only good part of you and now that he's gone all of Heaven will see you for the mean, vindictive Angel you really are!"

Anifiel's face went still. "You do not know me," he growled. To Ryan's surprise, he took two great steps onto the grass and launched himself into the air.

"The truth hurts, doesn't it?" Ryan yelled after him. But as soon as he said it, he felt awful. This was Heaven and yet he was acting more terribly than he had at any time during his natural life. What was going on?

"Say no more, Ryan."

Ryan turned guiltily to Vithius, but the Angel looked more sad than angry with him.

"You misunderstand Anifiel and I can see why that is, but I pray that your feelings for our Commander will change. He hurts and he is frustrated. I am sorry he is using you to assuage his pain. You do not deserve it, Ryan."

Ryan's lips still tingled from their contact with Anifiel's foot. As strong as his shame over what he'd done, he held an equal amount of desire and *that* he couldn't deal with.

"Maybe I do deserve this," he said in a dull voice. He yanked at his arms and laughed when the cord binding his wrists fell loose almost instantly. "The fall to the Beneath may be closer than I thought."

Vithius' brows drew down. "No! Never think that, Ryan. You are good and strong and it is as I told you—"

The dark-haired Angel broke off with a gasp at the sound of trumpets blaring across the land. It sounded like a thousand trumpets braying at once, reaching every ear in Heaven.

Ryan's heart jumped. "What is that?" He instinctively sought the safety of the Angel. "What is that sound?"

Vithius' face was grim. "That, my friend, is what I wish you would never have had to hear." He ran out to the grass with Ryan following anxiously at his heels. The Angel turned to Ryan and embraced him hard. He pulled back to hold Ryan at arm's length and said, "Stay in the Middle Tier, Ryan. You will be safe here. Do not leave here!"

Ryan gaped as his friend released him and jumped into the air. "Wait! Where are you going?"

"To join my battle companion," Vithius called back as he flew off. "The Eternity War rages."

Ryan gasped in denial, but he couldn't deny the terrible truth: the normally quiet sky was suddenly filled with a thousand speeding Angels. They darkened the sky like an immense flock of giant birds.

"To Ambriel's Gates!" he heard one of them cry.

They were heading to do battle with the Demons.

6

Watching the Angels whiz through the sky overhead reminded Ryan of a mass missile attack. There were so many, and yet none of them were armed. He hoped someone was waiting on the battlefield with weapons for them.

He watched them fly for several minutes as his worry began to grow. He had sent off Anifiel and Vithius to fight while they were uneasy with their relationship. Would it affect their ability to defend each other?

"Ry, you have messed up big time," he muttered, gnawing anxiously on this thumbnail.

But he had to tell himself that this was the Commander of Heaven's Army and presumably the next best warrior in Vithius. They were professionals. They wouldn't let unrequited love and lust and a way weird threesome get in the way of business.

Would they?

Yet the more he thought about what had gone down by the stream, the more he stressed. Anifiel knew that Ryan and Vithius had conspired to trick him. Vithius had been point blank rejected by his object of affections. Both of those things were enough to distract them, even for a second. And only a second was all a Demon would need to come between the two Angels and do something terrible...

Sam! Eric!

Ryan concentrated on his friends the way he always did in order to contact the other humans. Finn, too. Unless the brother and sister were busy, they usually showed up right away. He also concentrated on regaining his tunic, which he'd left by the stream. He relaxed once he felt the familiar weight of the fabric magically materialize over his body.

"Ryan! What's up?"

Ryan turned and tried not to wince when he saw his friends running toward him, still naked as jaybirds. *I really gotta get used to this.*

"Dude, did you see all the Angels take off?" Eric said excitedly as he and his sister joined Ryan by the pavilion. "How rad was that, huh?" He stopped and looked at the pavilion. "Oh, wow, is that what I think it is?"

Sam clutched Ryan's arm as she, too, stared at the construction. "Is that the Commander and Finn's home?"

"Yeah." Ryan looked at it sourly, his experience with the place not as great as his friends apparently thought it should be. "But look, guys, I didn't bring you here to stare at their place." He waited until the two siblings gave him their attention again. "Do you know how I can get down to the Lower Tier and watch the battle?"

Samantha's mouth fell open. "Why do you want to go there, Ryan? You know we're supposed to stay in the Middle Tier during the Eternity War."

Ryan did some fast thinking. "There's something I need to do. Something that's important to helping me ascend to the Upper Tier."

Eric lifted an eyebrow, skeptic. "Something to help you ascend?"

"Guys, I was naked with both Vithius and Anifiel," he told them, receiving wide-eyed looks in response. "That's one step, but now I really have to do this next thing. I really do."

"But, isn't breaking a rule like this going to hurt instead of help?"

Ryan smiled weakly at Eric while his stomach did flip-flops. He knew he was buying himself another year in the Middle Tier with this stunt, but what was four years when he'd already been stuck here for nearly three? Besides, Anifiel had already warned him that ascension was going to be next to impossible while he remained on the Angel's hit list. Ryan had nothing to lose.

"It's okay, Eric. Trust me. I know what I'm doing." He studied the twins. "So how about it? Do you know how I can get there?"

As he'd hoped, they exchanged guilty glances. "Maybe," Sam hedged. "But, Ryan, an Angel told us that part of the reason we're getting closer to ascension is because we didn't explore our discovery. You're doing the exact opposite. Are you completely sure you want to do this?"

A sudden image of Vithius, falling to a Demon, made Ryan shiver with dread. "I'm sure," he told his friends. "I have to get down there."

Eric and Sam shared more silent communication before Eric finally nodded. "Okay, come on. We gotta hurry if you want to be there before the action starts. Or maybe it already has."

"I hope not," Ryan mumbled as he joined his friends in a run.

Distance, like Time, had no real measurement in Heaven. A mile could be as short as a foot or as long as a marathon. Ryan didn't know how long to expect to run, but it didn't turn out to be for very long. He followed the twins over a tall hill and found himself facing a small pool with a short fountain of bubbling water in the center.

"What's this?" He looked around. His friends were standing on the edge of the pool, looking at him expectantly. Was there a magic ladder he was missing somewhere?

Samantha pointed at the pool. "Eric was curious to find out why it was bubbling like that so he dove in there." She grinned. "Guess where it goes?"

Ryan didn't bother debating the physics of what they were describing. "It drops down to the Lower Tier?"

Eric nodded. "It freaked me out at first. I fell out onto a cloud. It's a trip, man." He studied Ryan critically. "But Sam's right—you shouldn't do this unless you're sure. Accidentally breaking a rule is one thing; breaking it on purpose...I dunno."

"It's worth it," Ryan assured them. Or maybe he was reassuring himself. He suddenly wasn't so sure this was a good idea.

But it's for Vithius and he's worth an eternity in the Middle Tier, isn't he?

Of course he was.

He looked down at his tunic, briefly debated removing it, then decided to leave it on. He wasn't about to watch the great Eternity War while he was bare-assed naked. He turned back to his friends and gave them a crooked smile he hoped didn't look as nervous as he felt.

"See you later, guys. I'll give you a play-by-play of the action when I get back."

The twins just watched him with identical looks of worry on their faces as he jumped into the water. The pool was maybe double the size of a hot tub. Ryan immediately swam to the bubbling water in the middle. He took a deep breath and dove beneath the surface, fighting the upsurge. The pressure was surprisingly firm and for a second he thought the twins were wrong and he was going to be spat back up to the surface.

But then the water pressure gave way as if there was a hole in the current. Ryan swam downwards and slipped through the calm center. One minute he was swimming, the next he was falling through the air.

He yelled as he fell about six feet, landing on the softness of a cloud.

"Holy cow!"

He immediately looked up. The pool of water shimmered in the air above him like a translucent rain cloud. He could see the sky through it. He stood up and extended his hand. His hand sank into the bottom of the water up to the wrist. When he retracted his hand, it was dry.

Wow.

He raised his hand again, but the sudden trumpeting of horns made him jump. The horns held an unmistakable tenor of urgency. They were extremely loud; the gates and the Army must be close. His heart pounding, Ryan began running in the direction of the fading notes.

It hadn't occurred to him that the Lower Tier wasn't made up of grass, only clouds. When he'd been down here before, he'd been flying with Finn or Anifiel, and hadn't paid much attention. His focus had been on the Earth below.

Running wasn't easy. The first time he needed to leap across a gap to an adjacent cloud, his heart was in his throat. It didn't get better. As he leaped from cloud to cloud, his feet landing on the odd sponginess of cloud, he could see the air between. Far, far below was the Earth. And farther down lay the Beneath. He tried not to think about the consequences of a misstep. That was a long drop.

At least it was a danger he could see, which wasn't always the case. The clouds occasionally billowed up and over his head, forcing him to cross his fingers and run through them blindly, praying he wouldn't run through and off the end of a cloud. An especially dense cloud ahead was all but impenetrable. Sweating in fear, he held his breath and ran through, waving his arms before him to dispel the mist as quickly as possible.

He emerged at the gates of Heaven.

He skidded to a stop as he stared in awe at the gleaming golden gates. He was sure he'd been in this area with Finn and yet he'd never seen these gates before. They extended for miles as far as he could see. They were swallowed by clouds at either end and disappeared up into yet more clouds overhead to form more of a golden wall than a gate. The posts comprising it were as thin as his wrists and looked too delicate to hold back a human being, much less a horde of Demons. Yet the gates were doing exactly that. A swarm of Demons was stretched along the length of the gates. They threw their bodies against the bars, trying to breach them. Sparks would flare up, sending the Demons screeching away, presumably burned or electrocuted.

Ryan took an instinctive step back as he studied those twisted, black and white shapes. Whenever he thought of Demons he pictured the creatures of movies or books: gnarled, disfigured creatures with thick, veined limbs. But these things looked like humans. Sort of. They were definitely humanoid, but their thin bodies were as white as maggots. Pitch-black hair streamed from their heads, matching the thin, leathery wings that protruded from between their shoulders and the snake-like tails whipping between their legs. They were all males that he could see, the sight of their stubby, knobbed organs making Ryan temporarily heterosexual. From their foreheads sprang pairs of white, blunted horns.

They hummed, not like a person would in the shower when they were happy. Oh, no. This seething, ominous hum reminded Ryan of a swarm of bees, except there was an undeniable intelligence behind this, as though the hum had been pitched at the precise octave to terrify. The sound made his insides shrivel and brought a cold sweat to his face. For some reason he thought of being devoured alive.

Fortunately, facing the Demons on the other side of Ambriel's Gates were the Angels. The sight of them inspired a feeling similar to slogging through mud and muck to be suddenly doused with the purest of spring waters. Ryan's heart swelled. He stood straighter, his eyes drinking in the sight of the beautiful Angel warriors of Heaven. Their gleaming brightness made him feel confident and strong. They made him feel he could face down the Demons himself.

His confidence was short-lived, however, when he saw movement among the swarming Demons. A single Demon separated from the ranks and Ryan knew right away that this was a leader of some sort. He was as slinky as his fellows, but his skin was mottled with red spots. Ryan guessed it was a symbol of rank.

"Pitiful Angelsss of Heaven, sssee how you cower behind your gatesss. You are cowardsss!"

Ryan moaned in fright and stumbled backward

as that horrible, hissing voice slithered through his ear canals. He screwed his fingers into his ears, seized with a desperate urge to clean them out. He felt filthy just listening to that terrible voice.

"Come out, Angelsss. Show usss you are not cowardsss," the Demon continued, adding a grotesque cackle at the end.

Ryan shuddered and fought not to vomit. The Angels came to his rescue. Or at least one did.

Anifiel flew forward from the gathering of Angels, hovering just a few feet from the gates. Ryan dropped his hands from his ears, transfixed by the sight of him. Anifiel was dressed in shining silver armor, from a brilliant breast plate to shin and arm guards that winked like diamonds every time he moved. Even his hair seemed brighter, streaming down his shoulders like glowing gold. His huge wings, still larger than any Ryan had yet seen in Heaven, beat the air with powerful strokes. In his right hand he held the staff of a glowing silver spear—the Spear of Righteousness, given to him by the Creator.

Whatever animosity Ryan had felt for this Angel vanished. Anifiel was the most glorious being Ryan had ever laid eyes on. He was the type of being for whom religions were formed. Anifiel was in his own way a type of god, for Ryan knew without question that the humans and other Angels would gladly worship him if Anifiel asked it. He was the type of figure who could inspire followers to attempt the impossible.

"Demons, begone!" Anifiel bellowed. For once, Ryan was proud of the Angel's intimidating manner of speaking. Ryan wanted to cheer when he watched the Demon leader cringe at the sound. "Return to the Beneath for you will not enter the domain of Heaven now or ever!" Anifiel pointed the Spear at the Demon host. "Begone!"

"In time you will come to realize what the majority of Heaven knows: Anifiel is the glory of Heaven."

Ryan did see. Vithius had spoken the truth.

As if summoned by Ryan's thoughts, the dark-haired Angel disengaged from the amassed Angels and hovered at Anifiel's left flank, away from the Commander's spear arm. Again Ryan was struck with amazement that he been permitted to speak with these two magnificent Angels and, incredibly, to touch them.

Vithius was dressed in bronze armor, which complimented his dark skin and made him the perfect foil for Anifiel's light. His sensuous face was firmed with determination as he faced down the Demons. Ryan's feelings of love and lust for the two Angels were so powerful at that moment that he wanted to cry.

I've been so lucky, and I never even realized it.

"The disssloyal Commander and hisss catamite fear usss," the Demon leader announced for the sake of his fellows. "They do not wish to fight. Why not fight usss, Commander? Are you content to wallow in your bed of sssin with your dirty catamite?" When Anifiel stared back haughtily, the Demon leader grinned, bearing a mouthful of curved, ivory teeth. "Where isss your consssort, Commander?

Where is the deliciousss whore, Finnian? Or do you not care when you have your dirty catamite to ssswallow your cock?"

"Do not speak my consort's name!" Anifiel boomed. "You do not deserve to think of him, much less speak of him!" Ryan's heart ached to hear the Angel defend his lover with such intensity.

"Pretty whore called Finnian," the Demon leader purred. Ryan realized with dismay that there was a certain amount of relish in the Demon's voice. The creature knew something. He knew something bad. "The Commander'sss whore isss now a whore of the Demonsss."

Ryan's horrified gasp echoed those of the gathered Angels.

"Oh, yesss! We share hisss pretty face and hisss tight Angel asss. We have usssed hisss preciousss body to sheath our nasssty Demon cocksss. Ssso many timesss we have ssspilled our tainted Demon sssseed on hiss lipsss. Do you ssstill want to kisss your consssort, Commander, now that he tastesss of Demon sssseed?"

"You lie!" Anifiel surged forward, only to be stopped by Vithius, speaking urgently into his ear. Anifiel's face blazed dark red in his fury, but he remained where he hovered, held back by his battle companion's restraining words and hands.

Ryan, standing unnoticed on the side, shoved his fist between his teeth. All of this time he'd told himself that Finn was fine and could take care of himself. All this time Ryan had been soothing his guilty conscience by choosing to believe Finn wasn't in danger. But Finn was not alright. The

Demon leader could be lying just to goad Anifiel, but Ryan didn't think so. If the Demons had learned that Finn was no longer in Heaven, it didn't take a genius to figure out that they would have immediately gone looking for him on Earth.

And apparently, they'd found him.

"Leave this place," he heard Vithius speak for the first time. The Angel's voice shook with emotion as he stood beside his embattled companion. "You cannot overtake Heaven, nor will you succeed in corrupting any Angel here. Your lies fall on deaf ears, heinous beasts!"

"Catamite!" the Demon leader hissed. "How do you enjoy the great Commander'sss cock up your asss? Isss the Creator pleassed by how well you sssuck his favorite Angel'ssss cock?"

The Angel army murmured with outrage. Ryan's hands curled into fists. How dare they speak of Vithius that way? He opened his mouth to yell something but Anifiel beat him to it, shouting furiously, "Lower the gates!"

The gates of Heaven began to sink into the clouds. More than fifty feet of it was swallowed by the clouds before the finial tops of the gates came into view. As soon as they did, Anifiel flew over the top, Vithius following close behind, the dark-haired Angel's face reflecting the concern that Anifiel's did not.

Ryan knew why Vithius worried. Finn had told him how the Angels defended Heaven. It was just that: a defense. The Eternity War had raged for century upon century and it always unfolded the same way—with the Demons attacking Heaven in the hopes of breaching the Tiers, of course, but also seeking to goad the Angels to do more than defend their home—to take the offensive. Because once an Angel did more than defend, once he or she actively attacked, that Angel was corrupted and the Demons scored a significant and terrible victory.

The result was battles which were more often about taunting than physically harming the Angels. The Demons wanted an Angel to lose self-control and strike back. Anifiel's task was to keep the Angels focused and prevent them from taking anything that the Demons said or did on a personal level.

But here, before Ryan's very eyes, Anifiel was succumbing to the weakness he tried to spare his army. The Commander had been under great stress lately and it was little surprise that the attacks on his two closest companions had pushed him over the edge.

"Please be careful," Ryan whispered. The plea was for all the Angels, but mostly for the dark and light males who led the charge.

The two forces met on the outer side of the gates. Ryan noticed belatedly that the Angels were, in fact, armed, but only with long metal poles with blunted ends. Vithius carried two shorter poles, one in each hand, which he used to deflect the lashing tails and clawed fingers of the attacking Demons.

Vithius fought back-to-back with Anifiel, who used the glowing blade of the Spear of Righteousness to fling the Demons away from him. They were an incredible sight with the Demons flying around them in a blur of white and black. All of the Angels were engaged in driving the Demons back from the gates, but clearly the heaviest action was around the Commander and his battle companion.

The sight was jaw-dropping and Ryan needed to see more. There was a mound of cloud, like a foggy mole hill, which he thought he could make his way to and crouch behind for a better view. All the Angels and Demons were occupied in a frenzy of attack and counter-attack; none of them would notice him.

He had gotten halfway to the mound of cloud when he heard the ecstatic cackle.

"Ssstupid human cannot ressist curiossity."

A single Demon hovered in the air above Ryan. The creature looked like every other Demon he had seen, but having him this close made Ryan's skin break out in goose flesh. He prayed he didn't wet himself.

The Demon licked his lips with a black tongue. "There isss much more interessting sssights in the Beneath to sssee. Thingsss you won't find in Heaven. Exsssiting thingsss. Thingsss that will amaze you. Come with me, little human and I will ssshow them to you."

Ryan couldn't speak. Terror had robbed him of speech. He finally unlocked his frozen feet and started stumbling backward. The Demon grinned maniacally and followed him.

"We have Angelsss in the Beneath," the Demon told him. Ryan nearly tripped and fell in his shock.

The Demon cackled and nodded his head excitedly. "Yesss, yesss! Many Angelsss to sssee in the Beneath. Come with me and I will ssshow you. They will keep you sssafe."

A sick feeling of dread filled Ryan. What if the Demon was talking about Finn!

"Ryan!"

Anifiel's shout spun both Ryan and the Demon back to the battlefield. The golden Commander sped towards them, his spear pointing the way. Ryan's limbs turned watery with relief.

Then the unthinkable happened. A Demon darted in from the side and clipped Anifiel across the wings. The Commander tumbled out of the sky, landing face first on a cloud. Ryan screamed, but it was a whisper compared to what came out of Vithius' throat.

Roaring, the dark-haired Angel launched himself at the Demon that had attacked Anifiel. Vithius' twin poles whirled like helicopter blades in his hands. The Demon screeched in pain as the poles struck him in the chest and abdomen. Tail lashing fitfully, the Demon somersaulted backward through the air to get away.

The Demon with Ryan cackled gleefully and hissed, "Yesss!"

It wasn't until Anifiel regained his footing and looked up at his battle companion incredulously, that Ryan realized why the Demon was so pleased.

Vithius had done what he must not do—he had attacked.

The Demon nearest to Ryan flew back to the battlefield but didn't engage any of the Angels. In fact, all of the Demons pulled back, leaving their Angel opponents panting in confusion.

The Demons retreated until their red-skinned leader again hovered at their head. The Demon leader pointed at Vithius.

"The Commander'sss consssort fell to usss. Now hisss catamite doesss the sssame. Sssoon the Commander will fall, too, and the ressst of Heaven after. Prepare yoursselvess, Angelsss, for we will have you all!"

Cackling and screeching like a pack of hyenas, the Demons dove beneath the layers of clouds. Ryan watched them only long enough to ensure that they'd really left, before his attention swung immediately back to his friends.

The crowd of Angels was silent as Vithius touched down on the cloud where Anifiel stood. The dark-haired Angel didn't look at his companion; he covered his face with both hands. Anifiel staggered toward him and stopped just behind his companion's drooping wings. A mournful howl shook the Heavens as Anifiel reached forward. He plucked a single gray feather from within Vithius' pristine wings.

~~~~~~

Ryan sat hunched over like an ape, his arms extended between his bent knees, hands clutching his feet. But he didn't feel like an ape. More like an armadillo, trying to give the impression of being impenetrable and not worth the effort of provoking.

It was all an illusion, though. He was shaking, badly, and if someone were to poke him in the shoulder with just a finger he would roll over and collapse onto the grass.

Delayed reaction was setting in and it was setting in hard. The battle repeated in his mind like a historical documentary set on replay. He saw Anifiel coming to save him, leaving himself open to the Demon who swooped in like a hawk. Then he saw Vithius, doing the unthinkable with a cry of un-Angelic anger.

The Commander'sss consssort fell to usss, now hisss catamite doesss the sssame. The Demon leader's words of triumph made Ryan sick. He wanted to cover his ears, but the terrible words could not be banished that easily.

"Look at me."

He shuddered, squeezing his eyes tight as he felt Anifiel's burning presence standing before him.

"I said look at me!"

The booming command made Ryan gasp. His eyes shot open, his tear-blurred eyes focusing on the golden Angel. With the exception of his absent silver armor, Anifiel looked as he had in battle, his glorious hair tumbled recklessly across his forehead and his cheeks still flushed with passion.

In his hand, he held Vithius' tainted gray feather.

"I'm sorry," Ryan whispered, the shaking of his body only increasing as he stared at the embodiment of his friend's corruption. "I'm so s-sorry, Anifiel. I never meant for Vithius to get hurt. I'd rather be dragged to the Beneath by a thousand Demons. I'd rather you drive the Spear of Righteousness through my chest." His voice trailed off until it was the barest of whispers, "Please believe me. Please. He's my friend."

Anifiel threw the feather at Ryan's feet. "So you claimed of Finnian," he hissed. "Pray spare me the honor of being your friend lest you corrupt me, also." The Angel's expression twisted with such pain that more tears gathered in Ryan's eyes in sympathy. "Vithius is my battle companion! He has fought at my side for centuries. For him to become tainted over an insignificant human—" Anifiel turned his face away, his hands flexing impotently as if he wanted to strangle Ryan but couldn't.

Ryan's shoulders convulsed with sobs he couldn't seem to release. Vithius' feather lay like a fallen soldier at his feet. No, it looked more like a sacrifice. The sacrifice of Vithius' innocence.

"Just kill me," he choked out. "Go ahead and kill me. And if you can't do that again, then send me to the Beneath. I know I don't deserve to be here. I don't deserve anything I have. I know it!"

He surged to his feet and started to run in the direction he thought the edge might be. A large hand caught his shoulder and spun him around so hard he fell to his knees. The hand shifted to the back of his head and pushed him down. Ryan didn't attempt to resist. His forehead hit the top of Anifiel's foot. His lips immediately pressed to the Angel's hot skin.

"I'm sorry," he moaned as he covered Anifiel's foot and ankle with sloppy kisses. He tasted salt on his lips and the skin beneath his mouth became slick with his tears. "I'm sorry, Anifiel. So sorry..."

He welcomed the Angel fugue as it distorted his senses and rearranged his priorities. Nothing mattered except submitting to Anifiel, pleasing him. Ryan wanted to with every ounce of his being. He was grateful to the Angel for giving him this opportunity to make amends. Ryan would do anything for him.

He moaned as he clutched at Anifiel's ankle and dragged his tongue up the other male's shin. Golden blond hairs curled around his tongue and he caught some between his teeth and gently pulled. He heard a startled gasp from above and the sound filled him with joy. He continued his upward trek, kissing and licking the strong calf muscles. He bent his head around Anifiel's knee and licked the softer skin behind the joint. He heard something that could have been a moan.

"Just let me. Let me," he repeated in between his oral worship.

He moaned as fingers carded through his curls. "There are many ways to send a human to the Beneath," Anifiel murmured, the thick tips of his fingers rubbing behind Ryan's ears as if rubbing a cat. Ryan pressed his hot face to Anifiel's thigh, his mouth open as he gasped for breath. "You shall help me explore those ways, won't you, little human?" Ryan moaned as Anifiel caught the top of his ear between two fingers and sensuously rubbed.

"Yes," he groaned, his entire body vibrating like a struck lightning rod. He would have agreed to anything at that moment, his lust for Anifiel was beyond blinding—it was total. "Whatever you want of me. Anything."

As he slid up Anifiel's leg, his forehead brushing the hem of the Angel's tunic, he could smell the Angel's sex. Ryan's eyes widened in shock. He trembled. His hips bucked forward as that delicious musk filled his nostrils. My god, was there anything more intoxicating? He grew dizzy as that potent scent dragged across his senses like seductive fingers. His cock became swollen to the point that it hurt him. Whining low in his throat, he humped forward. His cock brushed against the tips of Anifiel's toes. The contact was sizzling.

He heard Anifiel murmur to himself. The Angel's fingers continued to drag lightly through his hair. "The instrument of your turning is awake I see," he whispered in a thick, raspy voice that came straight from Ryan's wet dreams. "It is so easy to rile you, little human. You cannot hide your weakness from me however much you try."

If he were lucid, perhaps Ryan would have taken it as a threat. But now, caught in the spell of the Angel pheromone or whatever it was, Ryan only became more aroused. He wanted Anifiel to use his lust against him. He wanted Anifiel to take advantage of him sexually. Oh, yes, he did. *Use me. Make me your slave.*

"Let us see how little control you hold," Anifiel went on ominously.

Ryan gripped Anifiel's leg tighter, his face crushed to the Angel's powerful thigh as Anifiel flexed his toes. The strong digits brushed up the underside of Ryan's scrotum, gently shifting the orbs. The single, teasing touch made Ryan cry out and then orgasm a second later.

He whimpered, hanging onto Anifiel's leg as tremors of pleasure ripped through his body. In the midst of his Heaven-shaking climax, he heard Anifiel say, "This will be too easy indeed."

Ryan opened his mouth to make a retort, but Anifiel lifted him up and crushed him in a bear hug. Ryan gaped into Anifiel's handsome face. The Angel's strong, broad chest was as hot and hard as a sun-baked stone wall, making Ryan hyper aware of his erect nipples rubbing against that unyielding surface.

"Ready for more, little human?" Anifiel smirked knowingly as he studied Ryan's flushed face. "Or should I call you Pet from now on? Which should it be?"

A small voice in the back of Ryan's head screamed in outrage at the nickname. Ryan tried to listen to it. He knew, deep down, that this was wrong. What had happened during the battle was an accident. Anifiel had no right to exact such a price from him. But the Angel fugue was powerful and demanded that he surrender to it.

Anifiel leaned forward, blowing air across Ryan's throat. It sealed Ryan's fate. He moaned, his eyes rolling up into his head as lust shivered through his spent loins. "Pet," he groaned, arching his head back submissively. "Let me be your pet."

"Very good," Anifiel whispered in a deep voice. His lips were a warm tickle against Ryan's throat. "You will find yourself in the Beneath soon enough, wretched human, but you will go there my way. Let us begin...my pet."

Anifiel launched them into the air, still holding Ryan in a bear hug. Ryan closed his eyes and tucked his face against the Angel's strong neck. He let Anifiel's scent overthrow all rational thought.

He kept his eyes closed when, after several minutes of flying, they touched down again. Anifiel released him, but didn't move away. Ryan felt something close around his neck. He opened his eyes and felt for his neck. The cord that had bound the Angel's tunic was now wrapped around his throat like a collar. But there was more to it than that—the free end of it rested in Anifiel's hand.

"On your knees, Pet."

Ryan sank down, staring at the bulge where he knew Anifiel's cock to be. The mound was soft. Anifiel wasn't attracted to him at all.

Finally, humiliation began to clear Ryan's mind of lust.

"Vithius, I have brought you a gift."

Ryan sucked in his breath and turned his head. Vithius sat upon the grass, huddled much like Ryan had been earlier. The Angel's wings were out, but they drooped from his shoulders, the white bottom feathers dragging on the ground. Vithius' head had been bowed, but at Anifiel's words he tilted his face up. Vithius looked defeated and beaten. The sorrow on his face tore Ryan's heart.

Vithius studied him, but the Angel didn't appear surprised or even unhappy to see Ryan on his knees and at the end of a leash. Vithius acted as though he barely recognized Ryan.

"I am not in the mood for games," Vithius said tonelessly. His dark eyes were dull and flat. "Play with Ryan elsewhere, Anifiel."

"This is no game." Anifiel stepped toward the other Angel. The leash pulled taut until Ryan had no choice but to crawl after him to avoid being strangled. "He has agreed to be our pet, Vithius. It is how he shall make amends for his sin against you."

At this, Vithius' dark brows creased. "His sin?"

"You are corrupted," Anifiel whispered, and here, his pain seeped into his voice again. "This human led to your corruption, Vithius. He sinned against you by breaking the rules of Heaven."

Vithius dropped his head again, his shoulders heaving with sorrow. "Corrupted..." he gasped brokenly. "Anifiel, my feathers—"

"Give me your hand," Anifiel commanded softly, but his voice was choked with emotion. "Please, my friend."

Ryan's entire body broke out in a sweat. *Vithius won't do it. He knows I'm not a pet!*

The dark hand extended slowly. It trembled. Anifiel caught it in his own. As Ryan watched with a sinking heart, Anifiel pressed the end of the leash into Vithius' palm.

Ryan shook his head in denial. The leather chafed his neck. This couldn't be happening. Not in Heaven. Not with Vithius.

"His name is Pet," Anifiel whispered. "He is yours, or we shall share him."

Vithius raised his tear-streaked face and studied the leash in his palm as if it were an alien artifact.

Then he looked at Ryan kneeling before him. Ryan could read nothing but immense loss in the dark-haired Angel's face.

"Pet," Vithius repeated, sounding sad. His fingers folded over the leash. "Thank you, Anifiel."

"You are welcome."

7

Anifiel called him Pet. The Angel used the humiliating moniker every chance he could:

"Pet, sit beside that pole and do not move one scheming finger."

"Do not give me that glare, Pet. You look as though you are entertaining thoughts of mutiny."

Ryan, tethered and collared, had no choice but to grit his teeth and bear it.

He glared a lot.

But as awful as it was to be at the blond Angel's beck and call, it was ten times worse to see what had befallen Vithius.

Anifiel had coaxed his companion to return with them to the pavilion. But although the dark-haired Angel was there in body, he most definitely was absent in spirit. Ryan's heart ached to see the handsome Angel sitting cross-legged upon the grass and staring off at the purple mountains. He looked empty. Vacant. This was not the cheerful, optimistic Angel Ryan had become friends with.

Ryan consoled himself with thoughts of how Vithius had been before, and he told himself that Vithius would be that way again. He basked in the fantasy of him and Vithius having dinner by candlelight. When Vithius recovered, Ryan promised himself he would show the Angel what he had withheld before. He would show Vithius pleasure. He would give Vithius every reason to abandon his futile interest in Anifiel and allow himself to be loved by Ryan. Whatever Vithius wanted, whatever he desired, Ryan was confident he could find a way to give it to him.

If Vithius recovered. Ryan worried that Vithius had fallen into some sort of coma. He thought he'd read somewhere that the longer a coma patient stayed unconscious, the more damage was incurred to the brain. Could Angels get brain damage? It didn't seem likely, but then again, Ryan hadn't thought that Vithius' current state was likely, either.

Corruption changes everything. It was a lesson Ryan wished he'd never had to learn. He feared more than ever for Finn, trapped on Earth.

Angels flew overhead with increasing frequency. They had witnessed what had happened on the battlefields and all of Heaven, Angel and human alike, knew that the Commander's battle companion was now corrupted. The Angels called to Vithius, sharing their well wishes for his recovery. If Vithius heard, he didn't respond. He sat as still as the statues on the Path to Inspiration, doing such a convincing job of mimicking them that Ryan brushed against him when given the chance, just to assure himself that the Angel remained warm flesh and had not become bronze.

Vithius' condition also greatly disturbed Anifiel. Ryan knew he was getting a rare glimpse of the Commander suffering from the dual stresses of a missing consort and a corrupted battle companion. Confusion and darkness hovered in Anifiel's eyes. The wide slashes bracketing the blond Angel's mouth grew deeper with worry. Though Anifiel made sure to give Ryan the most scathing of looks, those he turned upon his morose fellow Angel were heavy with sadness and helplessness. Anifiel had not left the pavilion for a long time. Ryan had slept fitfully, so he was unsure of the days, but he was pretty sure that at least a week had passed since the battle. Anifiel had been chained here as much as Ryan.

"Not even the best warrior of Heaven can defeat what you face now," Ryan said to himself as he watched Anifiel pace restlessly behind Vithius. It was like watching a lion endlessly circle a pit into which a fellow had fallen. Strength and bravery were useless, yet they were all Anifiel had.

Under other circumstances, Ryan might have found pleasure in Anifiel's distress. But it was impossible to find any pleasure when it came at Vithius' expense. Ryan wished for the hundredth time that the Demon had succeeded in luring him away without the Angels knowing. Ryan would rather be in the Beneath where he was heading anyway, than watching the slow destruction of a beautiful Angel.

He watched Anifiel come to a stop directly behind Vithius. The Commander dropped his hand lightly atop his friend's shoulder. Vithius didn't react. Ryan waited, breath held, for Anifiel to do what *he* would do: fall to one knee beside the despondent Angel and offer physical comfort in the form of a hug.

"Vithius, my friend...please."

The dark-haired Angel showed no signs of awareness.

"Vithius..." Uncertain, Anifiel lifted his hand.

It was all Anifiel could give him. Ryan shook his head. It wasn't enough.

~~~~~~

"Vithius has been corrupted."

The white-haired Angel named Camael thoughtfully studied the Lower Tier where the battle had occurred. Nothing remained as evidence of the conflict. Ambriel's Gates were unseen when Demons were not near. But the air held the unusual specter of sorrow. The Angel frowned, not used to the feeling, and clearly not liking it.

"The Commander will see him through it," spoke up another Angelic voice. "They are as brothers. Vithius will recover with his aid."

"Will he?" Camael arched a snow-white eyebrow. "If you had seen Vithius' face, you would not be so certain, Tofiel."

Tofiel knew to be wary of the introspective

look on her fellow Angel's face. This was no ordinary Angel she stood beside, after all. Camael was the next greatest Warrior Angel in Heaven after Anifiel and Vithius.

Tofiel used the moment of silence to admire Camael while his back was turned. The white Angel was the truth of Heaven. To look upon him was to be cast into the light of introspection. Tofiel often wondered if the Creator had designed Camael to be a literal light should the light of Heaven ever fail. The Angel glowed like a star. Darkness could not take hold where Camael boldly stepped.

Physically, the Angel was a sight to behold: pure white tufts of hair grew down the center of his head like the flared crest of a magnificent bird. His hair was long and extended down his bare back like a peacock's tail, ending in a point at the cleft of his buttocks. The sides of his skull above his ears were smooth, and he was hairless but for his eyebrows and a small patch of hair around his sex. His pale skin was luminous, as if it were lit from within. He was an odd-looking Angel but Tofiel did not think any Angel or human in Heaven thought Camael anything other than mesmerizing.

And intimidating. When Camael turned to prompt Tofiel for a response, the brunette Angel swiftly raised her eyes, afraid to be caught in her perusal. Camael understood his own beauty, but he did not tolerate fools who saw nothing but that. He was a warrior with a warrior's body and a warrior's impatience for anything which could not be swiftly solved with action. Tofiel often wondered if her friend wished he were an Angel of War, rather than of self-awareness.

"If Vithius does not recover, certain changes will be required," Camael said, watching Tofiel's face for reaction. "A corrupted Angel may not be strong enough to defend the Commander's back."

Tofiel blanched when she realized what the other Angel was saying. Camael only laughed at her expression.

"Do you realize that when you do that, the freckles on your face become very, very bright?" Camael's feet left the ground as he reached up and did what Tofiel hated: he mussed Tofiel's reddish-brown hair. The longish strands poked into her brown eyes. Camael glanced down Tofiel's body, a white eyebrow arching once again. "Yet your other freckles do not change color elsewhere on your body. Very interesting."

Tofiel frowned, pretending she didn't care how Camael's eyes, which were the color of robin's eggs, felt as they looked her over. "Do not tease me. What are you saying about Vithius? Surely you are not contemplating what I think you are? Anifiel will not abandon his companion. Not even after what has happened. They were made for each other."

"No, they were not," Camael said very slowly and very carefully. For all his visual magnificence, he was much shorter than Tofiel, a fact which did nothing to dampen the effect his personality had on the taller Angel. He stepped up to Tofiel and stabbed her in the shoulder with a finger. "Anifiel was given free rein to choose his battle companion. He chose, not poorly, but he could have done better." The Angel unfurled his wings and began to ascend to the Middle Tier.

Tofiel had heard this declaration before and it worried her now just as it had the previous times Camael had expressed his dissatisfaction with the Commander's choice. Camael might be purity—to look upon him inspired the humans to search their souls for truth—but he held a flaw just as Tofiel was beginning to suspect all Angels held in some form or another. Camael's was ambition.

She flew after Camael until she was side by side with the other Angel as they rose to the Middle Tier. The explosion of greens and blues settled Tofiel's heart somewhat. She had always found peace in this tier. Like most True Angels, she rarely ventured lower unless called there by the horns of war.

"Camael, word has spread of your brave showing in the battle," called an Angel who held court with a handful of tunic-clad humans.

The white Angel waved a hand and smiled. "It was not bravery, Cassiel, but faith in righteousness. I was inspired as we all were by the Spear of Righteousness and our Commander who wielded it."

"Indeed," Cassiel agreed, turning to make sure his human charges listened. "There is no room for pride or hubris in Heaven," he told them. "Though Camael is indeed great, he does not hold vanity in his heart."

Camael inclined his head.

"I'm so embarrassed!" one of the humans suddenly exclaimed. She ducked her head shyly.

"I'm vainer than I thought. I wanted him to notice how pretty I am. People always complimented me about my looks on Earth. Why did I just realize that? "

"Camael is the light of self-awareness," Cassiel said gently, waving the two Angels on. "His presence is meant to spur introspection, Angela. Tell me what else you have learned about yourself?"

Tofiel smiled as she and Camael left Cassiel and his students. The two Angels continued onward to the stream beside which they kept their 'home'. Though none of the Angels were 'lovers' as Anifiel and Finnian were considered, most had paired off with their battle companions. Tofiel was pleased that she and Camael had found a common bond away from the battlefield. It allowed them to sit beside this stream and discuss countless subjects and find mutual enjoyment from the other's company.

"Cassiel is a good teacher," Tofiel remarked as she settled upon the grass. A single perpetually blooming cherry tree stood beside the stream. As Tofiel was one of the tallest Angels in Heaven, she had to stoop deeply beneath the tree limbs before lowering herself to the grass. Delicate pink petals sprinkled her bare shoulders and breasts. "It is important that he teach the humans what is truly important and what is not. There are many humans who look to Angels as sources of worship and adulation. You and Anifiel are two of them."

"And many humans lust after and covet

Finnian," Camael said absently. "Or did." He stood beside the stream, letting the water run over the tips of his toes. He turned his head slightly, the long tail of his hair swishing across his shoulder blades. "And there are some who yearn to share your inner peace."

Tofiel chuckled. She ran her fingers through the grass. "Of you all, I sound the least interesting."

She watched Camael's lips carve into a smirk. "Which shows how very little they know you, my friend."

Tofiel said nothing. She had learned to still her tongue when Camael said or did something which caused a vague, unexplainable disturbance in her belly. It was not an unpleasant sensation, but Tofiel was certain it was not normal. She kept it a secret from Camael, which was not fair of her, but Tofiel was concerned. The feeling had been growing of late. It was especially strong when she and Camael were in the presence of the Commander and his consort. Something about the connection Anifiel and Finnian shared left her unsettled.

She doubted the great Camael had ever known such a feeling, thus she kept it to herself. And with Finnian trapped on Earth, Tofiel was curious to see if she continued to feel this odd feeling when she was next in Anifiel's presence.

"Cassiel spoke the truth about your valor on the field," Tofiel said, forcing her thoughts to another subject. "You made my position as your battle companion very easy. You did not need my protection."

"The battle did not progress as it should have,"

Camael said, subdued. Tofiel wished she could see her friend's face, but Camael had turned back to face the stream. "One mistake made which could have turned the tide for the Demons. What if it occurs again?"

Tofiel fidgeted. "It will not."

"All of Heaven knows what a warrior I am," Camael continued, the Heavenly light making his white hair blaze like colorless flame. Tofiel felt the pull of Camael and she tried to resist, but she knew she would lose. "The Commander of Heaven's Army requires protection. He cannot be allowed to fall, else Heaven itself shall fall. Only I should be the one to take on that burden. Only I am equipped to."

Tofiel swallowed. Camael was right, even if he was wrong. Camael did deserve to fight at Anifiel's side.

"But only if Vithius cannot," Tofiel reminded him gently. "He remains Anifiel's battle companion."

Camael turned around and smiled. Tofiel went temporarily blind. "Of course. That is what I meant."

But she did not think so.

~~~~~~

"I thought having you as his pet would rouse him from his grief, but it appears you are not interesting enough."

Ryan kept his chin raised, proud that he didn't

flinch. The weight of the leash around his neck was negligent, but mentally it felt like a chain of guilt. He wouldn't admit this to Anifiel, however. He glared back at Anifiel, acting as though he would attack the Angel if given the chance.

Anifiel smiled. "But you mean nothing to him, I see. A mere plaything cast aside. I could have told him that humans are not worth the bother of his time."

"You're not doing much better yourself," Ryan retorted. "You can't even show him that you care. What's wrong with *you*?"

That failure clearly troubled, Anifiel, too. He turned his head so that only his profile was given to Ryan. "If what is necessary to rouse him is the granting of a love I do not feel, then Vithius is lost to me. I will not engage in deceit to raise his spirits. I am not like you."

Ryan flinched. Attempting to seduce Anifiel through trickery had been wrong. But there was little he could do to erase that mistake. And besides, it didn't compare to what Ryan was asking for.

"You don't have to give him a blowjob," Ryan said, exasperated. When Anifiel looked at him blankly, Ryan shook his head. "Never mind. Just— why can't you hug him? Or-or say something nice to him? Isn't he your friend? Don't you want to see him recover?"

Anifiel stormed up to him so quickly Ryan fell back onto his elbows in apprehension. "What kind of a question is that?" the Angel boomed. "I would gladly trade places with him if it would clear his eyes of this self-imposed blindness!"

Ryan trembled. Having Anifiel this close, close enough that the Angel's sweet, apple-scented breath filled Ryan's nostrils and the Angel's heat warmed his own skin, made Ryan yearn to surrender. But he knew he couldn't. He shouldn't.

"He's not the one who's blind," he said in a voice that shook. "You are. Why can't you see him for who he is?"

Anifiel narrowed his eyes. "And why can you not?" He stepped back, allowing Ryan to sit up. "Vithius is what he is and has always been. It is you, meddling human, who wishes to change the way things are."

"No way. I didn't make him lust after you," Ryan argued more boldly now that Anifiel was out of his personal space. He felt his tongue beginning to flap on its own and that was probably a dangerous thing, but things couldn't get any worse, could they? "Vithius loves you. He's always felt that way for you. I just helped him recognize his feelings for what they are. And I didn't make Finn go searching for something that he couldn't find with you. That was his own choice. This situation has always existed, Anifiel. But you're like the jilted boyfriend. You just won't accept it."

Anifiel's face shuttered. "What do I fail to accept?"

Ryan gripped the grass with his fingers, expecting the worst. "You can't accept that Heaven isn't perfect. And neither are Angels."

Ryan waited for Anifiel to explode in rage. Or for the Creator to reach down and pluck Ryan from the grass and flick him over the side.

Neither happened, much to his surprise.

Anifiel simply watched him. A breeze came up, ruffling his golden hair. An unexpected longing welled up in Ryan as he watched the waving strands. He wanted to touch Anifiel's hair. He wanted his fingers to replace the wind.

He was going crazy.

"You will return Vithius to his former state." Anifiel held up a hand when Ryan began sputtering. The handsome Angel's expression was like granite. "You were the cause of his corruption; therefore you will provide the solution. You are his pet. And like a good pet, you will entertain him, you will roll onto your back, you will wag your tail if need be. You will do whatever is required to bring him back to me."

"But he has no reason to come back. Why should he want to?"

"Because I demand it!" Anifiel roared, the veins jumping out in his neck.

"Holy cow, how can anyone be such an ass?!" Ryan cried out without thinking.

Anifiel leaped upon him in an instant. Ryan yelled and tried to scramble away but Anifiel surrounded him on hands and knees. He grabbed the middle of Ryan's leash and pinned it to the grass, yanking Ryan's head to the ground. The cord cut into Ryan's throat. He had to raise his chin to prevent the leash from choking him.

"You insult me," Anifiel growled. "You dare insult the Commander of Heaven's Army? You, a measly human, who has corrupted my battle companion and lured away my consort? How dare you!"

"You're full of yourself," Ryan panted back. "If you were such a great Angel, Finn wouldn't have left and Vithius wouldn't have gotten hurt trying to protect you."

Anifiel growled again. Ryan shut his eyes. He had no idea what had come over him to provoke Anifiel like this. He'd been so easy-going on Earth...why had he become this terrible troublemaker in Heaven? He didn't think he was self-destructive. He didn't honestly want to be send to the Beneath. Did he?

No, because he loved Finnian and he was growing to love Vithius. He would miss them. And the twins, too. He would miss them all.

"Do you require another lesson in obedience?"

Ryan's eyes snapped open as cold dread flooded his body. "No!"

He watched Anifiel's lashes lower, the golden fringe doing little to disguise the unexpected eagerness in the Angel's green eyes. In a strange, low voice, Anifiel purred, "I think you do, little human."

Ryan shuddered at the way Anifiel's voice had changed. What did that change mean? He twisted his face away as Anifiel settled himself on Ryan's stomach, both strong thighs bracketing his body. Through his tunic, Ryan could feel Anifiel's powerful buttocks. And he could feel more than that...

"Stop it...you big bully," Ryan groaned. The

Angel fugue was rolling in. His hands fisted in the grass. The knuckles of his left hand rubbed against Anifiel's knee. Without wanting to he opened his hand and caressed the Angel's skin. Anifiel was hot. "I don't want you...pawing me."

"You desire a lesson in humility," Anifiel whispered.

In the back of Ryan's mind he questioned if this was the first time the mighty Commander had ever whispered anything. He forgot the question, though, when he felt Anifiel's golden hair spill across his collarbones. Anifiel's face was mere inches from his own. Ryan lost his breath at the handsome vision above him.

"Say it," Anifiel commanded softly. "You desire a lesson in humility."

Ryan could only stare up helplessly. His cock was hard and it had to be sticking straight up. He could feel the blood pulsing in it, a dull throb that was echoed in his ass. The skin of his face blazed like a sunset.

"Say it," Anifiel repeated. He shifted his weight. Something heavy and cylindrical rolled across Ryan's stomach. He bit back a whimper.

"I—"

Anifiel pulled on the leash. "Say it."

The constriction around his throat worked like a cock ring around Ryan's erection. He was so hard he wanted to cry. "I...desire," he gasped. He couldn't make himself say anything more.

He'd said all he needed to.

Anifiel grinned. Even his dimples looked smug. "Yes, you do, little human. I can smell you." As

Ryan moaned, Anifiel leaned down and sniffed the skin of his neck. "You smell of lightning," the Angel murmured. "You smell hot."

The fog enveloped Ryan completely. He was lost in it and he didn't care. It felt so good to give in, to let desire race through his veins and set his skin on fire. He wanted Anifiel all over him and inside him. He wanted the Angel to absorb him because that was all Ryan was—a part of Anifiel that yearned to be reunited with the whole.

Ryan could feel every inch of Anifiel, hard angles and soft, mysterious bulges. He whispered, "I need you."

He slid both hands up Anifiel's thighs, no longer shy, only hungry for the touch of the magnificent Angel. Crisp golden hairs curled around his fingers as he slid them up the thick, muscled thighs toward the hem of Anifiel's tunic. Ryan's cock twitched in anticipation. He heard himself panting. He could feel moisture dampening his own tunic. He was on the verge of coming, but he wanted to touch Anifiel before he did. He wanted to know if he was the only one who felt this way—

"Human," Anifiel rasped against his ear. The Angel's voice was ragged. "What are you doing to me?"

Ryan's fingers slid beneath Anifiel's tunic, rising towards the heat. "Anifiel—"

"Commander!"

Faster than he had pounced on Ryan, Anifiel leaped off of him and onto his feet. He put his broad back to Ryan, denying him a view of what he needed to see, to know.

"I sought to teach the human obedience," he heard Anifiel say, and it sounded completely different this time—no suggestion of sexual innuendo, no sensual promise. Anifiel nearly sounded defensive.

Ryan groaned as he rolled onto his side and pulled his legs up to his chest. He wanted to touch himself and release the pressure that cramped his groin and stomach. But he knew he couldn't. Not with an audience. Sweating and red-faced, he looked past his knees at who had interrupted them. His eyes widened.

Two Angels stood there and they were an odd pair. One was an extremely tall and gangly female; she could have played professional basketball with her long arms and legs, and large hands. Under a scarecrow's mass of reddish-brown hair her face was long and freckled. She was rather plain-looking, but she had kind brown eyes that studied Ryan curiously. Ryan returned the look, his anxiety melting away the longer he looked at this Angel. A queer sort of peace settled over him. He smiled. The Angel smiled back.

"The human appears to like you, Tofiel."

Ryan reluctantly pulled his gaze from the Angel to settle it on the new speaker. This Angel was quite different from the other. He was shorter than the other two Angels, probably Ryan's height, but his hair granted him an extra six inches. Ryan gaped. Since when did Angels have white mohawks?

As unexpected as the hair was, the Angel was

still stunning. Unlike Tofiel, this white Angel possessed beautiful, if sharp, facial features. His nose came to a diamond point. His lips were thin but very wide, and his eyes were periwinkle. Ryan couldn't take his eyes off him. The Angel was like a torch of white light with brilliant blue eyes shining from within. Those blue eyes were unnerving, though. Ryan sat up, suddenly uneasy. He realized how shameful he looked, and how sexual his thoughts had been just a moment ago. He'd practically begged Anifiel to take him. He'd wanted Anifiel to be his. He'd wanted Anifiel to make love to him, and to love him and hold him, and—

"No!" Ryan choked out, jumping to his feet. "I didn't!"

"The light of self-truth often burns," the white Angel remarked, amused. "Your human has been singed."

Anifiel looked over his shoulder at Ryan. The Angel's expression was full of contempt. It seemed impossible that he could be the same Angel who had been gasping into Ryan's ear just seconds ago.

"That human has many faults. I regret that we will be cursed with his presence in the Middle Tier for eternity." Anifiel's mouth twisted down. "Presuming he does not succumb to the Beneath first."

"Why does he have that collar and leash on his neck?" the mohawked Angel asked.

"He is Vithius' pet," Anifiel replied. He laughed, clearly enjoying his own joke. "I thought my battle companion could use a lap animal to lift his spirits." He glanced at the white Angel. "Do you like the human, Camael? I did not know you had a fondness for humans."

Ryan didn't think Camael was that interested in him at all after Anifiel mentioned Vithius' name, but the white Angel smiled obligingly. "I find him interesting. I have never seen a human pet in Heaven." He turned to where Vithius sat with his back to them all. Camael's expression became dim. "He is no better? Tofiel and I had hoped to find him recovered and eager to battle more Demons."

Ryan watched Anifiel's shoulders slump. It was a tiny movement that he doubted the other Angels noticed. But Ryan had had nothing to do but watch Anifiel lately, and he was beginning to notice the great Commander's weaknesses.

"Vithius does not speak, nor does he show signs of hearing what goes on around him. I do not know how to help him. The Creator has denied me an audience and I do not know why."

For the first time, Ryan heard fear in Anifiel's voice. Anifiel was beginning to think the Creator was punishing him for something, but he obviously had no idea what it could be. Ryan wanted to laugh at him. It served the big jerk right. What comes around, goes around, and all that karma stuff.

But if that were true, Ryan was in trouble, too. He'd done nothing but say and do the wrong things since entering Heaven. Sooner or later, his bad behavior was going to catch up to him, too.

"Do you mind if we linger?" Tofiel asked, breaking Ryan out of his anxious thoughts. To his surprise, he found the gangly Angel smiling at him.

"Perhaps Vithius can hear us and would enjoy our company."

Camael, who had approached Vithius and was studying him carefully, nodded his head in agreement. "Yes, Anifiel, let us stay. I would like to hear more on how this tragedy occurred." He looked to Ryan and Ryan felt like he needed to dodge a pair of blue bullets. "And you can entertain us with the story of how you came to acquire your human pet."

8

As Anifiel regaled his fellow Angels with the story of Ryan's screw-up, he stared at the grass and did his best to imagine he was somewhere else. He could feel the Angels, who were seated in a circle around him, studying him with varying degrees of curiosity and amusement. The amusement was purely Anifiel's. Camael and Tofiel simply studied him as if he were a new species of bug that had crawled into their midst. Ryan guessed that the two Angels, unlike Finn and Vithius, did not regularly spend time with humans. They were obviously True Angels, though whether they were as stuck-up as Anifiel remained to be seen.

"He still wears the full tunic," commented the Angel with the wild white mohawk. "He is new to Heaven?"

Ryan sighed. He didn't need to look up to know Anifiel was smirking like crazy.

"No, Camael, he is far from new. The human has been here for nearly three years. But as you can see, he has not ascended, nor do I expect him to. Ever."

"Three years?" murmured the female Angel who resembled a big scarecrow. Ryan couldn't resist sneaking a quick glance at her. The gangly Angel appeared sad for him. At catching Ryan's look, the Angel's expression brightened and she smiled warmly. "Three years is longer than some, but I have known many great Angels who required time in finding enlightenment. One remained in the Middle Tier for eleven of your Earthly years."

Eleven! Ryan's heart lightened at the news. He wasn't the worst!

"You speak of Sebastian," Anifiel said brusquely, "who spent ten of those years assisting in the construction of Ambriel's Gates. That human was remarkable. This human has neither the skill nor heart to accomplish anything so great. He remains here not because he is needed, but because he cannot go elsewhere. He is flotsam, Tofiel. Do not be fooled by his pathetic expression."

"Why can't you give me a break?" Ryan snapped suddenly.

"I told you to remain silent," Anifiel said stonily. He shook his head at the other Angels. "You see now why he will never find enlightenment."

The Angel called Camael nodded pityingly.

Ryan was fed up. He was sick of sitting here while the Angels talked about him as if he were a doll without ears. He glared at Heaven's Commander. "You make me sound like I'm some reject but I'm not, otherwise I wouldn't have gotten into Heaven in the first place!" He rose up onto his knees as he built up steam. He wanted to look down at the high-and-mighty Anifiel just once.

And what a view it was. Anifiel might have the personality of dirt, but he sure did earn the title of Heaven's Most Studly. Oh, man, those molded cheekbones. That iron jaw. That demanding yet sensual mouth! Ryan mentally shook himself. *Beauty is only skin deep and here's a perfect example of that! Be strong!*

"If I'm some colossal mistake, why am I sitting here?" Ryan challenged. "Why did Finn want to be my friend when he had all of Heaven to befriend? Why did Vithius? If I'm the worst thing to happen to Heaven why hasn't the Creator done anything about it? You just like bullying me around because it makes you feel more important, not because I deserve it. You're a jerk!"

Anifiel smoldered where he sat. His fingertips whitened as they dug into his knees. Ryan gulped and began scooting backwards. Anifiel looked like he was going to blow like a volcano.

"I believe this is the first time I have heard a human call one of us a 'jerk'," the Angel Tofiel mused in her calm, warm voice that made Ryan think of a flannel blanket on a cold night. "You are to be lauded, Anifiel, for inspiring such passion in him. I can see from the look in this human's eyes that he has discovered a side of himself he had not known existed."

"Indeed," added Camael, watching Ryan shrewdly, "he sees himself taking a path which he had shied from walking while on Earth. A path of boldness."

Why were they still talking as if he couldn't hear them? And what in the world was a 'path of boldness'? Was that anything like a path of idiocy? Ryan was pretty sure he was leading the charge on that particular trail.

"This human," Anifiel said very, very slowly as if releasing steam from a pressure cooker so it wouldn't explode and kill everyone, "believes he possesses the right to challenge Heaven. He believes that he alone knows what is right for the Angels and he has taken it upon himself to meddle in their affairs to satisfy his own whims."

"I do not!"

"It is this human," Anifiel, continued, his eyes burning into Ryan, "who coaxed my consort into the embrace of soiled Earth. It is this human who distracted my battle companion and led to his corruption. This human—" he all but spat the word, "—is little more than a Demon cloaked in deceptively pleasing flesh!"

Demon. Anifiel thought him a Demon, one of those horrible, evil monsters that wanted to destroy everything that was good. A creature of despair. Of unhappiness.

Something died in Ryan then. Being called a Demon by Heaven's greatest Angel was worse than being a failure. This was being unwanted. Hated. He'd had enough of that while he lived. He wasn't about to endure it while he was dead.

When Anifiel began to blur, Ryan scrambled to his feet. He sprinted away from the Angels before they could see the tears that spilled onto his cheeks.

Heaven worked on wishes. Wish to see his friends and they would magically appear. Wish for a tunic to replace the one Anifiel had ripped off him and a new one immediately hung from his shoulders.

Ryan wished. He wished for the edge of Heaven where wishes no longer made a difference. He wished for the border of happiness and goodness because he no longer deserved those things. He wished for the very last cloud in Heaven so he could launch himself over its billowy softness into flame and damnation where he belonged.

"Foolish human!"

A freight train bowled him over, knocking him to the grass where his face proceeded to dig a trench in the soil before his momentum finally slowed.

"Your desire to be saved from yourself is growing tiresome."

Ryan spit out dirt and grass, absently noticing how sweet both tasted. Anifiel was crouched over his back, crushing him to the ground, which was fine; Ryan had no intention of getting up unless it was to try jumping over the edge again.

He shivered when Anifiel's breath rushed over the shell of his ear. "Do you do this for attention, little human? Are you hoping one of us will save you and prove that you are worthwhile?"

Ryan closed his eyes and kept his face pressed to the grass. "I don't want anyone to save me," he muttered, emotionally exhausted. "Just let me do what you want me to do. Let me leave. Turn around, Anifiel, and I'll do it while you can't see me. That way your conscience can be clear."

"Do not presume to know what I want," Anifiel growled. His knees tightened around Ryan's hips as if he expected him to bolt.

Ryan opened his eyes. "What are you talking about? All you do is yell about how you can't wait until I get pulled to the Beneath. Don't try and tell me you were only joking."

"You will go to the Beneath in good time, little human, but not before I learn all I need to learn of your kind. And not before you return both my consort and my battle companion to me."

Ryan closed his eyes again. He'd heard all this before. He was trapped until he saved both Finn and Vithius—*blah, blah, blah*. Maybe this was Ryan's Beneath: hounded by Anifiel for eternity since Ryan had no idea how to save his friends. This would be a hundred times worse than enduring Hell in a woman's shoe store. This included possible violence thanks to Anifiel's short temper.

Not to mention my own habit of getting a hard-on at the worst possible times.

He dug his fingers into the soil as that familiar, unwelcome tingle began to invade his brain. "I won't try to jump. Please get off me."

"You will restore Vithius?" Anifiel murmured against his ear.

If you lick me, I'm gonna come. "Yes. I promise. Now get off. Please."

Anifiel climbed off him. He grabbed the end of Ryan's leash and used it to tug him to his feet. Ryan nearly choked since both his hands were busy covering his tented groin area.

Anifiel's eyes flicked curiously to the position of his hands. Then the Angel slowly smiled. "You are too easy to rile, little human."

"Yeah, yeah, whatever," Ryan mumbled, blushing. "It's not like you don't get a kick out of making me 'riled'."

Anifiel's expression went blank for a moment. Then he scowled and tugged on Ryan's leash. "You will not provoke me. Let us return to the others where you will revive my battle companion."

Ryan followed like a dutiful dog but Anifiel's words rang through his mind. He provoked Anifiel? Well, yeah, Ryan had been spouting off at the mouth a lot lately but he was pretty sure that wasn't what the Angel meant. As he stared at the back of Anifiel's thighs and admired the golden hairs and the bunch and flex of his muscles, Ryan recalled that split second before Tofiel and Camael appeared. Anifiel had been...different. His voice had been strained in a way Ryan had never heard from him before. Had Anifiel merely been disgusted that Ryan gave in to the Angel fugue? Or had his reaction been due to something else? Finnian and Vithius had discovered physical pleasure. Could the great Commander?

Don't go there, don't go there, don't go there, Ryan told himself quickly. With his luck, Anifiel would rip both his arms off the moment he attempted to put the moves on the golden Angel.

But what about that crack about Ryan being a Demon cloaked in 'deceptively pleasing flesh'? Was that the ultimate backhanded compliment or was Anifiel poor at choosing his words?

I don't care! Anifiel's a jerk. It's Vithius I want to care for, remember?

It was all so confusing. The Creator was a cruel, cruel...well, whatever *It* was.

As they returned to the others and Ryan's gaze fell on his comatose friend, he revised his purpose. If he must remain in Heaven he would save Vithius both from his pain of corruption and from his feelings for Anifiel. Both could only hurt the Angel. Ryan would make Vithius happy by showing him that true love wasn't to be found with Heaven's Commander—it could be found with a weak little human who was imperfect, but had a ton of love to share.

And that might be the lamest greeting card ever.

"Are you alright?" Tofiel asked him with what sounded like real concern.

Ryan nodded at her. "I'm fine. Thank you...Tofiel."

The tall Angel smiled. "You have not shared your name with us. What is it?"

"Ryan. My name's Ryan." He glanced at the mohawked Angel, Camael, but the Angel didn't look nearly as friendly as Tofiel. He looked bored, if anything. Ryan wondered why he was here.

"Pet, do as you have been instructed," Anifiel boomed as if he were addressing someone standing in China. Ryan rolled his eyes at the Angel's obvious attempt to show off for his friends. Angels really weren't that different from humans. What a disappointment.

"Yes, Master," Ryan drawled, rolling his eyes. He wanted to smack himself in the forehead when Anifiel's head whipped around, a heated look in the Angel's eyes. *Ryan, why do you have to push, you idiot!*

Chastened, he kept his eyes down as he settled cross-legged before Vithius. Anifiel gave an unreadable huff and joined his Angel friends a few feet away.

"Training a human pet is not easy, I see." Tofiel smiled sympathetically at Anifiel. "It might be wiser to set him free, Anifiel. Why torture the both of you? It is clear in his heart that he loves Vithius. You do not need a leash and collar to force him into our friend's company."

Anifiel gave Ryan the closest thing to a dirty look that he'd seen yet from an Angel. "Perhaps so, but it pleases me to see him humbled. He needs much humbling."

Talk about the pot calling the kettle black! Ryan had to bite his tongue to keep himself silent.

"Tofiel is ever generous," spoke up Camael, who frowned as he looked over at Ryan and Vithius. "She holds a fondness for humans much as Finnian did. Does," he swiftly amended, shooting an abashed look at Anifiel. As if to recover from the faux pas, Camael straightened where he sat, looking much like a bird preening for a mate. "Do you believe what the Demons said of Finnian? That they have corrupted him? I, for one, do not believe your consort has succumbed to anything they might have done. I am sore pressed to believe they have even located Finnian. Your consort is far too resourceful and intelligent to be turned by the Beneath. His heart is as pure and beautiful as the Middle Tier."

What a suck-up, Ryan thought.

Sorrow and gratitude mixed on Anifiel's handsome face. "I thank you, my friend. Truly. Finnian is indeed far cleverer than the Beneath realizes. I must believe that he has evaded their clutches while awaiting my rescue."

Tofiel leaned forward in concern. "Do you know why it is he went to Earth?"

Anifiel's eyes slid to Ryan, but to his surprise, they slid away again. "Curiosity has ever been my beloved's bane. This time it was his undoing."

Ryan's jaw dropped. Anifiel wasn't blaming him? Anifiel was admitting that Finnian might have contributed to his own downfall?

"My Finnian wished to explore the unknown and the new. His love of all things human was the impetus to lead him to Earth."

A smile crossed Anifiel's face. It probably made him appear brave to Tofiel and Camael, but to Ryan it revealed how helpless and worried Anifiel really was if he had to resort to a smile, rather than the action he craved. "He is most likely engaging in much mischief on Earth, making the humans fall in love with him as we love him here in Heaven."

"I am sure he is," Tofiel said gently. "No one can resist your Finnian."

Ryan swallowed, suddenly regretting everything he had done. Anifiel's love for Finnian survived their separation. Ryan's theory that their artificial Heavenly bond would fade with time apart was being shot to shreds. Anifiel was an Angel in torment without his consort. He needed Finn. Ryan was very ashamed that he had tried to interfere by setting Vithius and Anifiel up as lovers.

And yet, along with the shame was something he had not expected: jealousy. The haunted look in Anifiel's eyes made Ryan ache to have someone feel that strongly about him. Anifiel wasn't a girly man. He was as macho as they came. For him to be brought down because of a broken heart...

What I wouldn't give to be Finn, Ryan thought, and have this magnificent Angel yearn for me like this.

It didn't even occur to him that in wishing such a thing, it would mean Anifiel would be his.

"What if we spoke of the battle instead?" Camael spread his hands in his lap, looking uncomfortable with the emotion in the air. "I know thoughts of Finnian are trying for us all. Perhaps a discussion of the battle would fare us better?"

Ryan was annoyed by the suggestion, but Anifiel embraced it with obvious relief. Typical male, he didn't like dealing with his emotions. The big baby, Ryan thought fondly. Again, he wanted to smack himself in the forehead for being fond of an Angel who had slapped a collar around his neck of all things. He decided to tune the Angels out and concentrate on his friend. At least his feelings for Vithius weren't confusing.

Ryan shifted across the grass so he sat at Vithius' side, their backs to the other Angels. What Ryan had decided to do probably wouldn't go over very well if the others saw it. He needed to be careful.

His plan was simple and risky but Ryan didn't think Vithius' situation could get much worse. The Angel's dark eyes stared at something only he could see. His beautiful broad chest rose and fell with breath but he may as well have been a statue on the Path to Inspiration for all the life he exuded. Ryan wasn't sure if Angels could waste away, but he wasn't about to sit around and find out. Anifiel should be proud. Ryan was taking a course of action.

Yeah, right. He's gonna be proud of me for molesting his battle companion. Keep dreaming. Ryan was still determined. He would risk getting pounded into the dirt by Anifiel if there was a chance he could revive his kind friend.

"Vithius," he whispered, gazing at the aquiline features of the Angel. "Vithius, it's Ryan. I'm here. You can come back now. I'm right here."

Vithius didn't react, which Ryan had expected. This would take more than words.

He reached up and brushed back a strand of obsidian hair. Vithius' hair was soft. Ryan could imagine rubbing his cheek against it as the two of them cuddled in bed. Vithius would be such a gentle, respectful lover. He would be attentive to Ryan's needs and be passionate in satisfying his own. Ryan felt his own cock slowly stiffen and lift as he continued to imagine himself in bed with this gorgeous Angel. Yes, he didn't want Anifiel. He desired Vithius.

"Remember when we were at the stream?" Ryan continued to whisper as he brushed the backs of his fingers across a high, dark cheekbone. "I touched you for the first time, Vithius. Do you remember how that felt? I do. It was amazing to me. Absolutely, undeniably amazing. And that's how I think of you, Vithius. Undeniably amazing. You are my dream come true."

He hoped he didn't sound stupid. He'd gushed over girlfriends in an attempt to falsely prove he was interested in them, and he had once done so in a letter to a boy who turned out to be straight. All of those experiences had left him embarrassed and bitter. Rejection was his middle name and yet...and yet he didn't think it would be that way with Vithius. Even if the kind Angel let him down, Ryan was certain he would not be ashamed of himself for having tried. Nothing about wooing this Angel seemed shameful. It seemed right.

Ryan let his hand drift lower, skimming fingertips across Vithius' collarbones and the swell of his pectoral muscles. His fingers hesitated above a dusky nipple. "I've never been allowed to touch anyone so handsome," Ryan breathed, watching his fingers caress the aureole. He gasped when it drew into a hard pebble. He could feel his own nipples react by tightening beneath his tunic. He wished for a moment that he was as naked as Vithius and could rub their bare chests together.

"I like that your skin is the color of a chai latte.

My favorite, by the way. It makes me want to lick you." His face flamed at the admission but with no one to see him, Ryan was able to forge on. "I want to taste every part of you, Vithius. Rubbing that oil into your skin at the stream wasn't enough for me. It left me wanting more. It's left me dreaming of all the things we can do together. All the things I can show you about loving another person..."

He flattened his hand and ran his palm slowly down Vithius' chest, down to the rippled plane of his abdomen. Ryan breathed faster. Touching this magnificent body was turning him on like crazy. Knowing this body belonged to Vithius, someone as beautiful in spirit as he was in body, made it even more intense for Ryan.

He rubbed his palm over Vithius' abs, lightly at first, then with more pressure as the need grew to become intimate with him. Ryan dipped his forefinger into the Angel's navel and thought of how sexy it would be to stick his tongue in there.

"Vithius..." Ryan moved his free hand to his own lap and wrapped it around his clothed erection. He shuddered. "I remember how it felt to have your hands on me," he said raggedly. "I still feel them."

He wasn't exaggerating: Vithius' hands had left an impression on his skin which hadn't faded with time. They had also left an impression on his mind. The magic of the Angel's touch was in knowing it was the first time Vithius had physically explored a human. Vithius had touched, and he had enjoyed. His pleasure had been Ryan's.

"I want your hands on me again," Ryan panted.

He looked up at Vithius' face and thought he saw one of the Angel's eyelids flicker. Excitement seized Ryan. "You want that, too, don't you, Vithius? You want to know what passion and lust feels like. You want to know what you've been missing all these years."

Ryan leaned forward, his breath streaming across Vithius' neck. "I can show you. I'll show you everything. Please come back to me, Vithius. Please let me show you." He kissed the Angel's neck before carefully taking hold of Vithius' soft cock.

It twitched against his palm.

Ryan nearly fainted. "That's it," he whispered. "Feel me. Feel how good it is to be touched this way."

He looked down as he gently squeezed and pulled on the Angel's sex. He watched with joy as the organ stiffened and fattened. It was hot in his hand. It was hard and perfect. He caressed the spongy head. Ryan stroked himself and Vithius in sync, using long, slow strokes from base to tip to torment them both.

"Feel it," he chanted. A bead of sweat rolled down his temple. It was all he could do not to drop his head into Vithius' lap and swallow him whole. "Feel what you could have if you return to me, Vithius. Come back and I'll give you this whenever you want. I'll give you more—"

"More corruption?"

If Ryan was a girl he would have shrieked. He nearly did anyway as Anifiel slapped a hand on his shoulder and yanked him backward away from Vithius. The blond Angel's eyes widened as he took in Ryan and Vithius' matching conditions.

"What were you doing to my battle companion?" the Angel gasped, scandalized. "You assaulted him while he cannot defend himself? What sort of demented coward are you?"

Ryan threw up his hands to ward off the blows he knew were coming. "I was only trying to help him!" he cried. "Honest, I wasn't molesting him!"

"You had your hands on him while he was unaware," said Camael, who stood just behind Anifiel as though he were guarding the Angel's back. The mohawked Angel's peacock blue eyes looked down at Ryan with condemnation. "You seek to further harm the Commander's companion? You seek to weaken Heaven's defenses?"

Ryan gasped. "Of course not! I-I was only trying to—"

"Awaken me in a most pleasant manner," a soft voice cut in.

All eyes shot to Vithius. The Angel smiled ruefully at them before looking down at his erect cock. He frowned in confusion. "Am I meant to do something with this?"

Ryan covered his face and laughed.

~~~~~

Anifiel banned them all from the pavilion while he spoke quietly and urgently to his battle companion. Tofiel watched the pair of Angels smile at each other as they talked. The strange feeling she had come to dread fluttered in her stomach once more.

"What ails you, Tofiel? I see by your face that all is not well."

Tofiel was upset with herself that she wished Camael were far from her. It was not the brilliant Angel's fault that she suffered a turmoil she could not explain. She made sure to have a reassuring smile on her face as she turned to face her companion. Camael's brilliance made Tofiel's smile become one of complete sincerity. She wondered if this was how Anifiel felt when he looked upon Finnian.

"I am well," she told the bright Angel. "I worried for Vithius and Anifiel, but I see that they are soon to be fully recovered. It is a good moment. One which we owe to the human, Ryan."

Camael's expression was stony as he glanced aside at the human who paced anxiously at the borders of the pavilion. "He touched Vithius in a way Angels are not meant to be touched. I will not give thanks for that."

Camael's stubbornness was not easily overcome. Tofiel decided to try, though. She liked the young human.

"He was able to awaken Vithius when all others had failed. Perhaps his unorthodox methods were the only choice."

Tofiel hesitated, and then lightly gripped her companion's shoulder. Camael's eyes shot to her, wide and shocked. Tofiel nearly retracted her hand, but she nervously kept the grip. Camael's skin, though stretched over hardened muscle, was far softer than Tofiel expected. It made the odd feeling inside her grow stronger. "Do not judge Ryan poorly for doing what he thought best to help Vithius. The human's intentions are good, I believe."

"What I believe is that Anifiel was right: this human has brought corruption to Heaven." Camael deliberately stepped to the side, breaking Tofiel's hold. "What has come over you?" he demanded of the taller Angel. Camael appeared rattled, something Tofiel had not seen before. "Angels do not derive pleasure or satisfaction from physical contact. The purity of our love is all that is required, not the carnal corruption championed by the Beneath!"

Tofiel's heart shattered. "Camael, please, you interpret too much—"

"I know what I see and what I feel." Camael's light blue eyes were cold but Tofiel thought she also saw the pain of betrayal in their depths. "Corruption has found its way into Heaven and it has touched my fellow warriors," Camael choked out. "I will not let Heaven fall because of a weakened Army."

Camael looked again to Ryan and his expression was not kind. Tofiel recognized the look from battle. What had she set in motion by daring to be bold with her companion?

"Camael, what do you intend?" she asked worriedly. She knew Camael well. Her friend had been robbed of his opportunity to replace Vithius when the dark-haired Angel had awoken. Camael would need another way to win Anifiel's favor.

The white Angel gave Tofiel a look shaded

with suspicion. "Heaven must be purged of corruption. Now that Vithius can protect the Commander, I will do my duty to protect Heaven, as well. I will cleanse it."

Tofiel stepped in front of Camael, deliberately blocking his view of Ryan. "Do not hurt him," she said firmly.

Camael only smiled. "I won't have to."

9

The moment Tofiel and Camael flew away wasn't soon enough for Ryan. While he felt reasonably comfortable with the tall Angel—Tofiel reminded him of a gangly puppy at times—Camael with his weird mohawk made Ryan decidedly uncomfortable. The white Angel was like a mirror placed in an unflattering position in front of the shower. The Angel had the uncanny ability to make him see just how screwed up and undesirable he really was. Ryan could do that well enough on his own without outside assistance, thank you very much.

Now that the two Angels were gone, Ryan could stop thinking about his own failings and concentrate on what mattered most to him in Heaven: Vithius.

Assuming Anifiel let him within two feet of his

friend.

"Come on, come on," Ryan muttered impatiently as he rose up to his tiptoes once more in a vain attempt to see beyond Anifiel's broad shoulders where he stood speaking with Vithius. Ryan had already tried changing positions to see around Anifiel but the blond Angel seemed to have some sort of radar: every time Ryan moved, so did Anifiel, so that the best Ryan could see of his friend was a glimpse of Vithius' shoulder.

"I'm gonna talk to him sometime, you big jerk. It's not like you can hide him forever."

He hoped Anifiel couldn't do that. In reality, Ryan knew how easily the Commander could take Vithius away and forbid Ryan from ever seeing his friend again. If Vithius didn't resist, Ryan would be left to his own devices once more because Sam and Eric were sure to ascend to the Upper Tier any minute now.

I guess I could always hang around the gates and try to pick up new friends there, he thought morosely. Yeah, that was a great idea. Grab the newbies before they realized Ryan was the social outcast of Heaven. Fantastic plan.

"—Ryan—"

He froze, ears straining. Vithius had just mentioned his name. Unable to stand it anymore, Ryan called out, "Vithius! Vithius, I'm over here!"

Anifiel whipped his head around. "Silence, human!" he barked. "You are not wanted!"

Ryan cringed and shrank back. Anifiel had the power to make anyone cower. A voice in the back of Ryan's mind pointed out that that was a good thing, what with Anifiel being the Commander and all. Another voice suggested it was sexy in a demented way. But yet another voice sneered, *He's just an excellent bully.*

"All these voices in my head must mean I'm going crazy," Ryan moaned, flopping down onto the grass to wait. "Surely I was normal at one time in my life?"

He rolled onto his back and watched the clouds moving in gentle swirls overhead. He had been normal once. Mostly. He'd watched clouds like this with a boy, back on Earth. Granted, they'd been best friends at the time and Joey had no idea that Ryan was curious about what being more than best friends might be like. But in Ryan's mind at the time it had been an almost intimate afternoon.

Joey had a girlfriend and Ryan had been trying unsuccessfully to date for about a year. Ryan hadn't been clicking with girls. His awkwardness around them seemed especially acute. More than typical nerves, anyway.

But when he hung out with Joey, things were different. Ryan didn't feel awkward, although he didn't feel entirely comfortable, either. He became nervous around Joey with increasing frequency. Sometimes an unexplainable tension would well up in him which only a nookie or an impromptu wrestling match would relieve. He started making up excuses to touch Joey.

"Hey, dude," Joey had said that afternoon when they were watching the clouds, "you need to hook up with a girlfriend. Like, soon."

Ryan had sighed. "There's no one I like. And the ones I have asked were too stuck up or whatever." Truthfully, the girls were nice girls but they simply hadn't been interested in enduring his awkwardness for the duration of a date.

"I know," Joey had replied, head on his hands, looking at the sky, "but you need to find one, cuz...you're weirding me out. I know you know what I mean."

Ryan's heart had stopped beating. "Not really, I—"

"Give me a break, Ry. I'm not stupid. Just get a chick or—someone else—and I'll drop it."

They hadn't said much after that, just talked about sports and TV shows to indicate everything was still cool between them. But things weren't cool. Not for Ryan. Joey had tried to remain friends, but Ryan couldn't. Not while Joey thought that about him.

"You knew before I did," Ryan said to the sky, wondering if conversations in Heaven made it into Earthly dreams. "You were right, Joey. I couldn't accept that about myself. I couldn't accept a lot of truths. I wonder if you'd still be my friend if you learned it wasn't just a phase I was going through. I wish I could go back to you and find out."

A shadow fell over him. "Will you settle for me as your friend?" Vithius smiled down at him. "I cannot guarantee I will inspire such wistfulness in you, but I am happy to listen to your stories of him."

Ryan rolled to his feet and launched himself at the Angel. "Oh, Vithius, thank god you came back."

Vithius chuckled gently and returned the

embrace. "If that is who you must thank, so be it. Yes, I am back."

Ryan leaned back and gave him a crooked grin. "Thank Creator just doesn't have the same ring to it." His smile faded. A lump formed in this throat. He hesitantly touched Vithius' face, grateful when the Angel allowed the intimacy. "I never meant for you to get hurt, Vithius. It was the stupidest thing I could have done to go onto the battlefield. I swear I never would have done it if I thought it would put you in danger. I swear it."

Vithius leaned into the touch. "I know, Ryan. I know you do not wish me ill."

"It's not even about intention, it's about me being stupid enough to do something that made you get hurt!" Ryan exclaimed. His emotions churned, all his pent-up fear and his guilt making a tumultuous soup in his stomach. "You're the only friend I have and I let them hurt you! I let them make you sad—" Ryan broke off, his voice cracking. "I made you so sad, Vithius. I'd rather go to the Beneath than make you sad."

"No!" Vithius' vehemence startled Ryan. "Do not say such a thing. The Beneath is a terrible place and you do not deserve to be there. Not even if I were turned would I allow you to follow me. Never say such a thing again, Ryan."

Ryan trembled against him. "I-I won't. I promise."

Regret immediately softened the Angel's face. He slid his palms up Ryan's back in a soothing gesture. "I did not mean to intimidate you, my friend. Understand that my feelings for the Beneath are strong, and I would not have you consider falling there so casually. You are my first and only human friend and I would not lose you even to spare myself, do you understand?"

Ryan felt his eyes begin to burn. "Do you really mean that?"

Confusion clouded Vithius' dark eyes and then he smiled, the understanding that bloomed over his face making Ryan look down in shame. "Whatever you have known before, do not bring those troubles to Heaven," Vithius said gently. "I am your friend and I cherish you greatly. The pain of losing you would be as awful as the pain of corruption."

"You can't mean that."

"I do."

It was the most amazing thing anyone had ever said to him, alive or dead. Ryan pushed forward, rubbing his face against Vithius' bare chest. When Vithius' arms enfolded him, he had to struggle hard not to cry. "I'll do anything for you, Vithius. Anything. I'll be the best friend you ever had and I'll be even more if you'll let me. I want to give you everything I have. Everything I couldn't give to anyone on Earth. In fact I'm glad I couldn't give it to them because I want to give it all to you."

"You are a wonderful friend, indeed," Vithius murmured against the top of his head. "To have you and Anifiel—I am blessed."

Mention of the Commander made Ryan pull away slightly and look to the side. Yes, Anifiel hadn't left. The golden Angel stood to their left, arms crossed, a look Ryan could only assume was jealousy marring his handsome features. A spike of triumph shot through Ryan. What he shared with Vithius was something Anifiel would never know.

He pulled completely from Vithius' embrace but kept hold of the Angel's hands. "Will you come with me?" Ryan entreated. "I missed you so much. I want to spend the whole day with you. Just you and me."

Vithius looked at Anifiel, too, a fond and thoughtful gleam coming to his eyes. "I cannot abandon my battle companion. I have hurt him with my absence as deeply as I have hurt you." Vithius cocked his head. "Perhaps I can divide my time between you. We will spend the 'day' together. At least until you both weary of me." He laughed.

Share Vithius? Ryan wanted to gag. He knew he didn't have much say in the matter, though. Vithius was apparently still hung up on Anifiel. For now, Ryan would have to take what he could get.

"Alright." Ryan reluctantly glanced again at Anifiel. "The three of us will have a great time together."

~~~~~~

As expected, Anifiel was just as unenthusiastic about the idea. Ryan watched and tried to eavesdrop as Anifiel dragged Vithius aside and attempted to convince him to change his mind. Ryan heard Anifiel's favorite words like "interloper", "corruption", and "evil influence" bandied about.

But Vithius didn't look swayed by his fellow Angel's appeal. Eventually, Vithius laid his hand upon Anifiel's chest and said loudly enough for Ryan to hear, "You both are my dearest friends so I cannot and will not choose between you. If you insist and would like to visit me alone later, I would be happy to see you then."

Of course allowing Ryan first shot at Vithius was out of the question for Anifiel, so the Commander had no choice but to give in.

"I hope you're not the jealous type," Ryan said conversationally to Anifiel as he looped his arm through Vithius' and started walking.

"Ryan..." Vithius shook his head, smiling knowingly.

Anifiel, for his part, looked ready to beat someone.

"Where would you like to spend time with me?" Vithius asked as they walked. Anifiel trailing behind them like a petulant child who hadn't gotten his way.

Ryan thought about it. "Can we go to a pool? Finn liked to swim a lot and he always took me to them. But I never joined him in the water. I'd like to try swimming this time, though. With you."

"That sounds delightful. Come, hold on to me."

Ryan wrapped his arms round Vithius' forearms as the Angel hugged him from behind. A flap of the wings lifted their feet from the grass.

They didn't fly far, only a few hundred yards, before they came upon a collection of pools fed by a brilliant blue waterfall.

"How do you guys always manage to find ones

that are empty?" Ryan asked as they settled lightly onto the ground again. "It seems like these things should be crowded with people and Angels."

"If we had wished for company I would have imagined a populated pool and we would have found one," Vithius explained as if that explained everything. He approached the pool's edge and dipped a toe in. "Unsurprisingly, the temperature is perfect."

Ryan laughed a little until he heard the whoomp of another Angel approaching. He thought it interesting that the beat of Anifiel's wings sounded slightly different from other Angels'. Maybe because Anifiel had the largest wingspan of any Angel Ryan had seen so far. *You know what they say about Angels with big wings...*

He watched from the corner of his eye as Anifiel landed on the ground and took in the scene with a haughty scowl. On the flight over Ryan had made a hundred wishes that Anifiel wouldn't follow them, but apparently his wishes couldn't influence Angelic will. He kept one eye on Anifiel as Vithius slowly waded into the pool until the crystalline water rose up to just past his bellybutton.

"You said you will swim this time," Vithius reminded him, waiting expectantly in the water. A mischievous smile teased his mouth. "You cannot swim while wearing a tunic, Ryan."

"Heh. Yeah, I know."

Crap, was Anifiel gonna stare at him the whole time?

Unfortunately there was nothing Ryan could do

about it. He'd chosen to go swimming for a reason and he wasn't going to back down now just because Mr. Obnoxious was glaring daggers at him. Taking a fortifying breath, Ryan grabbed the hem of his tunic and whipped it off over his head. He ran forward and jumped into the pool as quickly as he could, cannonballing Vithius.

"There!" he said with fake confidence. "No big deal."

Vithius blinked water out of his eyes and grinned, while Anifiel chuckled where he stood. "Indeed, little human, 'little' fits you well."

Ryan's cheeks flamed. "Some guys are growers and not show-ers, alright? I mean, you've seen me get har—er, never mind."

To his surprise Anifiel looked away, a muscle jumping in his jaw. Was he embarrassed to be remembering how Ryan looked erect? Doubtful, Ryan decided. Anifiel was probably just angry having to picture Ryan's "instrument of corruption".

"Much has happened while I was away?" Vithius asked with an arched brow. He swam backward through the water, his soft cock dragging through the water like a fin. "You and Anifiel interacted?"

"That's one way of putting it," Ryan muttered. He slowly swam after Vithius. "He's been picking on me, same as usual."

"Yes, I saw the collar and leash. I was not pleased by that. I chastised him for it."

That made Ryan laugh. "Good. That was really humiliating. I only left it on because I thought I deserved it."

Dark eyes bored into his. "I do not desire your humiliation, Ryan. Do not think that way again."

Ryan's cheeks flamed. "Okay."

Vithius swam to the waterfall. He ducked his head beneath it and quickly pulled out again. He smiled as water droplets dripped from his lashes. "I have never known Anifiel to take notice of another male's organ before."

Ryan shrugged as he joined him before the falls. "I'm not surprised. I'm the only one he wants to make fun of, apparently."

"You do not think it a sexual interest?" Vithius watched him closely.

Ryan shook his head, amused by the idea. "Hardly. While you were in your coma or whatever it was, Anifiel was mean to me the same as always." He didn't feel like elaborating on the occasional doubts he'd had about the nature of Anifiel's interest in him. Better just to forget them. Better yet—

He swam closer until he was treading water directly in front of Vithius. "The only interest he has is in Finn." He watched sadly as Vithius' face fell. "It's true," Ryan went on as gently as he could. "While you were gone I realized that about him. He really does love Finn. He misses him a lot. I was wrong this whole time. Anifiel *needs* Finn."

Vithius' attention drifted beyond Ryan to Anifiel. The longing in his dark eyes depressed Ryan. Still, it was better that they end this attempt to seduce Anifiel before Vithius' heart was broken so badly it couldn't be mended.

"I feared as much," Vithius said softly as he

absently dragged the tips of his fingers across the surface of the water. "I allowed my own desires to blind me to the truth."

"No," Ryan corrected him, "You allowed me to blind you. I talked you into this, remember? I came up with that dumb idea of trying to make Anifiel jealous. I was wrong about all of it. Anifiel needs Finn. And you—" he swallowed nervously before bringing his dripping fingers to Vithius' chin and tilting the Angel's face up. "You need someone who loves you to the bottom of their soul." Ryan mustered his courage and whispered, "You need me."

Vithius' breath caught. "I think perhaps you missed me too much, my friend. Your relief is confusing your emotions."

"I did miss you too much," Ryan agreed, "but I'm not confused. Losing you was the most awful thing that's happened to me in a long time. It made me open my eyes to what I want." He felt his cheeks heating as memories surfaced. "When I was alive, I chased after men who didn't want me. I made a fool out of myself by pursuing guys I knew were out of my league. I knew they'd reject me."

"Then why did you continue?" Vithius asked, perplexed.

Ryan laughed uneasily. "Because I'm human. Humans are weird that way. I went after guys who would never be in a relationship with me because it protected me. I never got to know them well enough to be hurt when they left me. Because...they would *always* leave me."

"They are fools," Vithius insisted.

"I think I was the fool, actually." Ryan caressed the Angel's chin. "But when you got hurt, it made me think about things. About how I want this experience in Heaven to be for me. I don't want a repeat of my life on Earth. It wasn't a great time. I want my experience in Heaven to be different, to be the best I can make it, and that means taking a chance on the thing I really want, which is you. I know you're an Angel and I'm just a puny human. You can hurt me. You can say no. But I have to try. I've never met anyone as kind and wonderful as you. You're the nicest person in all of Heaven, I'm sure of it. And you're beautiful. Yet you don't see it, which makes you even more beautiful. Believe me: this isn't some infatuation. I'm falling in love with you, Vithius."

Declaring his love hadn't been part of the plan but once he uttered the words Ryan knew they were right and true. Vithius made him feel like a great person. Vithius respected him and treated him as an equal even though they obviously weren't. How could Ryan not love him?

"If-If you give me a chance, someday I'll be an Angel, too, and we'll be more equal. You won't need to be embarrassed about being seen with me."

"Shush." Vithius caught Ryan's hand on his chin and squeezed it. "I have no reason to be embarrassed by your company. I am privileged to share it." The Angel looked down at Ryan's hand and tentatively brought it to his lips and kissed it. "This is right? I have seen human males do this to their lovers."

Ryan stared at Vithius' lips hovering above his fingers. He could still feel the soft impression of the Angel's mouth against his knuckles. "Do it again," he breathed.

Vithius arched a brow as he pressed his lips to Ryan's fingers once again. Ryan's knees shook under the water. He felt his cock begin to rise.

"Sometimes humans are unfairly affected by an Angel's nearness," Vithius murmured. "I think that is happening to you now."

"No," Ryan said quickly, placing his free hand on the Angel's shoulder. "I know what that feels like. This isn't it."

It was partially true. The fugue that came over him when Anifiel touched him was like being bowled over by a train. It was intense, powerful, and all-consuming. What he felt while Vithius touched him was different. It was a warm tingly feeling that made Ryan want to curl up with the Angel and pet him.

"This is different," he insisted. "It's good. I'm still in control of myself, and of how I feel."

Vithius nodded, looking relieved. "I have heard that the intensity of it is sometimes related to an Angel's bearing. But having never touched a human, I was not sure if I would have an effect."

"Oh, you have an effect on me, alright." Ryan smiled ruefully.

Vithius looked intrigued. "Do I?"

Ryan hesitated and then switched their grip so that he held Vithius' hand. He guided it beneath the water. With his eyes locked on the Angel's, he pressed Vithius' palm against his erection.

Vithius gasped, his eyes rounding. "But I did not touch you first to make it hard!"

"Sometimes you don't have to." Ryan laughed hoarsely and pressed Vithius' hand harder against him. He shuddered and tried not to hump against the Angel. "That's my body reacting to yours. That's how much I like you. I wasn't exaggerating."

"I did not even need to touch you," Vithius repeated, astonishment painting his face. "You are hard and yet so soft."

He curled his fingers, spreading them around the root of Ryan's cock, fingertips brushing his ball sac. Ryan gasped and bit his lip.

"This was how you reacted when I touched you in your secret place," Vithius whispered, awed. "I did not get to see, but now I feel how your organ must have been then."

Remembering the Angel's finger pushing experimentally against his entrance made Ryan surge toward orgasm. "It was because of you, Vithius." He groaned and clutched the Angel's shoulder tighter as Vithius began to explore the length and shape of him. "I can't help myself. Oh, please..."

"Your body wishes to join with mine, yes?"

Oh, my god. The image of that coupling was too much. Ryan thrust himself against Vithius' palm, whimpering at the friction. "Only...only if you want it," he gasped.

Doubt, however, came to Vithius' face. And to Ryan's dismay, a touch of apprehension appeared, also. "I do not know," the Angel said, carefully extracting his hand from Ryan's grip. Vithius gave him an apologetic smile. "I am not certain."

Ryan sighed and nodded. "It's okay. It's really okay. This is all happening fast for you. I mean, you're a virgin, after all. A really, really *virgin* virgin. It's okay to be a little confused and maybe scared. And, hey, you don't even know if you like me that way so I can understand that too—"

"You speak quickly when you are embarrassed," Vithius observed, amused.

Ryan blushed, wishing he could tie his tongue in a knot. "Sorry. Nervous habit."

"I find it endearing."

Again, Vithius managed to make him feel better about himself even with his faults. Ryan gazed at him with all the adoration he felt. He could not think of a more perfect partner.

"I meant what I said earlier," he said earnestly. "I think I'm falling in love with you. No, I *know* I am. I'd like you to at least think about being with me. I know I'm not the most attractive person in Heaven, or the wittiest or most intelligent, or, well, anything. But I care so much for you, Vithius. I promise you I could make you happy and teach you things that I know you'll love."

Vithius tilted his head back and admired the sky. "You offer so much. I would be a fool to refuse you." He looked down at Ryan again and smiled. "We are already friends. I am open to the possibility of exploring more with you."

Ryan shifted from foot to foot. "So, uh, is that a yes?"

Vithius laughed. "I admit my heart still pines

for Anifiel, but I possess much love and I would like to share it with you."

"I need to teach you how to give a straight answer," Ryan grumbled, but inside he was jumping for joy. Vithius hadn't rejected him, which was huge.

"Come. We should not leave Anifiel alone for so long. He misses me sorely, I think." Still chuckling, Vithius took Ryan by the hand and led him back to where Anifiel was now sitting on the ground.

With Vithius' hand holding his, Ryan felt on equal footing with the Commander for the first time ever. In fact, he felt to be just slightly Anifiel's superior.

"I guess it's your turn to hang out with him now," he said to the scowling blond Angel. Ryan made a point of quickly kissing Vithius on the cheek and smiling bashfully when the dark-haired Angel gave him a look of pleasant surprise.

"Indeed, if you are done mauling and corrupting my battle companion," Anifiel growled, rising to his feet.

"Ryan is my friend, Anifiel. Please treat him with respect," Vithius admonished.

"He led to your corruption!" Anifiel snapped. He spread his own wings and reached into the imposing field of dense white feathers to pull out a single loose feather. Ryan paled at the sight of it.

"This came from you," Anifiel snarled. He held out the tainted gray feather to Vithius. "The battle companion of the Commander of Heaven's Army has been corrupted because of this human's actions! I will never forget that! Nor will I forgive it!"

Vithius' fingers trembled in Ryan's grip. "I did not know my wings were tainted," he whispered.

Anguish twisted Anifiel's face. "I did not want to see it!"

Vithius took a deep breath and then shook his head. "But which pains you most? That it was caused indirectly by a human? Or that it happened to the one who reflects on your name?" Vithius' voice shook with passion. "Do you not think that I am the one who has suffered most grievously from this? Do you not think that I should be the one who decides what punishment should be meted out, if any?"

"Then punish him!" Anifiel boomed, pointing the soiled feather at Ryan. "The fault lies at his feet and you know it!"

But Vithius dragged Ryan against his side and wrapped his arm around him. "I cannot, nor do I wish to punish him when he has shown he would gladly take my place in the Beneath if he could. That is a love I cannot punish, Anifiel."

"You are nothing but a fool who has allowed carnal desires to cloud your judgment! I thought my battle companion stronger than that!"

Vithius tensed. Ryan held his breath in dread, knowing what the Angel was about to say. "I question if you would have made me the same offer that this human did, Anifiel." Vithius' body vibrated with tension. "Would you have taken my place in the Beneath if such a tragedy were to befall me? Would you?"

Anifiel's mouth opened and shut without sound. Slowly, as if looking at Medusa, his face turned stony. "You know I cannot offer that," he said coolly. "My position as Commander cannot be forsaken. All of Heaven would fall."

Ryan felt Vithius' entire body trembling with suppressed emotion. He himself was awash with nervous sweat.

"Then do not dare tell me to whom I may grant my affections," Vithius lashed out in a strained voice. "If corruption is my fate, I gladly walk to it with one who truly loves me."

Ryan gaped, but Anifiel's face reflected nothing. The golden Angel inclined his head. "I shall visit with you another time, Vithius, when reason rules you again." He beat his magnificent wings against the air until his feet left the ground. He flew from them without a backward glance.

Vithius released Ryan and pressed both hands to his face. Stunned by the confrontation, Ryan backed away. His eyes fell to the grass where Anifiel had been sitting while he and Vithius swam together. The soil was churned up in rows, as if the golden Angel had been clawing it.

10

"Your wings are still beautiful, you know. It was just the one. The one feather, I mean." Ryan chewed on a thumbnail as he looked down at Vithius lying on his back beside him. "Now that it's gone no one will ever know it turned gray."

Vithius had one arm slung across his eyes, the other resting on his stomach. He smiled faintly. "Unfortunately it will grow back. Corruption is not something an Angel may forget. An Angel is not meant to. The taint serves as a lesson to all."

"But that's not fair," Ryan argued. He stretched his legs out. Sitting cross-legged while he watched Vithius was giving him cramps. Especially since the Angel had been lying there for at least half an hour, ever since Anifiel flew off. "If humans can learn from their mistakes and still ascend, Angels should, too. Well, except the ascend part, of course."

Vithius lowered his arm. His dark eyes were

clear, but they were sad. "I am a True Angel, Ryan. The Creator made me to serve as an example to humans and to protect Heaven. A True Angel is not meant to 'learn'. We are not meant to aspire to anything."

Ryan gnawed on his thumbnail again as he thought over the words. "But didn't you tell me that Angels have the equivalent of a fatal flaw? You said that if Angels were perfect, then humans would give up trying because we'd realize we could never match up."

He saw he'd surprised Vithius. The Angel slowly sat up. "I did say that."

Encouraged by his response, Ryan went on. "We both know Anifiel doesn't like humans and is narrow-minded that way. That's probably his imperfection." *Though I could easily name a few more.* "So maybe this is your flaw, so to speak. You're too—I don't know, protective, maybe?"

Vithius frowned. "That hardly seems a flaw. My role as Anifiel's battle companion is to protect him. My purpose as a warrior is to protect Heaven."

Ryan slumped. "Yeah, I guess you're right."

"Unless...No." Vithius shook his head and turned away.

"What? Did you think of something?" Ryan leaned forward, trying to see the Angel's face.

Reluctantly, Vithius turned his head. Ryan blinked at the adorable blush on the Angel's face. "Perhaps my fault is that I love Anifiel when I should not. When I saw him about to be attacked by the Demon a terrible rage overtook me. I did not think. I wanted only to harm the creature for daring to put someone I loved in danger."

It definitely wasn't something Ryan was thrilled to hear, but he had to admit his friend was probably right. Vithius hadn't been saving *him* no matter how good it felt to think that.

"Maybe you're right," Ryan said slowly. Then he brightened. "But that's good. Now that we've established you're not perfect, that means you can learn and overcome your corruption! And the way to do that is to stop pursuing Anifiel and start pursuing me!"

Vithius looked at him blankly. "Pursue you?"

Ryan's grin wobbled. "Well, that part was kind of a joke. But the rest is true," he hurried to add. "It's obvious you're not supposed to love Anifiel because look where it got you. Maybe you're supposed to learn that humans are just as loveable. And then your feather will turn white again."

The Angel studied him for a long moment. He cocked his head to the side. "Do you truly think so?"

Knowing he'd better be honest or things could become even worse for him than they already were, Ryan raised his hands. "Admittedly I could be a little off-base. I'm not exactly an expert of Heaven. You're looking at a guy who's been in the Middle Tier for nearly three years. But, it's worth considering, right? I'm not trying to trick you or anything, Vithius. I'd never do that if that's what you're worried about."

Vithius' skeptical expression quickly softened. "No, I did not think that at all, Ryan. It is something to consider, certainly. If loving Anifiel is indeed my weakness, then I should concentrate on discovering my strength, yes?"

Relieved, Ryan nodded. "That's right. And who knows, your strength could be how well you end up loving me!" He gave a crooked, bashful smile. "Or not."

"It would be a wonderful strength to have," Vithius murmured, focusing on Ryan with new intensity.

Ryan plucked absently at the grass, his blush deepening and a funny little tickle stirring his belly. He couldn't remember anyone looking at him like this.

Vithius lightened the mood by smiling and standing. He reached down and helped Ryan to his feet. "Should we find Anifiel and soothe his ruffled feathers, do you think? Although I should not love him, he is my friend and my battle companion. I care very much for his feelings. I do not wish them to be bruised."

"I don't think you'd be a very good Angel if you didn't care," Ryan replied honestly even though he'd rather do anything than go find Anifiel. The blond Angel undoubtedly had it out for him after that quarrel with Vithius. Ryan was probably Public Enemy Number One.

"His frustration is not with you," Vithius said softly, as if reading his mind. The Angel kept hold of Ryan's hand and squeezed it. "I may have hurt him. It is not your fault."

"What about it being his fault, then? He's the

one who wouldn't agree to switch—"

But Vithius shook his head. "Hush, Ryan. Please say no more. I care for him dearly. I will not side with you against him."

Ashamed when he realized he was trying to convert Vithius at least subconsciously, Ryan squeezed the Angel's hand back. "I'm sorry. You're right. I guess I'm butting in. I won't say any more about him."

"Censoring yourself is not what I desire, either. I look forward to the day when you believe what you say, and what you say makes you happy."

As Ryan blinked, trying to figure out what that meant, Vithius tugged him forward. Ryan gladly fell against the Angel's hard chest and abandoned thinking. For a moment he closed his eyes, savoring the feel of the Angel against him. He realized he was breathing deeply, inhaling Vithius' crisp, pine-like scent. *Angels smell so good...*

"One day the words you speak will benefit not only yourself but those around you, Ryan. The day is coming." He turned Ryan so they were back-to-chest. Vithius held him securely before lifting off the ground. "Let us find our wayward Commander. I fear he is saddened."

Saddened. Ryan stopped himself midway through making a face. He really didn't have the right, he realized. He'd seen the proof that Anifiel had feelings. The Angel missed Finn. He'd been upset by and jealous of Vithius' relationship with Ryan. If he were honest with himself, Ryan didn't think Anifiel was heartless, just too obnoxious and bullying. If Anifiel had been a human he would have been the type of guy at school Ryan would have hated and yet secretly stalked. Anifiel would have gotten away with anything and everything and Ryan would have resented him for that. Just as he was doing now.

"I know Anifiel's not bad," he said aloud as Vithius flew them above the grass and over streams of gleaming turquoise. "He couldn't be an Angel, or the Creator's favorite, if he weren't inherently good."

"True," Vithius agreed.

"But he's just—I want to understand him, but he makes it so difficult, you know? I mean, if I walked up to him and held out my hand and said, 'You know, Anifiel, we got off on the wrong foot. Let's start over', he'd laugh in my face or worse, punch me in the nose."

"What foot were you on? I do not understand."

Ryan laughed. "It's a figure of speech. It's not literal. But you get what I'm saying, right? I don't think it's entirely me; it's him. It's like he deliberately tries to make me mad. Like, all the time."

"Well, he does hold you to blame for Finnian's defection," Vithius pointed out carefully.

"Yeah, but—" Ryan tried to shrug but it was difficult while being held aloft by an Angel. "I don't know. I get the impression it's more than that. He didn't like me from the beginning, Vithius. Back when Finn and I were friends. He didn't like me even then."

Vithius banked, taking them into a gentle turn.

Below them a game of soccer was being played by two teams of humans. Ryan had no idea you could get a soccer ball in Heaven, but he supposed he shouldn't have been surprised. Heaven wasn't all that different from Earth, really. In fact, he thought happily, it was like an improved version of it.

"Have you considered," Vithius began, "that perhaps Anifiel's flaw is not dislike of humans, but jealousy? If, as you say he did not appreciate your friendship with Finnian and he clearly does not feel comfortable with your friendship with me, an explanation may be that he is jealous."

How did Vithius manage to dilute everything negative about Anifiel? Ryan wondered. Anifiel deliberately intimidated him and all but ran Ryan off whenever the blond Angel found him and Finn together. And saying the Commander wasn't comfortable with Ryan's friendship with Vithius was like saying Ryan felt a little funny whenever Anifiel touched him.

Vithius' white-washing frustrated Ryan because it invariably left him feeling like he was the one in the wrong. Yes, he was aware he'd made a lot of mistakes in Heaven, but surely not all of his run-ins with Anifiel were his fault?

Were they?

"Anifiel defends more fiercely than any Angel in Heaven," Vithius continued, his words of praise only serving to make Ryan more depressed. "He would fight every Demon alone if he must; he would not quail from such a demand. That loyalty and protectiveness would extend to his lover and to his battle companion. Yes, I think Anifiel is jealous of you. He does not dislike you; he fears you intend to take away those who are important to him. I believe if he understood that you do not wish such a thing, his attitude toward you would improve greatly."

The sigh Ryan released was so deep it felt as though it came from his feet. "But I can't just say, hey, I'm not going to take Vithius away. He won't believe me. I think he actually likes not liking me. I think he takes some kind of perverse pleasure from it. I think if things are going to change the attitude adjustment has to come from him first."

"You are not willing to try?"

"Of course I'm willing to try. I've got more to lose than he does. I don't want to be in the Middle Tier forever. But I don't think it's going to happen while he hates me."

"Ryan, he does not hate you."

"I know, I know," Ryan sighed again. "He's just jealous. But that doesn't change his treatment of me."

Vithius' arms tightened gently around him. "I wish I knew better how to comfort you."

"Honestly? Just be my friend. Don't let him talk you out of it. That's all I beg of you." It was such a likely possibility that Ryan dreaded it like he used to dread the day after Thanksgiving sales.

"You are my friend because I like you, whether or not Anifiel approves," Vithius assured him. "You need not worry."

Ryan nodded, telling himself he should believe it. Vithius wouldn't lie, after all. He couldn't.

Turning his thoughts from what he couldn't control, Ryan decided to take in their progress. He'd been zoning out and he discovered he had no idea where Vithius had been flying him, not that Ryan had much of a handle on the landscape of Heaven, anyway. Everything he'd seen so far had, for the most part, been blue and green with the occasional distant purple mountain.

"Where are we?"

"On our way to find Anifiel."

"You know where he is?"

Vithius turned them in the air again. "He was not on the Path to Inspiration, nor at his pavilion. So I believe he has gone elsewhere."

"Wow, we already flew over those? Where was I?"

A warm chuckle ruffled the hair of Ryan's head. "You were deep in thought about our Commander. Yes, we have already flown over the places he frequents. But there is one other place where he might be."

Vithius made one more turn before leveling out. The view that was suddenly laid out before them made Ryan's heart skip a beat.

"What is that?"

He felt the Angel's lips against his ear. "That is the Dreaming Coil."

It was like nothing Ryan had ever seen, either in movies or in dreams. Ahead of them stretched a field easily as long as ten football fields; he couldn't see the end. For all he knew it extended for eternity. On either side of the field, sakura trees grew like living sidelines, providing a border. They were bright pink with cherry blossoms and Ryan knew without asking that they were perpetually in bloom.

In between the rows of trees milled tens of thousands of humans. It was the greatest concentration of people he'd ever seen in Heaven. Heck, it was the most he'd seen anywhere except in the movies, and even then they were computer generated. This was what he imagined ancient armies must have looked like, masses of bodies gathered for a battle of attrition. It was a literal sea of humanity.

The humongous field, the lines of trees, the extraordinary number of people—it was all amazing but there was more. Angels flew above the field, each holding what looked like giant combs made of whale baleen. As Ryan watched, the Angels flew slowly width-wise across the field, their baleen combs dragging gently through what looked like thousands of iridescent filaments that hung in the air. It was as though the field was a bald man's head and the Angels were performing a giant comb-over utilizing glowing strands of hair.

"Dreaming Coil?" Ryan repeated, feeling dumber than he ever had in his life. "I don't know what I'm seeing."

Vithius laughed softly. He adjusted the beat of his wings until they were no longer flying forward but hovering in the air several yards from the edge of the strange field.

"Look to the trees on the right," Vithius instructed. "Do you see them? Do you see the dreams as they burst over the tree tops?"

Ryan had no idea what the Angel was talking about but he looked to the tops of the trees on the right side of the field. Shimmering threads resembling glowing fishing line arched above the trees. Upon closer study Ryan realized the threads didn't sprout from the trees but came from somewhere on the other side of them. He watched as new threads suddenly shot from whatever was on the other side of the trees. The threads arched over the field of people. It looked, strangely enough, as though people were casting fishing lines from the other side of the trees.

"What was that?" he exclaimed, pointing at the glowing threads even though they were soon difficult to differentiate among the thousands of others threads that currently shimmered in the air. "They shot up from the other side of the trees."

"They came from Earth," Vithius murmured. "Those, Ryan, are the dreams of living humans."

The confusion that filled Ryan's mind was immense, almost mind-numbing. Those strings were dreams? From Earth? But how? What did it mean?

Frustrated, he continued to watch the area above the trees and sure enough he discovered there were hundreds if not thousands of flowing threads bursting from over the treetops. Some flew all the way across the field and disappeared into the clouds beyond the second 'sideline' of trees. But some threads only reached midway over the field and then began to curl and twine in the air just like snapped fishing lines in the ocean. Other lines didn't make it that far; they shot up over the first line of trees then seemed to wilt and sink back out of sight behind the trees again.

"How are those dreams?" he asked. "Why do they look like strings and why do some go all the way over and some don't?" His eyes alighted on the Angels flying over the field who were combing the threads with their brush-like combs. "And what in the world are those Angels doing?"

His ignorance had never felt so acute, so overwhelming. It was like he was in another world, an alien one where science meant absolutely nothing. His face broke out in a sweat. A point behind his left eye began to throb.

"It is alright," Vithius soothed, again somehow knowing exactly what Ryan was thinking and feeling. Ryan rolled his face against Vithius' shoulders, seeking comfort from his sudden stress, but he couldn't pull his eyes from the amazing, bewildering scene before him.

"I will tell you what is happening," Vithius went on gently. "When humans dream, those dreams do not always remain in their minds. Sometimes when their need is great, when they are desperate or their minds are full of anguish and question, their dreams streak to Heaven. That is what you see there at the trees. Those are new dreams as they are being created. See how they burst up? Humans on Earth have just dreamt them."

Ryan nodded. He told himself to go with it, to not try to find a logical explanation for what should have been impossible. "Why do their dreams come up to Heaven?"

"Their need is great. Their pain is great. Whether the humans know it or not they are seeking answers and some seek comfort. Like children, they seek those things from their Creator."

Ryan pointed at a filament that lost steam three-quarters of the way across the field. Like the others that had failed to make it across, it wilted and curled around itself there in the sky. "Why do some of them make it all the way and others only go partway?"

"Some dreams are not urgent enough to reach the Creator. You see the Coil Angels?"

Ryan nodded. "The ones with the weird brushes?"

"Watch as they comb through the dreams. They will be able straighten most coils and send them on their way to the Upper Tier. But some, as you see, cannot be untangled."

It was true. Though the Angels combed gently through the coiling dreams, some refused to unwind. They hovered in the air like tangled, slow-moving seaweed.

"What's wrong with them?" Ryan asked.

"Those dreams are not meant for the Creator. They are meant for *them*."

Ryan looked down at the sea of people again. It was easy to see them as a solid mass, but if he concentrated on small areas, he saw that the people weren't standing still; they were reaching for the dreams. Some had hold of the tangled threads and were simply holding them. Others were in the process of releasing straightened threads into the sky. These threads then sank back over the trees whence they had come, like snakes retreating into holes in the ground.

"When a human dies, sometimes those he or she left behind cannot accept the loss. They cannot move on. Their dreams are full of anguish. The tangled coils you see are the dreams of the ones left behind."

"Left behind," Ryan echoed, his throat suddenly aching. "The families you mean. The friends."

"While there is pain for all, for some it is acute. It prevents them from going on with their lives. It is these whose troubled dreams find their way here. See the female with the long fair hair just below us?" Ryan located her. She held a tangled, glowing thread in her hand and was gently stroking it. As he watched, the thread gradually unwound. She released it, and it slowly retracted back over the trees. "That human female came here because she heard the call of that troubled dream. They all have. For them, a dream calls their name and they find it. They soothe it so those left behind on Earth can then move on."

Ryan's vision began to blur, the shimmering threads blending into a sheet of pearl. "I never heard that call, Vithius. No dream called my name. Does that mean no one on Earth...missed me?"

He closed his eyes as Vithius pressed his cheek to his. "Do not think such a thing, Ryan. Please. It troubles me that you would believe something like this. If you did not hear the call it is because those you left behind were strong. As I said, not every human sends a dream here. Look how few humans are here to soothe dreams when there are trillions in Heaven, Ryan. Trillions upon trillions. Yet there are only these few here. You were missed, I promise you. Do not judge your worth by the pain endured by your loved ones."

Ryan forced his eyes open. He blinked rapidly. Vithius was right. It seemed like a lot of humans had gathered here but in the scheme of things this was only a tiny percentage of them. It wasn't even a half percent of all who had come to Heaven. His family and friends weren't the only ones on Earth who had found a way to go on without him. He wasn't the exception.

"Why did you bring me here?" he whispered. He wasn't angry, but he didn't understand and he was upset. "What am I supposed to learn from this?"

Vithius' voice sounded apologetic beside his ear. "This is not a lesson. Nor had I meant to upset you. I thought—I hoped Anifiel would be here. I thought maybe Finnian might have dreamed of him and thus Anifiel heard the call. It was a dim hope. Finnian is not human. I doubt his dreams would reach Heaven the same way, or if he can dream at all. I confess I do not know how such things work in a situation such as his. I am sorry if I hurt you by bringing you here, Ryan."

"You didn't hurt me," Ryan replied softly, watching the strange dance of glowing threads and the Angels who combed them. He compared the scene to that he had seen earlier of the humans playing soccer. There was no comparison. "You've reminded me how far I am from everything I know," he continued, wanting to close his eyes and turn away. "This really is Heaven. I'm dead. All of this is real and it will never be the way it was on Earth. I've lost all of that."

Vithius' wings flapped, turning them away from the Dreaming Coil. "Yes, Ryan. This is Heaven. Whether you wish it or not, this will be your home forever. Please believe me...it is not a bad thing."

Ryan finally closed his eyes. "I guess I'll take your word on that."

~~~~~

When Vithius took him back to Anifiel and Finn's pavilion, Ryan understood the dark-haired Angel's intentions. Ryan was glad of it. The place was abandoned and when he climbed onto the pallet within the "walls" Anifiel had built Ryan felt safe. He knew this place. It could have been a garden, or someone's backyard on Earth. He could pretend for as long as he liked that he wasn't far away from the place he had always called home.

But he didn't expect Vithius to sit on the pallet beside him and pull him into a loose, warm embrace. Ryan submitted to it readily. He felt strange, like he'd received an electrical shock, perhaps. While a part of him wanted to cry a little, another part was simply scared. In the years that he'd been in Heaven he'd seen only a small part of it, the soothing park-like aspect of it. But Heaven was more than a beautiful park full of glistening lakes and lazy streams. It was an alien world beyond his comprehension. It was a place that even imagination could not fully explain. If Vithius were to leave him, Ryan would be alone to figure out its mysteries on his own and that frightened him in a way he didn't think anyone should be frightened in Heaven.

He sensed apology in Vithius' hands as they cautiously stroked his bare shoulders. The touches were light. They made Ryan shiver. The longer Vithius touched him the more he forgot his fear and concentrated only on the hot skin brushing over his. This was the first time Vithius initiated such intimacy. Instead of relaxing Ryan it made him hold his breath, wondering if Vithius had the courage, the curiosity, to do more.

One of the Angel's hands drifted up his shoulder, skimming hesitantly across the fabric of his tunic. Fingers touched the side of his neck. Ryan dropped his hands to Vithius' thigh and held onto the firm muscles as his own heart began to thud painfully against his rib cage. Fingertips traced the chords of his neck, sliding to the underside of his jaw. One finger discovered the pulse racing beneath his skin and hovered there.

Yes, this was Heaven, not Earth, but at least this was the same. This excitement, this hope— Ryan had felt them before when he was alive but this was the first time he believed they might actually lead to something good and not leave him rejected, alone and aching. Only in Heaven could he have found someone like Vithius. Only with an

Angel could Ryan rediscover the innocent joy of falling in love. It erased the stress he had felt earlier. If this was the trade-off of being a stranger in a strange land he would gladly accept it. He must.

Vithius' breath stirred the curls at Ryan's temple. The Angel's fingers slid up until they cupped his chin. Ryan responded to the hesitant pressure and lifted his face.

Vithius' eyes were as dark as he'd ever seen them. Maybe it was because his pupils were dilated the way Ryan knew his own must be. The intense look the Angel had given him earlier had returned. It made Ryan's spine melt even as his cock began to rise between his legs. His instincts were to fall back and hope that Vithius would follow, hover over him, and do whatever he wanted. But this was an Angel. A virgin Angel. Ryan couldn't be passive to get what he wanted.

He slid one of his hands up Vithius' thigh. Though the heat of the Angel's sex was like a mini-inferno, Ryan resisted touching the flames. Instead, he let his hand rest close to the Angel's sex as a tease. When he glanced down quickly, his heartbeat spiked. Vithius was as hard as he, the Angel's magnificent sex a rigid column of dark flesh in search of release.

Ryan wanted to take hold of it. He wanted to stroke Vithius hard and fast and show the Angel what he was missing of human pleasure. But he forced himself to refrain. Vithius was initiating. Ryan wanted to see how far he would go on his own.

He didn't have long to wait. With his hand tipping Ryan's chin up, Vithius lowered his face. The inches separating them dissolved. Ryan closed his eyes and moaned softly before their lips even met. When the soft pillow of Vithius' lips finally did touch his own he wanted to moan even louder, but Ryan swallowed it down for fear of scaring the Angel.

Whether it was because of the fugue or Vithius himself, this kiss was like no other kiss Ryan had experienced. Soft lips sweetly compressed his own. After a few seconds they began a slow exploration of the curves and contours of his mouth. Vithius' lips massaged gently. They brushed back and forth across Ryan's, heightening sensation as if the Angel was a skilled Casanova who knew all the right places to touch Ryan to make him tremble.

Ryan's fingers dug into Vithius' thigh as he fought to control himself. He wanted so badly to launch himself at the Angel and devour him. On Earth he'd often been a little desperate and thrown himself at guys, but this was different. If he became aggressive with Vithius he was positive he wouldn't be rejected.

Still, he waited. The novelty of having Vithius be in charge was too much of a turn-on to interrupt. Though Ryan began to shift restlessly on the pallet, rubbing his butt and squeezing his legs, he didn't move his hands from the Angel's thighs. It was a wonderful sort of self-torture that soon had him humping the air. His breath puffed hard and fast against Vithius' lips until the Angel leaned back slightly in concern.

"Am I doing this to your enjoyment?" Vithius whispered. "You tremble and you breathe rapidly."

Ryan laughed hoarsely. "I'm so turned on I could burst, Vithius. I love the way you kiss. You're fantastic at it."

The Angel smiled shyly. "I confess kissing is a strange action but I find pleasure in the touching of my lips to yours." His eyes fell to Ryan's mouth. His eyes darkened. "Your lips feel like the wings of butterflies. But I do not believe kissing butterflies would inspire such a strange aching in my body."

Ryan groaned at hearing Vithius ached for him. "Kiss me again," he breathed. "This time open your mouth a little."

Vithius' eyes widened slightly, but he didn't argue. His lips found Ryan's again. Ryan opened his own lips and slid his tongue out to lightly stroke it across the Angel's lush bottom lip.

Vithius let out a gasp, his eyes shooting open. Ryan hadn't closed his, so he stared back into his friend's eyes, hoping to soothe him. It worked, because slowly the dark lashes fell. In the next second, the Angel's slick tongue slid out and touched Ryan's in a tentative hello.

Ryan whimpered like he had the first time a girl touched his penis. He tried to keep his tongue under control but Vithius became suddenly bold, wrapping his tongue around Ryan's. Once that happened Ryan gave up trying to hold himself back. He lifted his hands to the Angel's hair and clutched the soft strands as he deepened the kiss. He licked Vithius' mouth, stroking palate, teeth and tongue, delighting in the soft cries of surprised pleasure the Angel emitted. Strong arms wrapped around Ryan's back, pulling him closer as if Vithius needed more contact. When Vithius sucked experimentally on Ryan's tongue, Ryan nearly came.

Climbing into the Angel's lap seemed the next logical move but when he attempted to move his legs Ryan found them unexpectedly trapped beneath rough palms. He started to open his eyes, wondering how Vithius' arms could be around his back when the Angel's hands were on his legs but then his mind started to fog over in the most pleasant of ways.

His eyes rolled up into his head. His mouth fell open wider, which Vithius took advantage of to deepen their kiss. The hands on his legs began to slide upward. They reached the hem of his tunic and still they continued up. Arousal clouded Ryan's brain. He could no longer participate in the kiss, could only moan as Vithius kissed him regardless. Of their own volition Ryan's hips began to move, tilting into the hands that were high on his thighs. Hands he now realized were coming from behind him...

"He does not care who is touching him, only that it is an Angel," Anifiel purred.

Vithius gasped into Ryan's mouth and jerked backward, eyes round. "Anifiel! This is—What are you—" The dark-haired Angel floundered, his cheeks burnt with arousal and embarrassment.

Ryan wanted to help him but the fugue was thick, overpowering. Two Angels at the same time...He moaned softly, reaching for Vithius, trying to bring him back and complete the mind-blowing circuit they had begun. Vithius leaned out of his reach, looking mortified, but Anifiel gave Ryan the touch he craved. The hands on his thighs moved to his waist almost possessively. Ryan shuddered as Anifiel spoke against his ear.

"Tell him, little human. You troll for Angels. It does not matter which Angel you trap, only that he feeds your carnal desires."

Ryan opened his mouth to agree because he couldn't deny that he ached for an Angel's touch. It was the most powerful drug in existence. Heroin had nothing on this. But when he lifted his eyes to Vithius' face and saw the crushed expression there, Ryan fought the fugue that Anifiel was forcing on him.

"No," he whispered, though his tongue felt thick and sluggish. Words were difficult to form. Moaning was so much easier. "Not—any Angel. Vithius," he gasped. "Only Vithius."

Vithius' expression eased and Ryan congratulated himself on how strong he was to resist the fugue. But the next words out of Anifiel's mouth killed that elation.

"I think I should prove you wrong, little human. I think my battle companion should witness for himself how little you care about who satisfies your filthy desires."

Anifiel tugged him backward. Unable to resist, Ryan fell back against the golden Angel's chest. The increased body contact made the fugue too powerful to fight. Ryan melted within the circle of Anifiel's arms, burning with need, knowing Vithius was watching but unable to do anything about it.

"Admit what you want," Anifiel husked.

"No," Ryan moaned, but he turned his head to the side, opening his neck for lips or tongue to explore him.

Anifiel's breath fanned his cheek, the scent of green apples filling his nostrils. "Admit it, little human. Admit you need my touch. Mine alone."

Ryan closed his eyes. *I hate you.* "Please..."

11

It should have been the worst thing that could happen to him, being mauled by Anifiel while Vithius was forced to watch. But the Angel fugue as it intensified had a curious way of dissipating all the negative feelings and resistance Ryan had once possessed until all that was left behind was a haze of mindless lust and happiness. The longer Anifiel held Ryan pressed against him, the more Ryan wished to surrender. He needed this, desired it, and so what if Vithius was probably disgusted with him right now? Let Heaven burn down around them. He didn't care so long as this lovely, intense pleasure continued to inundate his senses.

He wanted to do everything Anifiel asked, wanted to please the Angel in every way possible. Just thinking about submitting to Anifiel's desires made Ryan arch back against the Angel, pressing his buttocks into the cradle of the other male's thighs in blatant invitation to use him. *Take me, he thought at him. Make my body yours.*

Lips brushed down the side of his neck, dragging an invisible trail of warm, moist air. Ryan shuddered violently and felt his rigid cock spurt a tiny bit of liquid into the front of his tunic.

"You smell sharp, little human," Anifiel taunted, breathing hotly into the junction of his shoulder and neck. "Your body leaks its corruption. You are strangely wet."

"Yes," Ryan panted, pressing his face into Anifiel's shoulder. "Talk dirty to me. Tell me what you want."

"Anifiel."

Even the censure in Vithius' voice could not break the fugue's hold over Ryan. If anything it stoked his desire, reminding him that he could be sandwiched between them. He imagined giving them pleasure by offering up his body to be penetrated at both ends. Afterwards, he would wait on them on his knees, attending to their every whim and desire. He whimpered as the fantasy heated his blood. He fumbled backward, his hands clutching the tops of Anifiel's hard thighs. He needed, oh, god, how he needed.

"You have been following us," Vithius continued. "We were worried for you but our search for you was fruitless all along, was it not?"

"I had to keep watch over you. I knew he would attempt to corrupt you once he had you to himself." Anifiel's hands tightened around Ryan's waist, the large palms holding him securely. Safely,

Ryan's addled mind purred.

"And I was not mistaken," Anifiel continued, smugly. "Once given the chance he sought to turn you."

"So you are here to save me from him. To save me from the feelings he engenders?" The tone of Vithius' voice pulled at Ryan. With a huge force of will he opened his eyes and lifted his face from Anifiel's shoulder. Vithius' gaze was narrowed as he stared hard at the Commander. The tone of his voice held an unexpected note of skepticism. "This is your method of saving me?"

Anifiel bridled at the other Angel's tone. "Of course. Look at him. See how he writhes in sin?"

Vithius' expression hardened for a moment, but then relaxed, becoming almost thoughtful. He crossed his arms over his chest. "You appear skilled at showing his weakness."

Anifiel snorted. "That is because I understand this human. I see into his soul and recognize the darkness within. I came to prove to you how fickle his attention, how base his interests. Look at him, Vithius!"

Anifiel slid a hand up Ryan's stomach and pressed it against his chest, one of his fingers resting directly over a ridged nipple. Ryan groaned softly at the teasing touch. He began lightly twisting back and forth to make the Angel's finger stimulate the hardened pearl of flesh.

The golden Angel bent over Ryan's cheek. "What are you doing, little human? Does this mound of useless skin on your chest arouse you?"

Ryan gasped and trembled when Anifiel experimentally rubbed his nipple. "Is there not one part of your body which you hold sacred?"

"No, touch me anywhere you want," Ryan whispered without shame, reaching up and trying to guide Anifiel's fingers against him. The Angel resisted him, making him whine. "My body is yours. Just touch me. Please." Ryan sucked in his breath hopefully. "Or let me touch you."

"He is caught under your influence." Dimly Ryan noticed that Vithius sounded unhappy. "He responds this intensely only to you, Anifiel."

"That is nothing," the blond Angel scoffed. "Watch as I do this."

"Unnh!" Ryan all but melted into Anifiel's lap as the Angel touched the tip of his tongue to the pulse beating in his throat.

"You taste dirty," Anifiel whispered, his voice nearly inaudible, as if he were sharing a secret between them. All it did was make Ryan's ache grow to tortuous levels.

"He is nothing but the embodiment of carnal desire," Anifiel said in a louder voice for Vithius' benefit. "Watch and see how corrupt he is."

Strong thighs bracketed Ryan's hips. Though he was too far from the Angel's groin to tell if he was aroused or not, Ryan was convinced Anifiel must be. Anifiel rocked against him, a strange, awkward movement, almost like he was trying to nudge Ryan off the pallet. Anifiel might not know exactly what he was doing, but Ryan understood the Angel's novice attempt to mimic the sex act. It sizzled all the synapses in his brain, making them fire at the same time as he thought of Anifiel pushing inside him...

He yelled as orgasm rushed through him, "Anifiel!"

Strong arms held him in place as he drenched the front of his tunic. He slumped, face hot, breathing hard, but his damp tunic dragged over the tip of his cock, proving the organ had not deflated. His body continued to hum as if his orgasm had merely been part one of a sequel.

Someone should bottle and sell the Angel fugue, he decided dreamily. Eau d'Anifiel.

Still hungry, he turned his head, nearly bumping noses with Anifiel and making the Angel rear back, startled. Ryan happily nuzzled into the thick stalk of the Commander's neck, inhaling his masculine scent, pressing his cheek to the hot skin of the Angel's exposed collarbone. He wetly kissed Anifiel's throat and felt a tremor run through the large body. "Let me please you," he whispered as he twisted around to face him. Panting, he slid down the Angel's body until he came to a kneeling position between Anifiel's legs, his hands covering the tops of the Angel's feet.

He looked up and saw Heaven embodied in the Angel above him. Strength and courage gave Anifiel his firm, square jaw. Purity and faith made his verdant eyes glow as if beacon-lit. His golden hair fell over his shoulders in a spill of beauty and grace. Anifiel was perfect in Ryan's eyes. He was the male of Ryan's dreams, someone powerful and manly enough for him to worship and serve without shame.

"Look at his actions," Anifiel gasped as Ryan rubbed his face, cat-like, against the Commander's golden-haired legs. "He is shameless."

"He does not respond that way with me, Anifiel."

"Exactly!" Ryan let out a pained cry as Anifiel fisted a hand in his hair, jerking his head away from the Angel's skin. Anifiel glared down at him with a fierceness that bordered on frightening. "He responds to me," the Angel snarled, "and yet he claims to care for you. What does that tell you, Vithius? It tells me that his affections are driven by lust and can be satisfied with any Angel in passing."

Ryan shivered, torn by fear and desire that muddied his senses yet also served to heighten his arousal. It was too easy to convince himself Anifiel's fury was the flipside of a reckless, dangerous passion. The Angel could hurt him...and it would feel exquisite.

"No. I think not." Vithius' voice pulled Anifiel's attention, making the Angel break the hard stare at Ryan. "If he cared only for physical satisfaction as you claim he would pressure me more insistently. But he does not. He is passive, allowing me to explore as I feel comfortable. He does not force his attentions on me, nor beg that I satisfy his needs."

"It is nothing but an act to lure you in!"

"Have you considered the possibility that he has lured you?"

Anifiel stilled. The air became tense, as if thunder were about to rattle the skies. "What do you mean?"

"Look at what you are doing, Anifiel. Your actions, your words—they are carnal. You are deliberately goading him to respond to you. Why, you even mimicked the humans' mating act just now!" Vithius' voice became hushed, his eyes soft and round with question. "I wonder...I wonder why you do this. It is not normal for an Angel."

The hand in Ryan's hair tightened as the two Angels stared at each other. The grip continued to tighten until he couldn't stand the sharp pull against his scalp any longer, forcing him to cry out in entreaty. Green eyes flashed down at him. Ryan's cry died in his throat as he looked into Anifiel's eyes and saw what he never thought he would: fear. But like the snap of lightning it disappeared and in the next instant was replaced with an anger that made Ryan tremble where he kneeled.

The hand in his hair jerked, and Ryan was sent flying out of the pavilion to tumble across the grass.

"Anifiel! You treat him poorly!"

Ryan rose onto his hands and knees, sickness welling in his body as the Angel fugue fled his body. He sank back down as he recalled the way he had acted just now, the way he had thought.

"What's wrong with me?" he whispered as he pressed his forehead to the grass. Blades pricked his closed eyelids. "Why do I let him affect me so much?"

Though the fugue had dissipated as soon as he lost contact with Anifiel, some of the neediness still lingered in him like the residual odor from a fire. How much of that was from the fugue and how much was his own desire?

"I treat him better than he deserves," Anifiel growled from the pavilion.

Ryan lifted his head slowly, glaring at the golden Angel, the bane of his existence in Heaven. But Anifiel ignored him. He squared off with Vithius, both Angels standing tensely as if on the verge of launching at each other.

"This human has taken everything from me," Anifiel went on, his large body actually trembling from the force of his passion. "How you cannot see him for what he is confuses my mind and pierces my heart. You side with him against me. You choose a human over your battle companion!" Anifiel turned his head, briefly locking gazes with Ryan. "I see I was too late in coming here. He has already taken you from me, just as he drove away my beloved."

"No, it is you who are forcing the choice," Vithius argued. "You say you will keep my friendship only if I sever his? How fair is that, Anifiel? The Creator does not condone such exclusion. Nor would the Creator condone your recent actions. You behave in a contradictory manner, which makes me believe you are responsible for losing those whom you love."

"I see the truth now. You question my behavior while I question your loyalty," Anifiel declared, but he spoke softly, which was scarier because the Angel loved to bellow like he was shouting down mountains. For him to speak like this must mean he was beyond furious. "The Commander of Heaven's Army must know that those he depends on are loyal to him. That they will never turn on him when the moment is dire. You have shown where your loyalties rest, Vithius. I cannot accept this. I will see that things are set right to keep Heaven protected."

Vithius frowned, stepping forward. "What does that mean?"

But Anifiel didn't deign to reply; he stepped out of the pavilion and launched himself into the sky, beating his wings so powerfully they buffeted Ryan to the ground like a backhand of disgust. Ryan didn't bother watching him fly away; he looked to his friend instead. Vithius stood within the pavilion, hugging himself. He looked lost and confused and more than a little apprehensive.

"What could he mean?" he asked Ryan in a shaky voice. "What have I driven him to do?"

Ryan sat up, wincing at scraped elbows and knees. "You told him the truth. It's not your fault if he can't handle it."

But his face flamed as he said this. You're so full of b.s., he thought to himself. *Who are you to say that to Vithius when you can't own up to your own truths?*

Embarrassed, he dropped his head, inwardly cringing as he listened to the Angel approach across the grass. He felt a hand run lightly through his curls. He'd never felt so unworthy of the Angel's caress as he did now.

"You have difficulty resisting him," Vithius murmured. "Do not believe this to be a fault. The Angels' power over humans is not a power but a calling. You need something from Anifiel. It may surprise you to learn that the call is not one-sided. He needs something from you, as well. Your mutual need amplifies what you feel when you come together."

That caught Ryan's attention. He looked up to find Vithius studying him with curiosity. "Not one-sided? But...he doesn't act like I do. His personality doesn't turn inside out like mine does when the fugue comes over me."

"This fugue, as you call it, is not an effect to be abused as he does. As I said, it is a calling. For as strongly as it affects you, it does not leave Anifiel untouched. I see the change in him, even if you cannot."

It sounded pretty unlikely, so Ryan chose to ignore it. "What about when it happens between you and me? It's not as strong, but I still feel it. Do you?"

The smile that broke over the Angel's face relieved the tension Ryan had secretly felt. "Yes, Ryan. I feel the call with you and it is very enjoyable."

Catching the Angel's hand and drawing it to his cheek, Ryan asked, "What does it feel like for you? Is it good? For me, it's like I want to do everything I can for you, like my pleasure and happiness depends on yours." He carefully refrained from admitting that with Anifiel, he felt like the Angel's sex slave.

Fingers caught beneath his jaw, tilting his face up. Vithius ran his thumb gently across Ryan's chin. "It is like I am being swept along a rushing river to be tumbled over a waterfall that has no bottom. It is exhilarating and worrisome at the same time," he said with a small laugh.

Ryan grinned, thrilled by the description. "That sounds like falling in love," he said without thinking.

The thumb on his chin stilled. Vithius' eyes were dark and fathomless as they studied Ryan's face. "I do not feel that with Anifiel, though," the Angel admitted, looking troubled. "With him I feel great affection and yet at other times his very presence pains me. I ache yet I suffer no injury. He makes me unhappy without doing anything to hurt me. Why is that not like the feelings of falling in love?"

Ryan swallowed hard. "That's love, too. A different kind. On Earth we call it unrequited. It's when you love someone who doesn't return the feeling." His lips twisted. "I know all about it. I know it hurts."

Vithius dropped to his knees, bringing them nearly eye to eye. The Angel cupped Ryan's face between both of his hands. "How can love feel so differently? It does not hurt with you. I like it better this way."

Blushing, Ryan nodded. "There are many kinds of love. Sometimes you have to win the other person over, so it's a struggle. Sometimes it's wild and passionate with lots of drama, like, say if Anifiel and I fell in love." He laughed at the ridiculousness of the idea. "But sometimes it's not any work at all. You fall into it and all you know is happiness and rightness. That's a nice kind of love to feel. That's how I think it'll be with you." He smiled shyly. "Because that's how I already feel."

Fingers tenderly stroked his cheeks. "A happy love is a good love to feel, I think. Does the feeling fade?"

"Not if it's true love. Not if it's real." Ryan reached up and cupped the Angel's strong shoulders. "I'm sorry about the way I acted with Anifiel. I swear I didn't mean any of it. I honestly couldn't control myself. He makes me go kind of nuts."

"The calling," Vithius murmured, as if to himself. "No, your behavior did not bother me because it was mostly beyond your control. I was upset with Anifiel's actions. Not yours."

Mostly beyond his control? What the heck did that mean? Ryan couldn't recall one second of that scene in which he'd had any influence over his behavior.

Bothered by the comment, but deciding he'd rather just forget it, he said, "I'm glad it's not that way with you. I'm glad it's just...good."

He loved the smile that curled Vithius' lips. He liked to think it held some pride and maybe a little possessiveness. "Indeed," the Angel agreed, "it is good."

Ryan moved one hand behind Vithius' neck, his fingers carding through the sleek, dark hair there. He felt tendrils of desire tickling his belly as he admired the dark skin of the Angel's throat and collarbones. He wondered if Vithius would mind receiving a hickey.

"So, uh, do you want to do it some more? Kiss,

I mean?" He flexed his fingers a little, applying light pressure to the back of the Angel's neck. "You're really good already but there's always room for improve—"

The horns that trumpeted caused him to fall back on his butt. He stared up at Vithius. "Not again!"

The Angel shook his head, although his face had drawn into tight lines. "Those are not the horns of war. You have heard these horns before, Ryan."

A memory leaped out at him. Ryan's eyes widened. "Anifiel is calling a council! But, why?"

Vithius stood and grimly held out a hand to help Ryan to his feet. "I do not expect we will be pleased with the reason."

~~~~~

Ryan had attended Anifiel's councils before with Finnian by his side. The councils were usually interesting to Ryan, likely because he was human and discussion of the condition of Ambriel's Gates and the Demons' progress on Earth was something he'd not normally hear except in movies. He was pretty sure from Vithius' mood, however, that this particular council would be enthralling for reasons other than Demons.

The dark-haired Angel flew them to the amphitheater where Anifiel held court. Already the huge grass semicircle facing the stone platform was thick with Angels. A large contingency of curious humans hovered at the edges of the group, too shy to fill in the gaps in the lawn closer to the stage.

Vithius led Ryan by the hand to the front of the crowd, an act which Ryan promised himself he would thank the Angel for profusely once they were alone. The act, done in front of everyone who was important to Vithius, made Ryan feel special. Proud. He alone held Vithius' hand and he noticed the new regard he was given by the others—mostly driven by curiosity, but some spurred by respect. Yes, he hadn't done anything to warrant it so it didn't really mean much, but after the verbal beatings he'd been suffering from Anifiel lately it was nice to finally have Angels look on him with something other than disgust.

Their trek to the front was slow going as every Angel in attendance made a point to greet Vithius and extend their condolences and appreciation for what had taken place on the battlefield. At times the remarks about his corruption, though well-meant, hurt Vithius. Ryan could tell because the Angel unconsciously tightened his fingers around Ryan's. When that happened, Ryan always squeezed back, reminding him of his silent support. He thought it helped, because Vithius would throw him small, secret smiles of thanks that made Ryan feel a hundred feet tall.

He looked for Sam and Eric, but couldn't make them out anywhere. He did see the Angels Tofiel and Camael thanks to Tofiel's tremendous height. The two Angels watched them from the other end of the stage, Camael smiling slightly as he looked at Vithius and Ryan's handhold. Is he happy for us? Ryan wondered. It seemed a bit odd since the white

Angel hadn't been exactly friendly with him. Beside the mohawked Angel, Tofiel smiled, too, though Ryan had a hunch it was simply something the easy-going Angel did often.

Finally they made it to a small patch of grass at the right of the soapstone stage. Anifiel was nowhere in sight but as soon as they sat down, the golden Angel strode onto the platform as if he'd been watching and waiting from the wings. The conversation in the crowd immediately ended when he raised both arms.

"Dear friends in Heaven," Anifiel boomed out, his voice carrying as clearly as if he held a microphone to his lips. "After the great defeat of the Demons in our most recent battle with them, one among us fell, as you all know. The Commander's battle companion, Vithius, while defending your Commander from the vile taint of the Demons, risked his own soul in an act of true selflessness. As you can see, he is here with us, not a victim of the Demons, but an Angel strong and hale."

Vithius, sitting cross-legged beside Ryan, glanced around and acknowledge with a wave the cheers that greeted his recovery.

"So far, so good," Ryan whispered to him, trying to diminish his friend's unease.

"I do not like having them remember that I am tainted," the Angel whispered back, sorrowfully.

It was then that the truth struck Ryan: the Angels hadn't been looking at Ryan with respect, but with bewilderment that the troublemaking human who'd caused Vithius to be hurt now held his hand remorselessly. Shame flooded him. He dropped his eyes to his lap, afraid to look up, afraid to see censure on the faces of Vithius' friends.

"As you know, Vithius was tainted," Anifiel went on more soberly. "He still recovers in heart and soul. It is a difficult task, but your Commander has confidence in his full recovery. But again, it is difficult. It requires much introspection, much searching of faith to resist that taint and rediscover the light. And so your Commander, with much love, is granting Vithius the gift of respite to do these things."

Vithius stiffened as if he'd been stabbed. Ryan looked worriedly between him and Anifiel. "What does that mean?" he asked, panicked by the look on the dark-haired Angel's face.

Vithius didn't answer, but Anifiel did it for him. "Taking Vithius' place shall be Camael. Camael shall guard the Commander in battle from this day forward until Vithius has sufficiently recovered to resume his place as companion. All hail Camael!"

The gathered Angels took up the cheer, by all appearances receiving the news with joy, as if they believed this was a good thing for both Vithius and Camael. Ryan gaped as he looked around him. How could they all go along with this without argument? Didn't anyone question it?

The crowd rippled with movement as Camael approached the platform. Ryan took some comfort in that the mohawked Angel looked as surprised by the announcement as anyone. But he also looked incredibly pleased, and once standing beside Anifiel Camael puffed out his chest and preened as if he thought he should have been there all along. Ryan knew he shouldn't, but for that brief moment he hated the Angel. He looked all wrong up there, so much shorter than Anifiel, his paleness making him looked washed out next to Anifiel's golden brilliance. And that Mohawk—Ryan wanted to run up there and rip it out of his head.

A warm hand closed around Ryan's bicep. "Do not hold Camael responsible." Vithius looked horribly ashen and his eyes shimmered with tears, but no anger hardened his expression. "This was Anifiel's choice alone. I hurt him, and now he is hurting me back."

"Since when is revenge okay for the Creator's favorite?" Ryan demanded, furious. Seeing Vithius this way made his heart feel bruised, like someone had kicked it into a wall and then stomped on it. "What kind of an Angel is he? He's horrible and vindictive. How can he be the best Angel in Heaven?"

"Not the best. The most important." A tear slid down Vithius' cheek as he gazed up at the congratulatory scene being played out on the platform. "Heaven will fall if Anifiel does. Nothing matters but keeping him strong. Perhaps this is indeed for the best, if it will keep his mind clear and his spear arm strong."

His attitude made Ryan feel like the only sane person in a madhouse. "How can you be so forgiving?"

Dark eyes snapped into focus and pinned him. "Would you prefer that I had been tainted further and lost my capacity to forgive? Would you prefer that I hold grudges which fester in my soul and cause me to commit harm against those whom I believe have done me wrong?"

Stung, Ryan shook his head. "No. No, of course not. I'm sorry. I'm just so upset by this. Upset for you. I don't understand how anyone could hurt you. You're so good. So kind. This is like kicking a puppy. It's just cruel."

"It proves how deeply Anifiel has been wounded, that he would do this," Vithius replied sadly. He brushed at his eyes, dashing away the tears that hadn't fallen yet. "We must congratulate Camael."

Ryan's mouth fell open, but Vithius only stared at him, wordlessly challenging him to blame the mohawked Angel for something he'd had no hand in. Nodding resignedly, Ryan rose to his feet alongside Vithius.

It was like walking to his own execution. Ryan couldn't imagine how terrible Vithius must feel. Vithius had loved Anifiel, maybe still did. And now this betrayal. Uncaring of any Angels watching, Ryan placed his hand protectively at the small of Vithius' back as they walked.

He leaned against Vithius and whispered into his ear, "He won't hurt you again. This is the last time. I promise you. Not while you have me."

Vithius didn't pause, but he turned and stroked the backs of his fingers lightly down Ryan's cheek. "Beloved."

That one word lifted Ryan to a place beyond Heaven.

Together they mounted the platform to where Anifiel and Camael watched their approach with wary smiles upon their faces. It was like approaching a pair of ex-boyfriends, Ryan realized. The scene was awkward and slightly hostile, with a veneer of politeness covering the edges.

"You have chosen well," Vithius said softly to Anifiel. "I am pleased you will be safe."

Ryan studied the Commander closely, looking for any sign of regret over what he'd done to his friend. After an initial glance at Vithius' face, Anifiel seemed uninterested in looking at his former battle companion. His green eyes moved constantly over the crowd. "It is to the advantage of Heaven," he replied shortly.

Vithius nodded, looking pained, though he tried to cover it with a smile. It made Ryan want to punch Anifiel in the face.

"Congratulations, Camael." Vithius extended his hand to the white Angel. "Of any in Heaven, I trust you most to protect our Commander from harm."

Camael took the offered hand in both of his, his expression neutral, which was a relief to Ryan. If the mohawked Angel had looked even the tiniest bit smug he would have said something nasty to him.

"You watched over him well," Camael conceded. "I will endeavor to live up to your competence, Vithius."

Vithius inclined his head. "You are a great warrior. I have no fears that this will be so."

The forced politeness made Ryan want to gag.

He turned away, unable to take it anymore, and found himself facing Tofiel. The tall, gangly Angel wore a smile, but her brown eyes held a shocking sadness. The display of grief, nearly as deep as Vithius', spun the wheels in Ryan's head. Why would Tofiel be so upset? How could her friend's good fortune hurt her?

"Come, Camael." Anifiel's curt command pulled Ryan back around. The golden Angel still wouldn't look at either of them as he motioned Camael off the platform. "There is much we must discuss of your new position as my companion."

Vithius' soft sound of distress prompted Ryan to spread his fingers on the Angel's back. Anifiel heard it and paused. Eyes still down, he murmured, "Please be well, Vithius." He led Camael off the stage, where they were soon surrounded by well-wishing Angels.

Vithius leaned heavily against Ryan as if his strings had been severed when Anifiel walked away. "I must leave this place," the Angel pleaded in a broken voice. "Now, Ryan."

He didn't need to be told twice. Working his free arm like a Secret Service agent, Ryan carved a path through the Angels and led Vithius out of the amphitheater. As soon as they were clear of the throng, Vithius changed their positions so he could wrap his arms around Ryan from behind. A hard flap of the wings and they were born aloft, speeding away from the excited crowd.

"I am not a good Angel," Vithius gasped in a wretched voice. "I wish Camael to prove himself poorly in Anifiel's eyes so that I may reclaim my place as companion."

"You're being—" Ryan caught himself from calling Vithius human. Still, it was not an outlandish comment. Vithius was more like a human than he'd been when Ryan first met him in the Forest of Contemplation. *Hopefully that's a good thing.*

"You don't need him," Ryan told him, squeezing the arms holding him securely. "Anifiel makes us both feel like crap. He hurts you and he humiliates me. We're better off without him. We'll make our own Heaven, where we'll feel nothing but good."

"Are you sending us into exile?" Vithius asked with a strained laugh.

Ryan turned his head and kissed a bulging bicep. "No, I'm giving us a chance to start over. You and I."

Vithius didn't argue. Nor did he cry. With steady wings he flew them far from the source of their mutual pain, and into the new life Ryan intended for them.

12

"Even after all this time, it feels weird living without a roof over my head." Ryan chuckled and scanned the perpetually blue skies. Strips of sheer clouds coiled above him, too fluffy and light to create a shadow, but pretty enough to watch as they swirled overhead. "I keep expecting something to fall on me."

"In the Middle Tier, rain and snow fall only in areas designated for such. We may visit those areas, if you wish. They are very beautiful."

The idea of visiting a designated snowfall area made Ryan smile. Only in Heaven. "Nah, it's okay. I'm not complaining, just observing."

Abandoning his contemplation of the sky, he rolled onto his stomach and propped himself on his elbows. He admired the handsome Angel lying supine beside him. "Is the Upper Tier like this, without any buildings?"

A breeze played with a lock of Vithius' black hair, making it curl and uncurl across the Angel's forehead. Ryan resisted the urge to brush it back with his fingers and instead concentrated on the crescent sweep of dark lashes, waiting for them to lift.

"The Upper Tier is unlike here," Vithius replied softly, eyes still closed. "It is the reward, whereas the Middle Tier is the task."

"So, it doesn't look like this?" Ryan pressed. He was having trouble imagining what the next tier looked like. Pop culture tried to convince him Heaven would look like Greece or Rome, floating in the clouds, but Ryan doubted it looked that way. That was Western civilization's view of Heaven, and after seeing the Forest of Contemplation and the Dream Coil, he'd learned Heaven operated on a far different wavelength.

"No fields of grass, no waterfalls and lakes?" he asked.

"If you wish for these things, you will find them," Vithius replied enigmatically.

Ryan huffed, blowing a strand of hair out of his eye in the process. "That's not answering my question. Does it look like here or is it different?"

A suspicious twitch of the lips preceded Vithius' answer. "They are two different places, Ryan. The Middle Tier appears the way it does to prevent distraction and to encourage self-reflection and enlightenment. In this tier you must understand why you should ascend and what it is that is preventing you from doing so."

"Okay, I got that part. And the Upper Tier?"

"The Upper Tier is the destination after the journey. There are no more trials to face. It is what you wish it to be. It is what will bring you most happiness." A more pronounced hint of a smile touched Vithius' lips. "I think you will enjoy what you find when you ascend. It is a wondrous place."

Ryan automatically snorted. "You're assuming—"

Black lashes snapped upwards. "I am expecting."

The mild chastisement in Vithius' steady gaze made Ryan flush and look down at the grass. "Sorry," he mumbled.

Fingers touched his chin. "Do not be sorry for what needs improvement. Be determined to change it."

Ryan stiffened, ice sluicing his veins. It was similar, too similar, to something that had been said to him by someone important while he was alive. Suddenly Ryan's eyes flooded with tears and he couldn't stand up fast enough. He heard Vithius call to him, concerned, but Ryan turned away from him and quickly strode away, trying to get his emotions under control.

He fought down the tears. He didn't want to be upset in front of Vithius. He wanted to be strong. Only a strong human could win Vithius' love and deserve it. Ryan needed to be that person.

A little over a week had passed since that awful day at Anifiel's Council. It had been a week initially fraught with sexual tension as the reality that they could be together without inference gave new weight to every word and touch. But the mood had quickly relaxed into complete ease with each other as they'd jokingly shared reasons why they were better off without the Commander. Jokes aside, it was just the two of them now, and Ryan understood very well how much Vithius had lost and what Ryan must now replace.

Vithius had been the battle companion of the most important Angel in Heaven, and now he was all but an outcast. Oh, sure, the other Angels didn't think that way, but Vithius did, even if he pretended otherwise. The Angel had lost not only his purpose, but his best friend and one-time crush. Ryan knew all of this. He knew that almost all of it was his fault.

But if he could make the sacrifice worth it by making himself worth it, then everything would be okay.

"Ryan." A gentle grip caught his arm, halting him.

By then he had the waterworks under control. He turned to face his friend.

"Sorry," he murmured, giving a self-deprecating smile. He shrugged, trying to look embarrassed. "A weird memory struck me for a moment but it's gone now. Didn't mean to worry you."

Though he hardly looked convinced, Vithius graciously let him get away with the attempted deception. He released Ryan's arm. "You have told me very little of your life on Earth, and you are my first human friend. I am extremely interested in hearing what your existence was like there."

Sweat beaded on Ryan's forehead. "I can't—I can't tell you how I died."

"Then tell me how you lived," Vithius said simply. "I am not like Finnian. My curiosity has only now been piqued. There is much of which I am ignorant, and I would like to remedy that."

Ryan rolled his shoulders, releasing tension. "I don't even know where to begin," he admitted. If it was a description of life as a human, he could give that to Vithius, but anything more personal...maybe another time. He searched his friend's eyes. "There's a lot to tell, especially if I start out with how we're conceived and born."

Vithius smiled eagerly. "As you have no doubt noticed by now, Time holds little meaning here." He dropped where he stood, folding his long legs Indian-style. He looked up much like a puppy Ryan had once owned. "Please? Will you tell me what it is like to be a human on Earth?"

Ryan good-naturedly rolled his eyes. "Do you honestly think I can refuse anything you ask for?" He dropped, too, mimicking Vithius' position so they were knee-to-knee. "Whatever you want that I can give you, I will," he said earnestly.

The warmth that softened Vithius' eyes filled Ryan with what he could only describe as peace. His love for this Angel was the purest thing he'd ever known. How could enlightenment feel better than this? It was inconceivable.

"You can do one thing for me," Vithius told him gently. The Angel abruptly turned sideways and patted his thighs. "Would you rest your head in my lap and close your eyes while you tell me of Earth?" Sunset bloomed across Vithius' cheeks. "I have seen the humans in this position before and—I thought it a pleasant and intimate form of connection." Shyness made his cheeks burn brighter. "I would like that connection with you."

Ryan stared at him. He would've challenged anyone at that moment to prove that his heart didn't beat out Vithius' name.

I love you more than I've loved anyone or anything. Dying was the best thing that could have happened to me.

Aloud, he said casually, "I can do that."

He stretched out over the grass and placed his head in Vithius' lap. And as the Angel combed his fingers hesitantly but lovingly through his curls, Ryan told his friend about life in a place far, far away.

~~~~~

He fell asleep to Vithius' fingers stroking his scalp.

He dreamed he could fly.

Ryan soared high through the sky, the air streaming effortlessly over the pure white extension of his wings. Flying required as little conscious effort as walking. He was a natural, soaring over the perfect greenery of the Middle Tier like a bird that had been born to it. He waved at Angels and human alike. Everyone he greeted knew his name and was excited to see him.

And why shouldn't they be? He was Ryan, after all. He was the human who had helped save Heaven.

He felt and heard the air pressure change around him and soon enough Vithius appeared on his right. The handsome Angel grinned at Ryan and tipped his wings in greeting. The single gray feather nestled within the white field of his wings no longer held negative connotations. It was a badge of bravery and honor, or as Ryan liked to think of it— proof of Vithius' overwhelming love for him.

"I told you you would be a wondrous Angel," Vithius called out, letting his eyes roam over Ryan's naked form. "I knew from the beginning that you would be my equal. Yet you have become even more than that."

Ryan opened his mouth to refute the claim but a second shift in air pressure caused him to smile instead. He looked over his left shoulder and there was Anifiel, his grin as brilliant as his hair and wings.

"You did not think you could enjoy the day without me, did you?" the great Commander teased.

Ryan smiled and winked at the blond Angel. "We do nothing without you, Anifiel. You should know that by now."

Having Anifiel appear in his dream—and enjoying his company—should have been grounds for Ryan to rush out of it, screaming. But what woke him was a delicate touch that made him think of a butterfly settling upon his lips.

He waited, curious, and the butterfly buzzed him again. It lingered slightly longer this time as if testing the danger of its human landing pad. The mystery dissolved into pleasure, and thoughts of Anifiel bled away. The next time he felt the brush of contact, Ryan parted his lips.

He caught Vithius' gasp between them.

He kept his eyes closed so he wouldn't scare his friend, and after a few seconds Vithius' lips returned to his, pressing down gently. A pleasant lassitude kept Ryan calm. Normally his heart would have beat a thousand beats a minute at having Vithius initiate a kiss. But this was different; the moment felt sweet, not overtly sexual. As Vithius' lips moved around the perimeter of his mouth, dusting his skin with light kisses, Ryan got the feeling Vithius was reassuring both of them that he'd made the right choice to be here with him.

As Ryan had related what it was like to be a human being, he'd felt Vithius studying him with increasing interest, maybe even respect. Ryan hadn't revealed much of what he'd gone through personally, but he hadn't needed to. The typical trials and tribulations of the average human being struggling with school and relationships had been more than enough to impress the Angel as to how difficult life on Earth could often be.

Vithius had even said something to that effect while Ryan had paused in the middle of explaining how homosexuality was still not widely accepted and that some gay men and women denied who they were to fit into the mainstream.

"Much of being a human is about suffering," the Angel had commented thoughtfully. "But I did not know of this deliberate creation of pain. I had thought the greatest sacrifice was leaving the Earth, but you have taught me differently."

The kisses moved to his chin and followed the line of his jaw. Ryan tilted his head back, inviting Vithius' lips onto his bared throat. The first hesitant kiss beneath his jaw made him shiver. When another one followed, ghosting over his Adam's apple, his cock stirred against his thigh. He tried to concentrate on safe things, non-sexual things, as Vithius kissed over and across his throat. But he enjoyed the soft touches too much. He enjoyed being beneath Vithius too much, and his cock began to fill.

It was another one of those times when he tried desperately to will down his response to Vithius for fear of scaring him off. Ryan moved his hands beneath his hips and fisted them out of sight. He breathed deeply and curled his toes as Vithius kissed up the side of his neck until his lips were gently touching the skin behind Ryan's ear. Don't, he thought, anxiously. But petal-soft lips caressed that oh-so-sensitive skin.

Ryan moaned before he could stop himself.

The lips stilled against his skin, just as he'd feared. Disappointed, Ryan sighed. "I'm sorr—"

A warm tongue laved the outside of his ear. Ryan stabbed his hips into the air. "Vithius!"

"Was that pleasurable?" Insecurity made Vithius' voice little more than a husky whisper against the whorl of Ryan's ear.

Ryan swallowed a moan as the air curled into his ear canal. "Ah—you could say that. My ears are pretty sensitive. They're one of my spots."

"Spots?"

Ryan really needed Vithius to speak—breathe—somewhere else if the Angel expected coherent answers from him.

He turned his head away, not realizing this only opened up more of his neck and ear to the Angel. "They're called erogenous zones," he panted. "If you touch them or kiss them it turns a person on. Er—arouses them, sorta like if you—oh, don't do that..."

Vithius chuckled warmly while his lips and tongue plucked at the lobe of Ryan's ear. "I believe I understand. When I touch your 'spot' it makes you act as you do when my finger is inside you." Showing unexpected forcefulness, Vithius caught Ryan by the chin, holding his face in place while the Angel nuzzled his ear. "You find both pleasurable, do you not?"

Ryan squirmed beneath him, drawing his knees up to hide how hard Vithius was making him.

"Your spot is here," Vithius plunged his tongue into Ryan's ear, making Ryan's eyes roll up into his head. "And your spot is inside you." The Angel's other hand settled on Ryan's heaving hip. "Would you like me to touch you there, also?"

"Vithius," Ryan panted, trying really hard not to think about that hand on his hip which was only a few inches from the center of his current universe. "I can't—I can't think when you—"

"My organ is like yours," Vithius murmured before he pressed his hips forward and a rod of what felt like solid steel jabbed against the side of the thigh.

"Oh, my god," Ryan moaned. He reached down and fumbled for Vithius' hand before finally dragging it between his legs. The Angel's fingers flexed with shock before curling around Ryan through the cloth. "Stroke me," he begged. "No sex this time—too soon. But we can...we can do this."

Vithius thrust against him. "But I should be inside you, should I not?" His voice was deeper, thicker. "That is what this is made for, yes? To be inside you. To fill you—" the Angel's voice caught, "—oh, it aches, Ryan. It hurts me!"

Ryan let out a strangled cry and jerked out from beneath Vithius, startling the Angel. Ryan didn't bother to explain, he quickly flipped around until they were head to toe. Completely shameless at this point, he yanked the hem of his tunic up around his waist, letting his cock spring free and nearly putting out Vithius' eye in the process.

"Do as I do," Ryan gasped, hungrily grabbing the dark cock bobbing in front of his face. "Trust me, Vithius. Just mimic me."

He could smell Vithius, clean but definitely musky. Ryan closed his eyes and sealed his lips over the spongy tip, eliciting a sharp cry from the Angel. Vithius instinctively pushed forward and Ryan relaxed his mouth to allow the Angel to thrust inside.

"R-Ryan!"

A grunt of understanding was the best Ryan could do with his mouth full. He closed his eyes and savored the liquid salt which leaked over his tongue. He hollowed his cheeks and sucked out more dew while his free hand came up and cradled two soft, warm balls, lightly sprinkled with hair. He gently massaged them while he pulled more of Vithius into his mouth.

He could feel air bursting across his own cock as Vithius panted for breath. Ryan pulled off of the Angel long enough to gasp, "Touch me."

He'd no sooner enclosed Vithius in his mouth again when he himself was enveloped in wetness. Ryan couldn't help it—he cried out like the Angel had done. The feeling was nothing short of incredible.

At first Vithius only held Ryan in his mouth, letting himself grow used to the heat, taste and sensation of a male's cock. But very soon he began to carefully mirror what Ryan did. With a hand at the base of his shaft and one cupping Ryan's scrotum, Vithius delicately began to bob his head. Once he did that, Ryan realized he was about thirty seconds from lift-off.

Where the heck did all my stamina go? he wondered wildly as he sucked furiously, trying to bring Vithius to the same point. Unfortunately the Angel did exactly the same thing, which made Ryan lose all hope of control. He thrust erratically past Vithius' lips, as aroused by the act as by the thought of having an Angel give him a blowjob.

He wanted this to last longer. He really, really did. But Vithius' Angel fugue worked against Ryan. It became nearly impossible to concentrate on sucking his friend when all Ryan wanted to do was jam himself repeatedly down the Angel's throat. He didn't do that, of course, but the effort required to hold himself back left him shaking.

Then Vithius did something purely experimental: he poked his tongue into the slit at the end of Ryan's cock. It was game over. Whimpering like a crazed animal, Ryan wrenched his hips back. The tip had barely cleared Vithius' mouth before Ryan lost control. Vithius let out a surprised yelp as moisture squirted across his face. Whether it was the strangeness of the act—or something more—the Angel's cock swelled in Ryan's slack mouth and began to return the favor. Ryan had just enough sense left to close his mouth around the head so he could swallow down everything the Angel gave him.

Vithius screamed as he climaxed. There was no other way to describe it. Two strong hands clamped on the back of Ryan's head, holding him in place to accept the onslaught as the Angel howled. It was a good thing that on Earth, Ryan had practiced with a lot of toothbrushes, otherwise it could've been ugly.

Despite the violence, or maybe because of it, it was the best blowjob Ryan had ever given. The taste of Vithius was truly the nectar of the gods. The Angel's ejaculate was thinner than a human's and reminiscent of salted peach juice. Ryan slurped it down as quickly as it appeared.

Moaning both from his own release and the luscious essence flooding his mouth, Ryan was all but boneless as he suckled at Vithius' cock. Even after he'd sucked the last drop out and Vithius' hands had fallen from his head, he continued to the mouth the softening organ, simply enjoying the feel and taste of it.

"Ryan..."

He moaned softly around Vithius in acknowledgement.

An amused chuckle over the head of his spent cock made him twitch. "Ryan, I do not think my organ will release any more of its treasure to you."

Frowning, Ryan let the flesh fall from his lips. "Why not?" he complained, only half-joking. He kissed the shaft with longing. "I'm still thirsty."

"Is this liquid truly so delicious?"

The curious lilt of Vithius' voice made Ryan roll backwards so he could better see his friend's face.

"Oh, no," Ryan breathed when he caught sight of the Angel. "Oh, wow, I'm really sorry I did that."

Vithius smiled a little uncertainly. He held himself stiffly, uncomfortable with the cooling white liquid that splattered his face. A pearly drop hung from the tip of his nose. "I do not think you had any control over it, just as I did not."

"Yeah, but still..." It's probably bad karma to give an Angel a facial, Ryan thought with a wince. "Come here. Sit up."

Knee to knee, he carefully wiped his friend's face clean with the edge of his tunic. Occasionally he caught Vithius glancing at the damp fabric as if he considered bringing it to his lips and tasting it. After a shiver, Ryan firmly steered his mind elsewhere.

"So, uh, did you like that? Well, besides the

coming on your face thing." Ryan smiled sheepishly. "What we each did to each other is called a blowjob. Doing it at the same time like that is called a sixty-nine."

"Such strange names," Vithius mused.

"Yeah," Ryan replied absently. He couldn't stop staring at Vithius. Or more specifically, at his lush mouth, which only moments ago had been wrapped around his cock.

"I have never experienced such pleasure," Vithius admitted shyly. "It was much like the thrill of flying through the Upper Tier, only a thousand fold."

"Uh huh." Ryan nodded, not really listening, too busy staring at the way Vithius' lips formed words.

"It reminded me of the feelings I often have when we battle the Demons, especially when Anifiel raises the Spear of Righteousness above his head and—"

Ryan blinked. "Wait—what? My blowjob made you think of Anifiel?"

Guilt darkened Vithius' face, his smile fading. "I-I should not have said that. Please forgive me." He offered up an apologetic smile as he laid a hand over Ryan's knee. "No one but you could have shown me this, Ryan. I know this."

The words should have comforted Ryan, but they didn't. Vithius' first thoughts during orgasm had been of Anifiel.

Ryan hated the blond Angel now more than ever.

~~~~~

Thoughts of the Commander dominated Ryan's brain from then on. He didn't want to think about Anifiel so much, but he had to because Vithius' feelings for his fellow Angel were apparently still strong enough to come between them.

Short of pushing Anifiel over the edge of Heaven, Ryan didn't know how to blot the Angel from Vithius' mind, though. How did you eclipse the greatest Angel in Heaven when you weren't even an Angel yourself?

His subconscious tried to convince him that sharing his life story—his personal one—was the key to winning Vithius' heart completely. It would be the ultimate evidence of trust, and Vithius would recognize that and be moved by it.

But the thought of it turned Ryan's stomach. He believed there was an equally strong chance that learning everything about him would turn Vithius off. There had to be a less risky course of action, something that wouldn't involve the old Ryan, but the new and improved one.

It came to him while watching Vithius practice his fighting maneuvers.

Harboring the belief he would return to the battlefields as either Anifiel's battle companion or another Angel's, Vithius practiced the non-aggressive moves he used to ward off Demons. It reminded Ryan of Tai Chi, done with weapons in hand. Vithius' moves were fluid and graceful, yet the strength was apparent in every move and careful placement of his feet.

"Could I fight in the Eternity War?" Ryan wondered aloud.

Vithius paused in mid-stroke, his brow furrowed as he looked over to where Ryan sat. "Why would you wish to? It is a very unpleasant affair, Ryan."

"Yeah, I know, but isn't it better to have as large an Army as possible? I'd think the more help you guys got, the better your odds." He began to warm to the idea, picturing himself in shining armor on the battlefields, fending off a horde of Demons. "I'm somewhat athletic. I bet I could learn how to fight pretty quickly."

Vithius lowered his twin forked weapons. "Humans do not fight Demons," he said sternly.

Ryan cocked his head. "Why not?"

Sadness flitted across Vithius' face. He flexed his wings. "Because of this."

The gray feather had grown back, just as Vithius had warned Ryan it would. Looking at it made Ryan feel ashamed.

"If you forgo peace, you step toward the Beneath," Vithius told him. "If faced with a Demon, humans are not strong enough to simply defend. Fear and loathing make them lash out. Anger makes them wish to hurt." Vithius re-folded his wings behind his back. "It is not your fault you are weak. You were not made to face down Demons. Angels exist to fight this battle for you, Ryan. You must accept this."

"Has there never been a human fighter?" Ryan asked, grabbing at straws.

"Never," Vithius said bluntly. "Since the creation of Heaven there never has and never will be a human fighting on the battlefields of the Eternity War. Banish the thought from your mind, Ryan. It is an impossibility."

Ryan nodded, but his heart was stung. He wished Vithius had forbidden him because he feared Ryan would be hurt, not because that was how it had been for eons.

~~~~~~

"Visit with your friends," Vithius encouraged him much later. The smiling Angel tousled Ryan's curls, an action he admitted he had grown fond of doing since it was a human act. In some ways, he was becoming like Finnian, eager to behave as humans did. "It is important that you have contact with other humans and not be isolated with me."

Less than enthused, Ryan nodded reluctantly. "Are you going to visit your friends, too? Other Angels?"

Eagerness briefly lit Vithius' face, which only made Ryan feel glummer. "Yes, I have been away too long. I fear they worry for me."

"Yeah, I guess you should go see them, then."

He thought he'd disguised his disappointment fairly well, but a hand on his shoulder stopped him as he was turning away. Dark eyes were soft with sympathy as they studied Ryan's face.

"We are two, but we exist within this world of many," Vithius said gently. "We must not forsake them, Ryan."

Ryan nodded. "I know. You're right. It's not healthy to hide ourselves away."

Though he spoke the words—and he even managed to make them sound as if he believed them—inwardly he felt like he was the only one in this relationship who truly cared about them as a couple. He should have been enough for Vithius. Ryan was willing to do anything for him. Why did Vithius need to go elsewhere?

But in the end, Ryan found himself waving as Vithius launched himself into the air. The only thing he took pleasure in was the happiness and excitement on his friend's face. But even that was tempered by the knowledge that that eagerness was to see someone other than Ryan.

"You are such a girl," Ryan muttered as he tromped across the grass fields. Though he could summon Sam and Eric with just a thought, he was putting it off, choosing to wallow in self-pity instead. "Vithius isn't going to want to come back to you if you let him see how needy you are."

There was no shadow to warn him, only a smug, hated voice from over his shoulder: "Indeed, he should already know this, but he has been blinded."

Ryan gasped and spun, but Anifiel was too close. A heavy wing knocked him backward off his feet. He landed on his back with a hard thud, the wind stripped from his lungs. As he lay gasping, the Angel landed on the grass near Ryan's head.

A sandled foot nudged his temple. "Come, little human, no proper greeting?"

A growl ripped from Ryan's mouth before he rolled to his feet. "Screw you. What are you doing here? You got what you wanted. It's not enough for you that you hurt Vithius and drove him away? You have to come looking for us?" He kicked the grass, wishing it was sand, because the thought of kicking it in Anifiel's face sounded pretty damn good right now. "You're acting exactly like a bully, Anifiel. You need a target to make yourself feel like a big-shot."

Anifiel's eyes narrowed and his nostrils flared. Ryan had a moment to notice that the Commander seemed to have grown more gorgeous since the last time Ryan had seen him before Anifiel began striding toward him. Ryan backpedaled as fast as he could.

"I have come because I expected Vithius to have found reason again," Anifiel snarled. "But how could he, when a foul-mouth, deceitful human has kidnapped him?"

"You forgot corrupted and carnal," Ryan baited him, his blood rushing so loudly through his ears that he could barely hear Anifiel, even with the Angel's loud voice. Adrenaline pumped through his veins. This was what he needed, someone on whom he could take out his frustration. "Go on, Anifiel. I know you're dying to: ask me if we've had sex yet. Ask me if Vithius has put his mouth on me because guess what: he has, and he loved it."

A veritable lion's roar was the only warning Ryan had before Anifiel leaped through the air and tackled him backward to the grass. His skull bounced off the ground, leaving him too dazed to fight as the Angel grabbed the throat of his tunic and tore it open down the middle. Ryan cried out in shock as the two shredded halves slid down either side of his body, leaving him completely bared to the Angel's eyes.

"He has not touched you!" Anifiel roared, yanking Ryan's limbs up and apart, pinning him spread-eagled to the grass. Fiery, verdant eyes raced over his naked body, looking for evidence of his fellow Angel's trespass.

Ryan shuddered violently beneath him, trying to convince himself he should feel violated by the treatment, but his body gave away the lie: his cock surged to life and his nipples contracted as if they'd been touched with ice. A flush swept his body, leaving his skin burning.

"You can't see it," Ryan rasped, staring defiantly up at Anifiel's face, "but his brand is now on my skin. On my soul. He wants me, and there's nothing you can do about it because it was your choice to turn him away. It was your mistake that gave him to me. How does that feel? How does it feel to know you finally screwed up, huh, Anifiel?"

"You are vile!"

With his hair mussed from the struggle and his eyes bulging, Anifiel looked like a madman. Too late, fear surfaced in Ryan. What the hell was he doing? When Anifiel's wild gaze latched onto his rigid cock, Ryan began to thrash like crazy, terrified the Angel would grab the organ and rip it off his body as punishment. When the Angel did grab him, Ryan let out a bloodcurdling scream of fright.

"You have taken everything from me!" Anifiel shouted, his fingers closing around Ryan's shaft. "You and your instrument of sin should be destroyed!"

Ryan cried out and tried to pull out of the grip. To his amazement, Anifiel's grip was actually loose enough for Ryan to pull back a few inches.

The problem was that they were the best few inches of Ryan's life.

His buttocks clenched and he pushed back up into Anifiel's fist without even thinking about it. The resultant explosion of pleasure made him cry out as if he were being tortured. He shut his eyes at the horror of the situation but he was too hard to stop himself. When Anifiel's fingers didn't pinch his dick off, Ryan withdrew and thrust up again into his grip. The Angel's calloused palm dragged fire over his engorged cock.

"You disgust me," Anifiel rasped. "You turn even punishment into carnal pleasure. Does your depravity know no bounds?"

Ryan shook his head, hating himself, but a voice in the back of his mind pointed out that Anifiel hadn't tightened his grip to stop Ryan from moving, nor had he simply let go. The Angel made the perfect circle with his fist for Ryan to thrust into. He was helping.

The Angel fugue was a veritable soup now. Ryan couldn't breathe without inhaling a lungful of Anifiel's scent and pheromones. He felt helpless and yet he was excited by that helplessness. His awareness narrowed down to where his cock slid in and out of Anifiel's curled hand. Ryan moaned and breathed deeper. He surrendered, because it always felt good to let Anifiel take control.

"Dirty little human."

Anifiel's voice was different, strange. Ryan cracked open his eyes to look up at him. With the sun behind the Angel's head it was difficult to tell if it was color or shadow which darkened Anifiel's cheeks. The intensity in his eyes could have been passion or disgust.

"If I'm so dirty," Ryan panted raggedly, "why don't you stop touching me?"

Green eyes snapped upward. The anger in them made Ryan swell within Anifiel's fist. The next thing he knew, the hand around his cock disappeared and he was yanked up by the hair and flipped onto his hands and knees. The hand in Ryan's hair pushed down, shoving his face to Anifiel's extended foot.

"You and your—foot fetish," Ryan moaned, but he didn't resist as Anifiel pushed his face to the Angel's strong, handsome foot.

"Thank me," Anifiel growled. "Worship me."

If he had more than three brain cells left Ryan would have asked what he was thanking the Angel for—this humiliating treatment or for Anifiel driving Vithius away? But caught in the fugue, Ryan could think only in basic terms. If Anifiel wanted thanks, he would get it.

He kissed the top of Anifiel's foot and flicked his tongue out to taste the Angel's hot skin. His own cock leaked profusely as he dipped lower and slipped his tongue between Anifiel's toes. He heard a gasp above him and it made him moan in return. He licked lovingly between each toe before returning to the thick, dominant digit. Moaning again, Ryan closed his lips around it and sucked.

It was wrong, this was wrong. He hated Anifiel. But Ryan couldn't deny that he was on the verge of orgasm because of everything that was happening. Every time he curled his tongue over the Angel's big toe Ryan took another step closer to the edge of climax.

When the fist tightened in his hair and Anifiel's voice husked out, "I said, worship me," Ryan humped the air and began coming.

Anifiel pulled his toe from Ryan's mouth. He released the grip on Ryan's hair. Ryan heard the Angel stagger backward and then the *whoomp* of his wings as the Commander launched himself into the air. Whatever else happened was lost to Ryan. He orgasmed all by himself, crouched in the grass where his enemy had placed him.

13

"You horn dog! You're doing two Angels at the same time?"

Ryan blushed madly at Eric's exclamation. "I'm not doing two Angels!"

"You just said Anifiel rubbed off on you and Vithius and you did a sixty-nine." Eric studied him with admiration. "That must have taken some serious sweet talking, man."

"It's not like I forced myself on him," Ryan muttered, embarrassed. "He was in the mood, too."

"That's Vithius. But you said you're also fooling around with—" Sam, gulped, her eyes as round as her twin brother's, "—with the Commander," she finished in a hushed voice. She quickly looked around. "Anifiel!"

"Yes, I know who he is," Ryan muttered, crossing his arms over his chest. "But I didn't choose to do anything with him. He keeps stalking me and attacking me. He's totally psychotic."

"You're talking about the Creator's favorite and the hottest Angel in Heaven!" Eric gave him a look of incredulity. "And he's the Commander of the Army! If he's psychotic, what does that mean about the rest of us? He's the ideal. He's perfect, dude."

"You don't even know him!" Ryan blurted in frustration. He'd called for his friends after he'd recovered from that humiliating foot licking session with Anifiel. Right now he didn't want to be anywhere near an Angel and their soul-stealing fugues.

"He's jealous of me so he attacks me because there's nothing else he can do," he told them. "If what Vithius and I are doing is wrong the Creator would have stopped it. But obviously there's nothing wrong with it and Anifiel hates that."

Sam plucked a stalk of grass and nibbled on it thoughtfully. "I'm having a hard time setting aside the mental image of you and Anifiel doing the horizontal mambo. It's really hot."

Ryan glared at her. "Please try."

She grinned and winked playfully at him. "Okay, I'll set it aside for later. So you're teaching Angels how to have sex. Well, you know Eric and I had fun teasing and playing around with Finnian. You were always there with us, so you saw what we did. But the thing is, we never went further than innuendo and teasing. Anifiel keeps telling you you're corrupting Vithius—I hate to say it but maybe he's right."

Eric nodded. "Yeah, man, you gotta think if the

Creator wanted the Angels to know about sex then they would know it already. Angels aren't supposed to learn. They're already perfect."

Ryan looked at his friends in exasperation. "How come you guys are about to ascend, and I'm still at the bottom of the pile? Angels aren't perfect. They're deliberately *im*perfect so we won't be intimidated by them. If the Creator could plan that, why couldn't he anticipate that someone would eventually teach them about sex?"

Eric burst into laughter. "Are you saying that's how you'll reach enlightenment? By teaching Sex Ed to the Angels?"

"No, that's not what I'm saying," Ryan gritted out. "Look, I really doubt I'm the first person to have fallen in love with an Angel. Think about Finnian. He probably had thousands of admirers, if not more."

"Yet no one dared touch him beyond what we did with him," Sam pointed out. "Humans know better. Sex is something for Earth. It helped us get through the bad stuff. Now that we're here we don't need anything so messy."

"Hey, when you put it that way I wish I hadn't died," Eric complained. "I like messy sex."

A goofy smile crossed Ryan's face as he remembered how he'd squirted on Vithius' face.

Eric, seeing it, chuckled. "High five, dude."

Sam rolled her eyes. "Yeah, that's all amusing, but we're still talking about sex with Angels. I mean, just the thought of asking one of them to— and kissing their—" she shuddered. "Playing with Finnian was just play. But to go all the way with an

Angel—it feels wrong. They're too innocent. I know it's completely different, but it makes me think of pedophilia."

Ryan blanched. "It's nothing like that! I'm not a pervert!"

"According to Anifiel you are," Eric pointed out, grinning. "That's so awesome that he said that."

"He's the one who gets off when I'm sucking on his toes!"

An awkward silence fell. Ryan groaned and covered his flaming face with both hands. "Pretend I didn't say that."

"So...why'd you call us?" Sam asked, finally breaking the silence. "Are you asking us for advice on how to get over them or do you want our blessing to have crazy, forbidden Angel sex? Ooh, that's sounding better and better."

Ryan pretended he hadn't heard the last comment. "I can't get over Vithius and I don't want to. I want advice on how to keep him interested. He's an Angel. By all accounts I'm the worst Angel candidate in Heaven. I want there to be some reason why he'd want me despite that."

"Can't he want you simply because you're you?"

Eric snorted derisively at his sister's question. "That's just corny and useless advice. Ryan wants specifics, like how to give the best blowjob and stuff like that, right?"

"No, that's not what I want!" Ryan insisted, embarrassed that he was a little curious if there was something more he could be doing in that department. "I don't want to talk about my sex life with you guys. I meant other things. Relationship things or-or personality things."

"But that's just it," Sam huffed. "He already likes your personality otherwise he wouldn't be doing something with you that he's never done with any human or Angel. Ryan, we all joke about hooking up with Angels but none of us expect an Angel to feel the same way about us. Yet, he does."

"It's like winning a date with a supermodel," Eric translated helpfully.

"But what if it's just the newness of what I'm showing him?" Ryan worried at his bottom lip. "What if it's not me that has him interested, but all these exciting new feelings he's having? Once he figures out he can get that from anyone else, he'll probably leave me, Sam."

"And that is why you're at the bottom of the pile when it comes to ascension," she declared flatly. "You don't even believe you're a decent human, much less Angel material." She scowled. "Why are you so down on yourself? You're cute, sweet and funny. Who told you that you aren't? Who made you doubt yourself?"

Ryan looked down and saw his fingers trembling. He hastily shoved them beneath himself before his friends could see. "It's just things I've learned about myself, things that—look, that's not the point, okay? I just want you to tell me how to make myself sexier or cooler or something. I need to be someone Vithius can't leave."

Sam began to tick off her fingers. "For one, Angels have no concept of whether you're 'cool' or not. For another, they can see right through humans, so any attitude or sexy makeover you adopt in an attempt to be more desirable is a waste of time. And don't even think about playing hard to get. Vithius'll see right through that, also." She sighed. "That's what being in Heaven is about, Ryan: it's being honest about who you are, seeing your flaws, and accepting them."

"But isn't it also about self-improvement? What if I realize I'm a social reject? I'm supposed to work to change that, aren't I?"

"How are you a social reject?" Eric asked. "We hang out with you."

"Yeah, but no one else does," Ryan mumbled, pretending a sudden fascination with the grass. "Finn's gone. When you two ascend I'll be here all by myself again. Vithius is all I have."

"You could always try meeting more people," Sam suggested.

"I could, yeah. But I'm not good at that. I don't have any clue what to say after 'Hi, I'm Ryan, what's your name?' I'm terrible at small talk. And I always feel—I always feel like people are looking at me and can tell that I'm not great at conversation and I'm not that interesting and if we hung out together they'd end up being bored. I can just feel that."

"You're a little paranoid, man. Lighten up. This isn't some pick-up scene at a club. This is Heaven."

"But it is the same," Ryan argued quietly. "All of my life I've been the one who chased. No one ever came after me. No one looked at me twice unless I threw myself in front of them. And it's happened here, too. That's not coincidence; that means something. It means I lack that special something. I'm ordinary and that's not good enough for an Angel like Vithius."

"Oh, Ryan," Sam sighed. She laid her hand over his knee in comfort, but her hand settled on the cloth of his tunic, not his bare skin, underscoring yet another area in which he wasn't comfortable with himself. "You were Finnian's best human friend. So what are you saying—he was desperate or something? You know that's crazy."

Ryan laughed. "Of course he wasn't. But it was the human thing again. I was the only one who treated him like a human and he liked that."

"I still say you're reading too much into all this." Sam withdrew her hand and grew thoughtful. "Who's another Angel that you've talked to that you like? Besides Finnian and Vithius."

Ryan sighed. "I don't know any—" He blinked. "Actually...there is one. I didn't get to talk to her for very long, but she seemed pretty nice. Like Finn, maybe, but not in a cute-and-chirpy kind of way."

"If you liked her, she probably liked you, too," Eric pointed out. "Good vibes travel in a circle, dude."

"Okay, but so what?"

Sam shook her head as if Ryan were completely clueless, which he pretty much was. "So, you should go talk to her and find out from her what Angels are attracted to. How are Eric and I supposed to know? We're dumb humans like you. And while you're talking to her, you can ask her what she likes about you."

"I can't do that!" Ryan's face heated at the thought of asking such a question.

"Dude, what Sam's saying is if you find out what this Angel likes about you, you can emphasize that more. You're not fishing for compliments. As an Angel she'll know that."

Sam nodded along with her brother. "We're no help to you in this, Ryan. You need Angelic input. And maybe if you're lucky this Angel will become a new friend, too."

Ryan thought it over. He supposed it sounded logical. The best way to win an Angel's heart was to learn what Angels wanted. There was a good chance Tofiel would be available to talk, too, since Camael was now Anifiel's battle companion and was probably spending a lot of time sucking up to the Commander and leaving Tofiel to her own devices.

"I think maybe you're right," he said slowly. "I think I will talk to another Angel and find out what they like." He smiled at his friends. "Thanks. Thanks for helping me. I don't have anyone else to talk to about this."

"Speaking of which," Sam began, leering at Ryan, "in payment you now owe us some dirt. Tell us what it's like to blow an Angel." She dropped her voice. "Is he sweet? Salty? Does he become gigantic when he's hard? What kinds of noises does he make?" She broke into a maniacal laugh. "Tell us everything."

As casually as if he were reaching for a banana, Eric dropped his hand between his legs and wrapped his fingers around his cock. "Yeah, man, give us details. I'm already throwing wood."

Ryan winced. "You two are so sick."

"Says he who's banging two Angels at the same time," Eric teased.

"For the last time, I am not banging Anifiel!"

Sam leaned forward, grinning. "Yeah, but I bet deep down you wish you were, am I right?"

Ryan wouldn't dignify that with an answer.

~~~~~

Assuming that calling any Angel worked the same way as when calling someone he already knew on a first name basis, Ryan stood in the middle of a meadow and concentrated on Tofiel. He was a little scared to do this, because what if calling an Angel without prior approval was considered rude or insulting? He didn't want to start off on the wrong foot with Tofiel.

After a few minutes, just when he was beginning to think this was an idea certain only to get him into more trouble, he heard the familiar cadence of wings beating the air. He watched as an Angel flew closer and even before he could see the Angel's face, Ryan knew it was Tofiel. The tall, gangly Angel was recognizable for miles. Relieved, Ryan waved to guide her in.

The scarecrow-like Angel smiled as she changed the angle of her descent and slowly settled on the grass. "Ryan," she greeted, a touch of confusion in her voice, "did you call for me?"

"Yeah," Ryan said shyly, "I did. Is that alright

or am I not supposed to do that?"

Looking up at Tofiel was like looking up to his dad as a child, if his dad were a woman, super tall and skinny and walked around naked, that is. And actually, Ryan couldn't remember his dad ever looking at him the way Tofiel did. The gangly Angel's gentle, almost goofy smile made Ryan relax. He could practically feel his stress melting out the soles of his feet.

"Few humans call us," Tofiel admitted, "but that is only because they are not aware they are allowed to. I am pleased that you did, and that you are in better spirits from the last time I spoke with you."

Ryan cringed. "Yeah, you didn't see me at my best. Anifiel's stupid collar—"

"He was grieving," Tofiel cut in gently, "and he did not know how to express it. It was unfortunate that Anifiel took out his pain upon you in that manner, but he did not mean you any harm."

He just wanted to make me feel like a dog, Ryan thought, but he didn't say it aloud. He wasn't here to badmouth Anifiel.

"Um, the reason I called you here was I was wondering if I could talk to you about some Angel things."

A brown eyebrow lifted, disappearing into Tofiel's ragged shock of hair. "Vithius is unable to help you with these things? I thought you two are very close?"

Ryan cursed the blush he could feel fanning over his cheeks. "We are, and that's why—the thing is—" He groaned. "Could I talk to you about some private stuff that I don't want him to know about? Are you allowed to do that? Keep secrets from each other, I mean?"

Tofiel's bemusement increased, although that only meant she looked more comical, like a dog that tilted its head when it heard a funny sound. Ryan was grateful he wasn't having this conversation with Anifiel. The golden Angel would have let loose a roar of annoyance and pounded Ryan's face in by now.

"I suppose it depends upon the secret," Tofiel said at last. "I cannot knowingly or willfully engage in deception that would harm another or this place—"

"Oh, no, no, of course not," Ryan blurted. "It's nothing like that—just personal, sorta embarrassing stuff." He tried to run a hand through his hair but his fingers got tangled so he ended up looking like an idiot as he had to yank his hand free. "Maybe this was a dumb idea. I'm sorry for calling you all this way, Tofiel."

"I will speak with you."

Ryan looked up uncertainly. "You will?"

Peace radiated from Tofiel and Ryan felt his breath leave him in a long sigh, his tension bleeding away. "Yes, Ryan. You are distressed and I would like to help relieve that if speaking with you of your secret will accomplish this."

"It might. I hope. I don't know." Ryan mentally shook himself. "Yes, I would really appreciate it, Tofiel. But, er, would you mind doing me one other favor?"

"I would not."

"Could we have this discussion in the Lower Tier?" Ryan had thought long and hard about this and the only way to keep this conversation secret from his stalker, Anifiel, was to hold it in a place Anifiel disdained from visiting except in times of war.

Tofiel's smile never wavered. "If that would make you comfortable, that is where we shall go."

~~~~~

Tofiel was a good flyer, just like Vithius. It seemed only Anifiel flew like a maniac. When they settled onto a cloud in the Lower Tier, Ryan felt completely at ease, as if he and Tofiel had been friends for years.

"Why do I feel differently with you than with—" he caught himself from saying 'Camael', "—other Angels? I don't know you any better than I know them."

"I am an Angel who inspires peace," she explained. She was turned perpendicular to Ryan so that her long legs extended in front of her while the Angel leaned back on her hands. It put Ryan a little closer to the Angel's groin and hip area, but her nakedness didn't bother him nearly as much as a male Angel's would have.

"As Camael inspires self-truth, I inspire humans to release their worries and concentrate on that which provides restful thought," Tofiel continued.

"That's a nice power to have," Ryan remarked.

She laughed. "It is not a power. Angels are like mirrors. Each will show you something different within yourself. We cannot produce what does not already exist within you; we serve only to help you reach self-realization."

"And being at peace will help me do that?"

"A mind and soul knotted with anxiety cannot focus upon anything else. Peace is necessary for true introspection."

Ryan glanced over the edge of their cloud. A larger one the size of a bus floated several yards below them. Six humans in tunics were stretched out on their stomachs on the cloud, watching the activities occurring below on Earth. A pang of sorrow echoed through Ryan's heart. He had once been like them, still caught up in life on Earth, too afraid to believe it was all over and he would never be a part of that world again.

"I prefer your power—er, essence or whatever you call it—to Camael's," he said, turning away from the cloud. "He makes me uncomfortable. And I know it's not his fault," Ryan hastily added. "Self-truth isn't easy for me to handle."

"It is not easy for any human, Ryan. Do not feel you hold worse secrets than others do."

That's what you think.

Tofiel looked at him oddly, as if she'd heard Ryan's thought. Panicked, Ryan hurriedly changed subjects.

"Speaking of Camael, how does he like his new job? That's a pretty big promotion, right?" He nearly said, "It broke Vithius' heart to lose it."

"It is Camael's fondest wish," Tofiel acknowledged. She smiled, but it was clearly tinged with sadness. Ryan was surprised, not that the Angel was unhappy— he had guessed as much after Anifiel's Council—but that the Angel would allow him to see such a private emotion. "I am pleased for Camael, for I wish him the best. It is unfortunate that we can no longer fight together, however. I will miss his companionship on the battlefield."

And off the battlefield, too, Ryan bet. The two Angels had seemed very close, or at least Tofiel had seemed close to Camael. The mohawked Angel struck Ryan as a little too self-centered to care much about what she was up to.

"But you did not bring me here to speak of Camael," Tofiel reminded him. "Or did you? What is on your mind, Ryan? Are you unhappy over Anifiel's decision to replace Vithius?"

Ryan looked down, combing his fingers through the gauzy cotton. "I am unhappy about that, but that's not why I brought you here. This is probably going to sound weird, or maybe kind of shocking, but—"

"You love Vithius." Tofiel broke out into a wide grin as Ryan gaped up at her. "Love is easy to see in Heaven, Ryan. At least it is for Angels to see. Your feelings for Vithius are obvious and very generous. You care for him a great deal, and I am pleased by that. Vithius is my good friend. I wish him to be loved the way he deserves to be loved. He has sufficed without for too long."

Ryan wondered if Tofiel knew about Vithius'

unrequited feelings for Anifiel. Were Angel feelings as easy to read as humans'? But then he realized he didn't want to know if Tofiel saw that kind of love for Anifiel from Vithius. He'd rather live in ignorance than know the Angel he loved was truly head over heels for someone else.

"Yes, I do love him," Ryan stated. It felt good to announce it; like he had a right to. "I want to make him as happy as I can."

Tofiel nodded. "And you believe I may be of help?"

"Well, I wanted to ask you for some advice on what I can do to make him like me more. Angels and humans are similar in some ways, but we're mostly different. I was hoping you could show me what you guys like and what turns you off, those sorts of things."

But Tofiel's smile fell. "I cannot make him 'like you more', Ryan. Vithius' heart is not human machinery which can be altered for better performance."

Ryan struggled hard not to laugh. Had Tofiel been spying on television commercials?

"And if you are suggesting artifice in order to please him, I recommend you rethink what you desire from him. Do you wish for a Vithius who loves Ryan, or a Vithius who loves Ryan who is playing the role of another person?"

Frustration began to mount in Ryan. He didn't understand why everyone was making such a big deal out of this. Why were there a million self-help books if improving yourself was such a bad thing?

"I'm not trying to play the role of someone he

might like," Ryan argued. "I just want to know if there are things that maybe Angels simply don't find appealing in humans. Like say Angels hate it when humans eat with their mouths open, or when they snore, or something like that."

"Do you truly believe Vithius would retract his love because you chew with your mouth open?" Tofiel asked with surprise.

Ryan suddenly felt stupid. "On Earth, yeah, that's definitely grounds for a break-up if someone's picky enough. But..." he sighed, "you're saying Angels aren't that petty."

"Or fickle," Tofiel added with an amused smile. "Ryan, if Vithius enjoys your company—and he has never spent any length of time with a human before you, which is a strong indication that he does—it is because he is pleased by who you are in your heart. He has seen who you are and compared it with who you will become and has decided he approves. You do not need to perform for him or change your behavior to suit him."

"But what about enlightenment and self-improvement? Isn't that why I'm here?"

"Yes, but those improvements are deeper, greater, than those which hold your present attention. They relate to your perception of yourself and of your role in the greater whole. They are profound changes made because you have decided they need changing, not because you believe they will positively affect the opinions of others." Tofiel gave him a quizzical look. "Have you no one to talk to about this? Most humans gather with Angel teachers and discuss the path to ascension. I am surprised Vithius has not begun this with you."

Shame made Ryan shift his eyes away. "I think maybe he has been trying to teach me in his own subtle way. I've been preoccupied with a lot of other things, I guess. I haven't really been listening." And it embarrassed him that those 'other things' involved sex, sex, and more sex. No wonder he was a terrible Angel candidate.

"I think, Ryan, you are placing too much pressure on yourself. Being loved by an Angel is cause for celebration, not stress and fear. You should speak to him of your worries. He will help you understand the reasons behind them and show you how to move beyond them. The changes he most wishes to see in you do not relate to how you appear to him, but in how you appear to yourself."

Ryan nodded and slumped slightly in relief. Although he hadn't learned anything specific from Tofiel, he felt better about his standing with Vithius. He just had to get over his hang-ups about Earthly relationships and accept that things worked differently in Heaven. Angels weren't potential jerks, waiting to break his heart when he did or said something wrong. They weren't straight guys doing a little experimenting who would dump him when their curiosity was satisfied. This was Heaven. Things were better here. *He* was supposed to be better here.

Ryan hesitated, and then tentatively touched Tofiel's shoulder. "Thank you for helping me, Tofiel. I know we don't know each other that well but I'd really like that to change. Maybe you could come and hang out with me and Vithius sometime?" *Because I think you might be lonely, too, now that Camael is no longer with you.*

Tofiel's puppy dog eyes and freckled cheeks endeared her to Ryan. When she smiled, the effect was doubled. "I would very much enjoy that, Ryan. And what of Anifiel?"

A kick to the head wouldn't have stunned Ryan more. "Anifiel? Uh, what about him? He's definitely not invited."

Too late he realized how bad that must have sounded to one of Anifiel's friends but Tofiel looked more confused than angry.

"Why would you not wish to invite Anifiel? Isn't he—"

"He made me wear a collar and called me Pet!" Ryan exclaimed. "I think those are two pretty good reasons."

"But—Anifiel does not normally speak to humans..." Tofiel trailed off, studying Ryan as if she thought he might be slightly brain damaged. "You truly dislike him?"

Ryan really didn't want to spoil a good conversation by talking about the Big Golden Jerk, so he forced a smile and shrugged. "He rubs me the wrong way, but I'm sure I'll get over it."

Tofiel blinked at him, still looking as though she were talking to an alien that spoke another language.

This was getting weirder by the second. Uncomfortable, Ryan smiled harder, hoping the brilliance of his grin would change Tofiel's train of thought. "I think if just the three of us got together—you, me and Vithius—it would be nice and intimate. It's easier to hold a conversation that way. Lots of people are great for parties and stuff, but it's difficult to talk and really get to know people. You know, the music's too loud, everyone's trying to be funny, someone gets drunk and keeps repeating the same story over and over. This'll be like a little tea party...er, without the tea." *I sound like an idiot!*

After a long, searching look which made Ryan squirm and turn two shades of red, Tofiel nodded. "You speak oddly when you become nervous. Yes, a tea party without tea sounds enjoyable. I would enjoy intimate conversation with you and Vithius. Camael and I often debated, so it will be refreshing to converse with new minds and explore fresh arguments."

Happiness lifted the corners of Ryan's mouth. "Awesome. Maybe you could come—"

The sudden scream of the war horns nearly sent Ryan tumbling over the edge of the cloud. He clutched at his chest, gasping, as his heart banged against his rib cage. He looked to Tofiel, wide-eyed. "Again? But they were just here!"

"Something is wrong," Tofiel muttered as she shot to her feet. "The Demons have not attacked this frequently in a thousand years."

"Why would that change?"

Tofiel looked grim. "I do not know." She pointed a finger down at Ryan. "Stay here. Do not venture to the battlefields again, Ryan. It is not a place for humans."

White-faced, Ryan nodded. "Be careful," he whispered.

Tofiel spared him a reassuring smile before launching off the cloud in the direction of Ambriel's Gates. Soon, more Angels shot out of the Middle Tier and zoomed through the air of the Lower Tier, heading for the battlegrounds. They looked like fighter jets scrambling for dog fights. Ryan watched, transfixed, until a familiar dark-haired figure dropped from the Middle Tier and shot forward to join the others.

Ryan leaped to his feet. "Vithius..."

The horns continued to blare, but now he could hear that hair-raising drone of the Demons again, along with a deep-throated chant that made him pale.

Anifiel. Anifiel. Anifiel.

The Demons called for the Commander.

Ryan's entire body shuddered and he scrubbed at his arms to try to rub away the goose bumps that had risen over every inch of his skin. Angels continued to buzz the sky, moving at incredible speeds as they hastened to defend the gates. Ryan looked over the edge of his cloud. The six humans he'd seen earlier were now huddled against each other, heads bowed in fear. Ryan knew he should be acting that way, too, but the fear he felt was different.

It wasn't for himself.

The longer he remained in the Middle Tier, unable to ascend, the more he had to lose. First it had been Finnian. Then it was Vithius. Now it was

Tofiel. And in a way it was Camael and Anifiel, too, for the loss of them would hurt those whom Ryan loved. Yes, he had more to lose now.

And more to defend.

He dropped his arms. He heard the horns in his ears but although they were supposed to act as a warning to humans and a calling to Angels, to his ears they now sounded like a summons. If he could not fight for what he loved, he would watch and lend silent support. He wouldn't cower on the comfort of a floating cloud and cross his fingers that the Angels would take care of him.

He ran. He leaped from cloud to cloud, which was still a harrowing affair even after having done it once. When he ran into the dense, moist cloud of fog that preceded the gates he flinched only slightly. And then he was through it, bursting onto the edge of the battlefield.

Again, the magnificence of Ambriel's Gates made him temporarily forget his purpose and simply stare. The sheer size of them made him feel like an ant gazing up at a yard gate. He stumbled forward and crouched down behind the small hill he'd found last time. The golden fencing remained in place, separating the writhing, black and white horde of Demons from the brilliant glory of the Angel warriors. Again, Anifiel was at the head.

But the Angel by his side was not Vithius. It was Camael.

The mohawked Angel was breathtaking, sheathed in white armor, his entire body glowing with a faint but unmistakable light. His hair stood up almost angrily, as if he had deliberately flared the white tuft to appear more imposing to the enemy. Ryan stared at him in awe, but he couldn't help questioning the wisdom of having Camael there instead of Vithius. He worried it might send the wrong message.

Apparently he was right.

"Where isss your dirty catamite?" called the mottled leader of the Demons in his terrible, slithering voice. "Can it be he hasss fallen from your gracesss ssso easssily? Ssso fickle, Anifiel, choosssing a new ssslut to replace your corrupted catamite. You have no loyalty to Heaven or to your fawning Angel whoresss. Your catamite sssought to protect you and for that you reward him by ssshunning him."

"He is not shunned!" Anifiel shouted. "Our Army defends with every wing in Heaven."

The Demon leader continued on as if he hadn't heard. "Firssst your dirty conssssort, now your ssslutty catamite—how will you ssshare your new white whore with usss, Anifiel? We wish to fill his every hole with our filthy Demon sssseed and make him grow pretty feathersss to match thossse of your consssort and catamite."

The Demons cackled with glee. Camael flared like a peacock. He started to surge forward, but Anifiel threw an arm across his chest to stop him.

You idiot! Ryan thought at Camael. *Don't distract Anifiel by taking it personally*!

"You vile creatures," Anifiel boomed, his voice so powerful Ryan was surprised it didn't rattle the gates. "You waste your disgusting breath with your taunting words. Heaven will not fall to you, nor will this army. Begone! Begone, before I burn your bodies with my Spear of Righteousness! Begone, before my companion blinds your eyes with the light of self-truth! You shall not prevail in Heaven, vile legion, not while a single white feather remains on my wings!"

"Yeah, you tell him," Ryan whispered, so thrilled he shivered. He loved Anifiel like this.

"You have stormed our gates a hundred thousand times," Anifiel shouted, "but you have never breached Heaven and you never shall. Those who fall to you are redeemed by the love of the Creator. There can be no victory over Heaven. There can be no victory over us!"

"That's right!" Ryan echoed, pumping his fist in the air.

"You cannot defend Heaven when you cannot defend your own catamite. And what of Finnian, whom the Demonsss have enjoyed usssing in all the dirty, nasssty waysss you fantasssize about but are afraid to admit? You cannot defend your ssslutsss, Anifiel. How can you defend the entirety of Heaven?"

"I can, because I am not alone," Anifiel declared.

Behind him, the Angels cheered.

In response, hundreds of Demons simultaneously threw themselves at the gates, sending up a shower of sparks so explosive it looked like fireworks had erupted.

"Let usss in," the Demon leader coaxed. "If you believe you can defeat usss, engage usss. Do not hide behind pretty words, Anifiel, when you have a pretty ssstick to ssstab usss with."

This time, what had to be thousands of Demons flung themselves at the gates. Ryan threw up his hands to shield his eyes from the blinding flare of light that burst up from where the Demons burned against the gates. As those Demons fell, another wave of creatures launched themselves at the gate. Then another, and another, until the sky ceased to be blue and instead burned a gleaming, phosphorescent white.

Ryan squinted against it, trying to see if the gates were still up. Could sheer force knock it down? Could enough Demons throw themselves at it to short-circuit it?

Whether his fears were legitimate concerns or Anifiel had lost his patience, the Demons' tactic had worked:

"Drop the gates!" Anifiel bellowed.

Light glinted off the notched top of the gates as they dipped below the line of clouds. Immediately Angels and Demons surged forward to clash above the finials.

Ryan searched desperately through the melee for signs of Vithius and Tofiel. He hoped they'd chosen to fight together since both had lost their companions. He hoped, too, that Tofiel was a good fighter. Vithius could not afford to be compromised again. The thought of another gray feather among his friend's wings made Ryan sick to his stomach, not for himself, but for what it would do to Vithius' state of mind.

Locating a particular Angel, though, was difficult in the surging mass of bodies. Since both Angels and Demons could fly, the battle was waged in the air as well as on the clouds. A wild, chaotic fight between birds of prey couldn't have been more dizzying.

"Ssso you come again to watch the battle."

Ryan cried out and spun around. This time three Demons crept toward him. Whether one of them had been the same who'd spoken to him last time he couldn't tell since they all looked alike to him.

He tried to tell them to back off but all that came out of his throat was a terrified squeak. Their eyes, including the sclera, were entirely black. It reminded him that these creatures were soulless. Evil. His bladder threatened to loosen. He stumbled backwards on trembling legs.

"Finnian isssuesss hisss greetingsss, human friend," hissed the Demon at the head of their triumvirate. "He asssksss why you do not fight for him."

"D-don't talk about F-Finn," Ryan finally managed to stammer. "You don't know him."

"Not only do we know him, we posssesss him," cackled the Demon. He and his fellows continued their slow advance, but now the two behind him began to separate. Ryan realized to his horror they were making a move to outflank him.

"Stay away from me!" he yelled.

"Better yet, why don't you come with usss? Come sssee Finnian and make him feel lesss sssad. He isss all alone without you. He criesss so piteousssly."

Ryan shook his head as tears sprang to his eyes. "Y-you're lying. You don't have him."

The Demon's lips split, revealing sharp, yellow teeth. "We have him and we are usssing him to sate our Demon lussstsss, but he hasss not gone mad, not even when we peel hisss pretty ssskin from hisss flesh. He callsss for hisss human friend in Heaven. He missssesss you. Will you abandon him to the Beneath? Will you leave poor, pretty Finnian to sssuffer alone?"

It was too horrible to imagine. They had to be lying. They had to. Ryan covered his ears with his hands, not wanting to hear anymore because his heart was going to shatter into a thousand pieces if he had to hear one more word about Finn suffering at their hands.

"Leave him alone," he choked out. "Let him go..."

"Come with ussss, human, and you can make him happy. Make Finnian sssmile. Pretty Angel hasss not sssmiled for a long, long time. He only weepsss like a tiny child."

A sob broke through Ryan's parted lips. "Oh, god, Finn..."

He took another step backward and hit something hard. Two somethings. Terror made his legs collapse beneath him. On his knees, surrounded by the three Demons, Ryan began to hyperventilate.

"Come with usss," insisted the main Demon. "We can take you to sssee him without pain. But if you fight usss we will hurt him and make him ssscream. He will ssscream for days unlessss you come with usss."

A sickly white hand extended down to him. Ryan looked through his tears at the clawed fingers and imagined the sharp nails dragging furrows through Finn's soft, untouched skin. "Don't hurt him," he whimpered. "Please don't hurt him."

"Come with usss, and we will ssstop hisss pain."

Bile rose in his throat. He couldn't think of Vithius or Tofiel or even Anifiel. The only Angel in his mind was Finnian, his best friend, his reason for hope. Twin tears dripped down Ryan's face as he raised his hand to accept the Demon's.

Before their hands could connect, a silver-garbed figure barreled into all four of them, knocking them asunder like bowling pins. Ryan tumbled head over heels before a muscled arm slid beneath his belly and hooked him like a piece of folded laundry. The air rushed hard and fast around his ears as wings bore him up and away from the sprawled Demons.

"Finn!" Ryan called out brokenly as he extended his hands to the Demons.

"I should have let them take you," Anifiel growled above him. "I would be better off without you, infernal human! Must you cause trouble wherever you go?!"

Ryan hung his head and wept. "I don't care if you hate me, but let me save Finn. Please let me help him."

The Lower Tier passed in a blur beneath them. Ryan continued to cry. When greens and blues exploded into view beneath them, he heard very quietly: "Finnian is not yours to save, little human. All of mine belong to me."

If Anifiel said more than that, Ryan didn't know. He zoned out on the Angel and on everything that was happening to him. He could not feel anything but sorrow, his mind tormented by images of his beloved friend, trapped in the horror of the Beneath.

14

Beep...beep.

He saw the light dancing behind his eyelids.

Beep...beep.

A slow spike that was supposed to indicate hope...

Beep...beep.

...or endurance.

The jumping ball of light didn't speed up nor slow down as unconsciousness released its hold on him. He kept his eyes closed. It was as if he'd been buried beneath sand for years; he could barely move.

And he suspected if he did, he would regret it.

"Do you ever wish," began a voice that spoke in low, hushed tones, "that it had been the other way around?"

Shame made the words timid, as if they wanted to hide rather than be spoken. He recognized the voice. He recognized the speaker. More than ever, he would not open his eyes.

Beep...beep.

"You mean, do I wish...?"

"Yes," replied the first. "I know it's awful of me, but—"

"Of course I do." He listened to the second person bite off an angry sigh. The sigh was a knife. It stabbed deep into Ryan's chest. "How could I not? How could anyone not feel that way? Jesus, what happened—"

"I know." The words were broken, sobbed out. "It would have—it would have been better for everyone, even him, if it had been the other way around."

"But he is alive, and we should be—thankful for that." Thankfulness sounded like resignation, though. Like disappointment. "It doesn't matter what they say. The rumors—he's still our son. We love him, even if-if..."

Beep...beep.

"Yes." A choked sob. "Even if."

Ryan opened his eyes. The ceiling wasn't white cork, it was Heaven glimpsed through the vines and flowers of the pavilion.

A single tear slid down his cheek.

"Thank god I'm dead," he whispered.

~~~~

He looked up hopefully at the sound of beating wings. The leash of the collar Anifiel had once again attached to him fell lightly across one shoulder and trailed down his spine before disappearing into the grass to whatever held it down. Ryan had made only one attempt to release himself before realizing the pointlessness of it. He didn't want to leave the pavilion. He needed to wait for the others to return if he wanted to learn what had happened to Finnian.

And he desperately did want to know. Since shaking off that unhappy dream/memory, he'd spent his time worrying and thinking about pain and suffering. He knew better than most people that there were worse things than death. He understood that Demons could and probably did lie all the time. But they could also tell the truth if that truth was horrible enough to hurt. Ryan knew all about truths that hurt.

If the Demons hadn't managed to physically capture the bright Angel, simply touching Finnian was grounds for revenge.

If Angels could seek revenge, that is.

"And if they can't, I'll do their dirty work for them," Ryan muttered angrily as the combined air pressure from four descending Angels stirred his curls around his face. He quickly scanned their faces and although all were grim—Anifiel looked like a pressure cooker about to blow as he glared at Ryan—no one appeared to have been harmed this time.

Vithius sent him a concerned, but encouraging smile as he landed. Ryan ran to him and discovered the lead on his leash barely allowed him to jump into the Angel's embrace.

"I am grateful that you are safe and well," Vithius murmured against the top of his head. His voice was rough with emotion. "I have not felt such fear in a century."

Ryan shut his eyes tightly, pushing back the sadness that had arisen in his dream. "I'm sorry," he whispered, pressing his face against the Angel's neck. "I'm sorry I scared you. I don't know how they found me. I tried to keep out of sight but they—"

"You should not have stepped foot on the battlefields to begin with!" Anifiel boomed from behind Ryan. "You were expressly forbidden, foolish human! You threatened the well-being of every Angel in Heaven. I left my army defenseless so I could save you!"

Ryan lifted his head and looked back over his shoulder at the golden Angel. He wasn't hurt by Anifiel's lack of concern for him; he expected it.

Like the others, Anifiel no longer wore his battle armor, but his body still seemed an impenetrable fortress. A wild, fleeting thought crossed Ryan's mind: what would it take to bring down those defenses? Then his gaze lifted to Anifiel's and the anger and near hatred in the Angel's brilliant green orbs dashed any interest in reaching the Angel behind the walls.

"I never asked you to save me," Ryan told him. "I was prepared to go with them and save Finn. I didn't take you away from the fighting. You did that on your own."

Standing just behind the golden Angel, Camael's white brows descended over his eyes as he studied Ryan with his penetrating blue gaze. "The Commander would never permit a human of Heaven to be taken by a Demon." Camael's tone was critical. "Your presence on the battlefield demanded that you be defended. The Commander was given no choice."

That is such a lie, Ryan thought, glaring at the two Angels. He hadn't cried out for help. If he'd been taken by the Demons no one would've known except Anifiel, and Anifiel sure as heck didn't care what happened to him.

"We would never allow you to be harmed," Vithius agreed, placing a hand on Ryan's cheek and bringing his face around. Looking up at Vithius' loving face was a million times better than looking at Anifiel's pissed one. The dark-haired Angel smiled. His gaze roamed hungrily over Ryan's face as though he'd feared never seeing it again. "Do not ever believe the lies of the Demons, Ryan. Going with them would not have helped Finnian, no matter what they promised you."

"But what if they do have him? I want to help him, Vithius. I'll do anything." Ryan gulped. "I'm partly to blame for him leaving Heaven in the first place. He's my responsibility." He half-expected an exclamation from Anifiel after that admission, but the Commander remained oddly silent.

"You have such a good heart," Vithius whispered, his thumb gently smoothing across Ryan's lower lip. "You will truly be a great Angel."

"I haven't done anything yet," Ryan protested.

"What you have done is cause nothing but trouble!" Anifiel butted in helpfully.

Ryan gritted his teeth and began to turn around, but Vithius held him firm. To Ryan's surprise, the Angel looked up over his shoulder at Anifiel with a stern expression on his face. "We discussed this, Anifiel. This might not have happened if your feelings are not as they are."

Ryan looked at his friend in confusion as Anifiel sputtered behind him, "It is a theory of yours and Tofiel's which holds no weight at all. It is preposterous!"

"I believe it does hold weight," Tofiel chimed in for the first time. The gangly Angel looked to the ground, avoiding meeting anyone's gaze. "The Demons have not attacked so frequently in a millennium, Anifiel. One must believe they have a reason for doing so. I, too, believe what Vithius believes."

"It is impossible!" Camael exclaimed, sounding as offended as Anifiel. He stared at Tofiel accusingly, making Ryan want to stand between the two Angels to protect his new friend. "Do you understand what you are saying?"

"She does," Vithius said very clearly, returning his gaze to Ryan. "It is not impossible at all."

Ryan had no idea what they were talking about, but he certainly liked the way Vithius currently looked at him. "What are you talking about?" he asked. "What theory?"

"Vithius, I warn you: do not speak of this to him."

Anifiel's order was like a thunderclap. Ryan resisted the urge to cower. What was so threatening to Anifiel that he felt compelled to threaten Vithius to keep it a secret?

Thick arms wrapped around Ryan as Vithius drew him against the Angel's chest. "He should know, Anifiel. This pertains to his safety, as well."

"He shall remain safe if he remains here," Anifiel retorted. The leash attached to Ryan's collar snapped against his spine as Anifiel jerked on it. "He will not return to the battlefields no matter how many times the Demons attack us."

"But that is no solution at all!" Vithius protested, reaching over Ryan's shoulder and yanking at the leash. "Ryan is a human, not a pet for you to torment. Shame on you, Anifiel, for preferring to treat him so cruelly rather than deal honestly with what is happening here. It is not his fault, nor is it yours. The Demons are taking advantage. We must work together to stop them, not place our loved ones in chains."

"He is the loved one of no Angel," Anifiel snarled so ferociously that Ryan was glad he had his back to the Commander. He shivered and burrowed into Vithius' chest. "Do not force your offensive theories upon me, Vithius. I will not have them!"

"Then the Demons will continue to torment you." Vithius' breath blew harshly against the top of Ryan's head. "They will continue to thrive on your denial and Heaven will fall because of it, Anifiel. I love you as no others do, but I cannot support you in this foolishness. Not while your blind eyes harm all whom I love."

"He is corrupting_"

"He is not."

Ryan stopped breathing. He'd never heard Vithius sound that way—as if he were one step from snapping completely.

"The only corruption here is that which is caused by fear. And its victim, Anifiel, is you alone." Vithius tugged on the leash again. "Release him to me. We are leaving."

"You cannot leave—"

"And how will you stop me?"

A long moment passed before the leash magically unclipped from Ryan's collar and fell to the ground.

"Go then." Anifiel's voice was a harsh whisper. "Take the steps which will take you not only from me but from Heaven. For if you go with him, Vithius, you turn willfully."

Vithius trembled with suppressed emotion. "At least I go there with my eyes wide open." He clutched Ryan to him. "Let us leave this place."

He didn't wait for Ryan's acquiescence. He lifted them from the ground and launched them into the sky.

~~~~~

Strangely enough, Vithius flew them to the stream beside Anifiel's hill, the same stream where they had first bathed and touched each other while the golden Angel watched.

They didn't land in the water, but beside it. Ryan looked to Anifiel's hill worriedly. There was a good chance the Commander would show up here to brood, so why were they here, too? But the tormented expression on Vithius' face kept Ryan silent. Vithius knew what he was doing, even if his decisions weren't consciously made.

"Lie down," Ryan urged, dropping down and stretching his legs in front of him. He patted his lap and smiled up at Vithius. "Put your head here. I want to connect with you."

It brought a small smile to Vithius' face, just as he'd hoped. Like a warrior finally relinquishing the battle, the Angel dropped tiredly to the grass and positioned himself so he could rest his head in Ryan's lap. He closed his eyes as Ryan gently combed his fingers through his ebony hair.

"Better?" Ryan murmured hopefully. He didn't like seeing Vithius upset. The gentle Angel should never have a reason to be upset, in Ryan's opinion. It was just wrong.

"The battle is over, the Demons repelled, and I am here with you." Vithius smiled and sighed. "Yes, Ryan, this is better."

"I love you," Ryan said softly as he stroked his fingers over the high arches of Vithius' cheekbones. "Don't ever forget that."

Dark lashes lifted and warmth bathed Ryan as the Angel looked up at him. "You glow with the love you hold for me, Ryan. It is impossible to forget. I am truly blessed." He reached up and caught Ryan's hands in his. "I should have been the one to save you. I should have sensed that you were on the battlefield, and that shames me. Please forgive me."

"You're joking, right?"

A puzzled look overtook Vithius' face. "I am?"

Ryan grinned. "You have nothing to apologize for. I was the idiot who went where I wasn't supposed to. I wouldn't have wanted you to be distracted by what I was doing. You and Tofiel had enough to worry about while defending each other. You guys did fight together, right?"

The Angel nodded. "Yes, we have paired off as battle companions. Tofiel is an excellent warrior. Her reach is unrivaled."

"I'll bet. She's like a giant tree." Ryan released a relieved breath. "I'm glad she can keep you safe. I worried about that."

"Do you not worry for Anifiel's safety, too?" Vithius' eyes were unwavering as they bore into Ryan with unexpected intensity. "He fought with a new companion, also."

"Yeah, but it's Camael. He's the equivalent of a Marine. Fighting is his life. Neither one of them will get hurt. Besides—" he added, when Vithius looked about to speak, "—I don't care about Anifiel, I care about you. You're my boyfriend."

Childlike joy suffused Vithius' face. "You call me by your human word for affectionate coupling."

Ryan rolled his eyes and laughed. "Way to make it complicated, Vithius. Let's just stick with 'boyfriend'."

"Boyfriend, it is," the Angel whispered and released Ryan's hands to reach up and tug him down. "I would enjoy kissing my human boyfriend now."

"What my boyfriend wants, my boyfriend

gets," Ryan replied with a goofy smile on his face. He closed his eyes and touched his lips to Vithius'.

Twenty-four years on Earth passed through his mind like the fanned pages of an illustrated autobiography. Sixteen years of good. Eight years of bad. But they were the pages of a story that had ended. Whatever had happened before—even if it had brought him here—meant nothing to him while he pressed his lips to this Angel's. In the velvet pillows of Vithius' lips awaited Ryan's future. Wherever he went, whatever he did, he wouldn't go there alone; he would have Vithius beside him.

The fugue began to soften Ryan's limbs. He felt himself lowering his head and deepening the kiss, his tongue teasing the seam of Vithius' lips. His hands slid down the Angel's muscled neck and over the sleek swell of his chest. Vithius' skin burned beneath Ryan's palms. His smell was intoxicating. Ryan pushed his tongue more insistently against the closed crease of the Angel's mouth, desperate to plunge inside and taste Vithius from the inside.

He couldn't stop the faint moan of disappointment when the Angel gently broke the kiss and pushed Ryan upward.

"You lose yourself in me," the Angel warned, but the rosy glow on his cheeks showed he didn't especially mind it. "I will not take advantage of that."

"Maybe I want you to," Ryan said, trying to twist out of Vithius' hands and return to their kissing. "I enjoy the way you make me feel."

"It is the same feeling Anifiel engenders in you."

Ryan groaned and sat up. "Thanks for the reminder."

Vithius sat up, too, and folded his legs Indian-style. Ryan darted a quick glance at the Angel's groin and smiled to himself upon seeing the swollen thickness of Vithius' cock.

"You wish to ask me questions, Ryan. I will not distract you from that." Vithius smiled to lessen the frustration they both felt.

Ryan sighed and nodded. "Fine, alright. No nookie until we talk." He tried to think about questions, even though it was difficult. All he wanted to do was jump Vithius and rut on him for an hour. "Okay, well, I guess I do have a question. I want to know what happened back there. What were you all arguing about? What's this theory of yours?"

Vithius became very serious then, so serious in fact, Ryan worried he'd asked the wrong question.

"Tofiel and I believe there is a reason for the Demons' repeated attacks upon Ambriel's Gates," he said.

Dread settled in Ryan's stomach, his arousal wilting. "What is it? Is it—is it because of Finn? Do you think they have him?"

Vithius reached over and entwined their fingers. "We believe they have been attacking us because of you."

Ryan's mind went blank. *Because of you.* The blame was his. Once again, he was the reason for the hurt, for the pain. *Because of you.* He tried to pull away.

But Vithius wouldn't release his hold. "Tell me

what you are thinking," the Angel demanded, brows furrowed. "Where has your mind turned? Your reaction is unreasonable."

"Easy for you to s-say," Ryan stuttered. "It's not your fault."

"And neither is it yours."

Stalks of grass pricked Ryan's thighs through his tunic. "W-what?"

"The Demons attack because of you," Vithius repeated, squeezing Ryan's hand, "but not because you have done something wrong. Some might say you have done something right, though I doubt it will be said for quite some time yet." A wry smile touched Vithius' mouth which Ryan didn't understand at all.

"You've totally lost me," he admitted. "They're attacking because of me, why?"

"Because when they do, Anifiel comes to your aid."

Vithius' meaning sunk in as pleasantly as an arrow shaft to the intestines. "No, you've got it wrong. The first time it was you who..."

Vithius nodded as Ryan trailed off in realization. "Anifiel's actions spurred my own. He acted first. Both times, Ryan, it was he who saved you."

Oh, no, no, no, no, no. Ryan's mind whirled, looking for another excuse. He found one quickly.

"It's his duty," he blurted. "Just like Camael said: as the Commander Anifiel can't allow a human to be taken by the Demons, and the Demons know this so they use me as bait."

"Possibly," Vithius conceded, but the doubtful

look on his face didn't encourage Ryan. "What concerns me greatly is that you continue to place the two of you in harm's way by venturing onto the battlefield even after you are warned not to. Why do you do this?"

"I sure as heck won't do it again!"

Vithius didn't blink. "How can you be certain?"

Ryan clapped his free hand over his face and groaned with dismay as the grasses stirred around them in a heavy wind.

"He cannot, for he is weak and without willpower or intelligence of any sort."

"Nice to see you, too, Anifiel," he muttered as the golden Angel settled on the ground before them. Ryan peered between his fingers at Anifiel and was surprised that the Angel didn't look angrier. Anifiel wore angry like other people wore white. Right now he looked only mildly ticked.

"I hoped you would come," Vithius commented lightly. "What we have to discuss should be for our ears only."

"My battle companion is my brother," Anifiel pointed out. "What you have to discuss should have been said in front of him."

"Has Camael changed his stance on the intermingling of Angels and humans, then?" Challenge rang through Vithius' voice. "You desire his respect, Anifiel. You know as well as I that what we say here will not endear you to him."

"He respects the Commander of Heaven's Army!" Anifiel roared, insulted.

"Will he respect the Commander of Heaven's

Army when he falls defending the one he loves?" Vithius asked quietly.

Lightning was supposed to strike. Ryan kept glancing at the sky, trying to figure out if it would strike him or Vithius first.

But the sky remained clear, and amazingly, Anifiel's head didn't explode, either.

Red-faced with fury, Anifiel glared at them both. "If I cannot chain the human like I would a misbehaving pet, what are my alternatives?"

Vithius smiled and clasped Ryan's hand, drawing him up as the Angel stood. "Ryan has already come up with a suggestion. Perhaps it is time we test it."

Ryan smiled weakly. He had no idea what his new boyfriend was talking about, and he wasn't so sure he wanted to find out. But surely anything was better than pursuing the topic of what compelled Anifiel to save him.

Anything but that.

~~~~~

"You may as well bind us together and throw us over the edge," Anifiel remarked caustically. "This plan is madness."

Ryan experimentally swung the metal shield Vithius had conjured from thin air for him. It was around the size of an extra-large pizza and though Vithius had assured him it was made of solid metal, it felt as light as, well, a pizza box. Two leather straps kept it in place against his right forearm as he swung the shield and sliced it through the air in a karate chop. He felt like Captain America.

"This shield is great!" he gushed. "Can I have another one?" he asked Vithius. "You know, for my left arm?"

"Then you will look like double the fool that you already do," Anifiel muttered. The golden Angel didn't hold the Spear of Righteousness, but was armed with the same long wooden pole that Vithius carried. The dark-haired Angel had explained that they were the Angels' training sticks.

"You need only one," Vithius told Ryan with a fond smile. "Your shield is for defense, not for offense. Two shields might encourage you to attack."

The outer surface of the shield was smooth, not a scratch marring it. Ryan ran the fingers of his left hand over the sleek surface, marveling at the lack of fingerprints or streaks left behind. "Is this like, titanium or something?"

"It is the same metal used to create the gates," Vithius said. "Your shield shall not break nor bend. It is excellent protection for you. I am pleased."

"I would be pleased if he did not trespass on the battlefields!"

Ryan threw back his head in exasperation. "Are you serious with this? I already told you I wouldn't go there again. I learned my lesson, okay? I don't want to run into those creepy things any more than you want to save me from them. Believe me, Anifiel, we're in *complete* agreement on this."

The golden Angel huffed.

"If my theory holds true," Vithius began

calmly, "we must prepare you for attack."

"I told you, though, Vithius: the Demons aren't calling me to the battlefields. I know what they sound like and I definitely don't hear them in my head." Ryan shuddered. Vithius stared patiently at Ryan until he gave a rueful smile. "But if you want to train me, I'd be stupid to refuse," he relented sheepishly.

He liked the pleased, approving smile Vithius sent him in return. I've got to make him happy more often, Ryan told himself. *It makes me feel so good.*

"It is important for you to learn how to defend, and how to resist responding," Vithius said as he raised his pole in both hands and faced off against Ryan. "The human instinct is to fight if one cannot escape and to take advantage of weakness in your opponent. This is not the way of the Angel warrior. To attack weakness is to embrace aggression. To inflict pain upon those who hurt you is to succumb to bitterness and hate. There can be no revenge. You must find no satisfaction in violence." His eyes softened. "It will be more difficult than it sounds. Do not be discouraged that you do not 'get it' immediately, Ryan. It is not an easy thing to think like an Angel. Most humans cannot, which is why they are forbidden from participating in the Eternity War. I expect you to fail many times, and then I expect you to succeed."

The brutal honesty appealed to Ryan. It made him more determined than ever to make Vithius proud of him, even if it took a hundred instances of being knocked on his butt. He raised his shield arm and took a wide-legged stance. "Okay. I understand.

I think I'm ready."

"You shall never be ready," Anifiel murmured darkly from where he stood to the side. His green eyes were narrowed with what Ryan could only take as gleeful expectation of Ryan's imminent butt-kicking.

"I'll be ready to make you eat your words," Ryan retorted, and then yelped and jumped back as Vithius' spinning pole flew at him like an out of control propeller.

The wood clanged against his shield, sending painful vibration shooting up Ryan's arm and into his shoulder. "Ow!" he cried out.

Bang! Bang! Bang!

"Hey, ow, wait! That hurts!"

Vithius acted as though he hadn't heard a thing. Expression grim, the Angel's pole continued to batter at Ryan's shield in a serious of teeth-rattling strikes. Startled and afraid of the sudden, vicious attack, Ryan used his shield arm to knock the pole away and then jumped forward to take advantage of the opening.

"Wrong!" Anifiel barked as Ryan chopped at Vithius with the shield. "You cannot attack! You cannot seek retribution!"

"Damn it." Ryan gritted his teeth and fell back, panting. Adrenaline surged through his veins, but he nodded. "Okay, okay. I won't. I've got it now."

No sooner had he said the words than Vithius swarmed forward again, his pole spinning so quickly it was nearly invisible. Ryan fell back, his heart in his throat, afraid of the impact of that expertly wielded weapon. When it struck it was as frightening as he expected.

Bang! Bang! Bang! Bang!

Ryan shut his eyes and held the shield over his face, cringing. A single crack to his skull would bust it wide open.

Bang! Bang! Bang! Bang!

"Move, you fool!"

Anifiel's voice gave strength to Ryan's shaking legs. He scrambled backward, gasping as he fled Vithius' spinning pole.

Then an impossible break came: Vithius tripped on the grass and sprawled forward, his pole caught beneath him. Without a second thought Ryan leaped forward, eyes wild, shield raised high—

"Wrong again! You cannot harm the fallen!"

Ryan staggered and fell to one knee, shocked at his actions. Vithius looked up at him from his sprawl in the grass and winked.

"You tricked me!" Ryan accused. "You fell on purpose. I could have hurt you! How could you do that?"

Perplexed, Vithius sat up. "Ryan, I am attempting to teach you. I will not allow you to be turned because I failed to prepare you for the Demons."

Ryan turned away, his cheeks burning. "I know," he choked out. "I know you're trying to help me. But this is harder than I thought. When you come at me I'm scared out of my mind and when I have the chance to strike back I can't help doing so. This is impossible. No human can only defend. It goes against our instincts."

"You truly are a pathetic little human."

His head snapped up as Anifiel stepped forward. The Angel's handsome face twisted into a mask of disdain. "You ask why you cannot ascend—it is because failure is all you accept. Just as you failed in everything else, so, too, do you fail in this. And when you sneak your way onto the battlefields again, you will bring harm to every Angel when I am forced once again to save your worthless soul. I should have turned my eye elsewhere when the Demons sought your hand. You are a disgrace to Heaven!"

"Anifiel!" Vithius snapped, shocked. "You go too far!"

"No, he knows it is true," Anifiel went on, his hard, cruel gaze fastened to Ryan like a wasp, stinging him again and again. "He recognizes the weakness and cowardice within himself, but he will not admit to it. Tell the truth, little human: my beloved Finnian requested that you accompany him to Earth but you refused because you were afraid of returning to the location of your failure. You forced him to go alone and thus left him vulnerable for the Demons to attack him!"

The rage that flooded Ryan was so strong it left him light-headed. "That never happened," he gasped, his shield hand curling into a fist behind the metal. "I would never have let him go alone if I'd known that was his intention. He's my best friend. I love him!"

"But you claim to love Vithius, too," Anifiel pointed out, smirking triumphantly. "Is there no end to the lies which spill from your mouth? Whom else will you claim to love? Will it be Tofiel? Will you convince her to break the laws of decency and join you in a disgusting orgy of—"

"Shut up!"

Anifiel's lashes dropped until only sickles of green could be seen behind the pale fringe. He raised his pole. "Do you think you can take me, little human? Do you think the force of your anger can defeat the Commander of Heaven's Army? Can a pitiful human like you ever be more than a space that should have been granted to another?"

Reason fled, if it had ever existed. Anifiel was more than his rival for Vithius' affections—he was Ryan's nemesis. The frustration of being unable to defend himself properly against Vithius blazed anew in Ryan, but this time it felt sweet because this time he could take out his aggressions on Anifiel. The bullying Angel expected him to fail, so what was the harm? *You want it, you big jerk? I'll give it to you. Gladly.*

Ryan charged him, yelling like he was storming the beaches of Normandy, his shield arm raised before him as if he could batter the Angel with the force of its reflected surface. He saw the expectation written all over Anifiel's face: he'd anticipated this very reaction. But also on Anifiel's face was a curious tension, as if he thought Ryan might, just might, change his mind at the last minute.

To Ryan's own surprise, he did. He leaped through the air. When he was within arm's reach of the Angel, instinct of another sort took over his body. Instead of bashing Anifiel's face in with the shield, Ryan tackled the golden Angel, wrapping arms and legs around his solid torso. Anifiel dropped his pole and staggered backward beneath the combined weight. When Anifiel's head hit the grass, golden hair splaying beneath his head, Ryan grabbed him by the sides of the face and crushed a kiss to his mouth.

The fugue exploded over Ryan's senses. He moaned like he was dying. He stabbed his tongue between Anifiel's lips in search of the most intimate touch he could find. The startled Angel didn't defend against him. He gasped as Ryan's tongue pushed into his mouth. Ryan ate at him, unable to get enough of the green apple smell and the dark, seductive honey-like taste of the Angel's mouth. Anifiel's tongue lay shyly at the bottom of his mouth, afraid of the siege, and it drove Ryan wild as he rubbed and slid his tongue over and under that tender flesh, dominating the Angel the way he couldn't any other way. He moaned again, hungry. He ground his rigid cock against Anifiel's stomach as his body temperature rose to that of a raging inferno. He needed more. He needed in...

Then the world spun and Anifiel was above him, one hand planted in the grass beside Ryan's head, the other fisting in Ryan's tunic and yanking hard enough to tear the fabric from his body. The primal action ripped a cry of lust from Ryan's throat. Air rushed over his tight, fiercely beaded nipples and tickled his sweaty chest. The first rough touch of Anifiel's palm to his belly made Ryan scream into the Angel's mouth. With his legs still wrapped around Anifiel's waist, Ryan lifted his hips and jabbed his swollen cock against the Angel's body in a mindless search for relief. When an answering hardness poked up beneath his scrotum mere inches from his hole, Ryan's eyes rolled up into his head and he came explosively all over Anifiel's tunic.

He didn't quite pass out, but he was orbiting another planet as Anifiel rocked awkwardly and uncertainly above him. Only after the Angel let out a keen of frustration did Ryan's senses clear.

Anifiel was hard against him. He was rock hard. His green eyes blazed like a madman's in his sweaty, flushed face, and strands of golden hair clung to his damp skin. He looked crazed, desperate.

As the Angel continued to tremble and huff like a race horse, Ryan realized the Commander didn't know how to ease the tortuous ache he felt which Ryan had given him. Anifiel was at his mercy. Anifiel felt the fugue just as Vithius had claimed he did.

And that tidbit of knowledge suddenly felt like a powerful weapon in Ryan's hand.

Ryan let his arms and legs fall haphazardly to the grass. His shield knocked sharply against his elbow, making a dull sound. Anifiel's wild eyes flicked to the metal circle.

"Never tell me again that I'm a failure," Ryan panted, staring in fascination as the Angel suffered the worst case of blue balls in Heaven. "I just defeated you, Anifiel, and I didn't have to hurt you to do it."

Something flashed in Anifiel's eyes, but before Ryan could identify it and prepare to be pummeled, familiar hands gripped him under the arms and slid him out from beneath the larger male. Vithius, blank-faced, looked from Ryan to his commander. Anifiel remained on all fours, head down and unmoving except for the occasional shudder that wracked his body.

"What did you do to him?" Vithius asked quietly as he helped Ryan to his feet.

The first sense of control where Anifiel was concerned made Ryan grin like the Cheshire cat. "I just kicked his butt, Ryan-style."

Then he let out a laugh because he figured it would be the last time he'd get the chance. The next time he ran into Anifiel, Ryan knew the Commander would make him wish the Demons had dragged him to the Beneath.

15

Vithius flew them to the Path to Inspiration and set them down on the white stones directly in front of the statues of Anifiel and Finnian. It wasn't Ryan's first choice of destinations, but anywhere far from the horned-up blond was a good choice.

He'd beaten Anifiel at his own game, given the Commander a taste of his own medicine. Ryan couldn't think of a better punishment for the arrogant, domineering Angel, and he didn't think what he'd done was particularly evil, either. It shouldn't add more than a few months to his sentence in the Middle Tier. Hopefully. And even if the punishment was another year, Ryan would take it. For once in his life—so to speak—he, doormat Ryan, had gotten one over on a hot guy who'd wanted to humiliate him.

But why does he want to humiliate you? Anifiel isn't dumb, and even though it's satisfying to say it, he's not cruel. Angels can't *be cruel. Vithius and Tofiel believe Anifiel is compelled to protect you not because he has to, but because he wants to.*

That means Anifiel cares.

Ryan shut his eyes. No, Anifiel had only proved he could lust after him. That wasn't the same as caring. Not by a mile.

"I have sometimes wondered," Vithius said as he paused before Finnian's statue, "whether Angels who love each other can experience what humans feel when they are overwhelmed by contact with Angels."

"You mean the fugue?" Ryan joined him on the path and reached out to run his fingertips down Finnian's cheek. The adrenaline in his blood thinned as he gazed upon his beautiful missing friend. "I think we saw proof that you guys can. Or at least, Anifiel can."

Anifiel lusts after me…

Had any human in the history of humanity ever said that before?

"Anifiel is capable," Vithius agreed with an enigmatic smile. "But my question was whether two Angels can experience such. For instance, did you ever witness it between Anifiel and Finnian?"

"I saw Finn and Anifiel kiss each other," Ryan told him. He smiled as he remembered the memory—not because he enjoyed the thought of Anifiel being happy but because Finn had been. "When they kissed...it was amazing. I could feel their love as if I had been included, as if I were part of their relationship, too. It was so intense. So pure and perfect."

"But that is what *you* felt. It was an extension of your 'fugue', as you call it." Vithius moved to stand directly before Anifiel's statue. His hand came to rest on the Commander's inanimate foot. "I have not known of an Angel who has lost reason because of another Angel...or because of a human."

Ryan laughed uncomfortably. "Anifiel lost reason over Finn a long time ago, though. He goes totally nuts whenever he thinks or talks about his consort. That's a form of fugue. It's affecting every decision he makes."

Vithius cocked his head quizzically as he regarded Ryan. "I have witnessed your fugue many times. Not once have I seen it cause you to behave with angry aggression, nor with anxiety."

"Look, I think I know where you're going with this and you're assuming the wrong thing." Ryan paced away, not wanting to be close to Anifiel's statue while they followed this line of conversation. "Anifiel didn't feel anything extraordinary just because *I* made him feel it. If Sam or Eric jumped him like that the result would've been the same. Heck, if you knew what you were doing and jumped him like that it'd be the same. It's the sex part that makes us all go a little nutty. It's not me with my super fugue powers or anything, because trust me, I have zero power in that department."

Every word seemed to burn his lips as they passed from his mouth. *You are not supposed to tell lies in Heaven...*

"But, Ryan," Vithius' voice was soft with disappointment, "I have not reacted that way with you or Anifiel, fugue or no."

Ryan blinked dumbly. *That* wasn't what he'd expected of this line of questioning at all.

Vithius shyly toed the ground. "Why am I different?"

"Is that what this is about?" Ryan asked in disbelief. "You think Anifiel and I have a better connection because of what I just did to him?"

The Angel's cheeks turned a dull red. "Yes."

"But—what about when we were in the stream washing each other? Or-or when we sixty-nined? Those times you became excited, too, remember?"

"Those times were amazing to me, yes, but the way Anifiel was just now..." Vithius trailed off, his blush increasing. "I have not known such temporary madness."

Ryan couldn't help marveling over his boyfriend's reaction. Vithius was insecure? How was that possible? How adorable was that?

Ryan moved to the Angel and cupped his chin, lifting it so their eyes could meet. "I can make you lose control like that if you want." He watched Vithius' pupils dilate. Ryan couldn't remember ever feeling sexier as he murmured, "I can make you forget your name and only remember mine. I can make you go crazy, make you go wild."

Vithius' lashes fluttered like the wings of a butterfly. "I wish to know this feeling," he husked. "I desire what you gave to Anifiel."

Ryan shivered as his cock swelled. "No, I won't torture you like that. I'll make it good for you. I'll blow your mind." He curved his arms behind the

Angel's neck. "Take us somewhere, Vithius. Take us somewhere private and quiet where I can hear you moaning as I touch you."

A soft sound escaped Vithius' lips as he wrapped his arms around Ryan's back and pulled him forward. "My body reacts strongly to your words," he whispered as he pushed his erection against Ryan's lower belly. "How is it that words from you make me feel excited? Your words make me ache."

"It's called dirty talk." Ryan groaned as he pushed his own hardness against the Angel. "A lot of sex is mental, and dirty talk is a part of that."

Fingers pressed urgently into Ryan's back. "Sex that is mental? How is that possible?"

Ryan kissed the underside of Vithius' jaw. "I'll explain when we get there. Just get us there. I want to attack every inch of you." He licked up Vithius' throat. "I want to stroke your cock...maybe touch you inside..."

"I am very excited," Vithius warned shakily. "I feel as I did when you took me into your mouth and I spilled my essence."

"Then hurry, Vithius." Ryan thrust against him. "Hurry."

"Yes." Trembling, the Angel held Ryan securely and launched them into the air.

This was the first time Ryan flew while facing the Angel who carried him and he took full advantage of the position to molest his boyfriend. He kissed across Vithius' throat and shoulders, his mouth opening to suck at hot, dark skin, his teeth nipping playfully at the Angel's taut muscles.

"You're so sexy," Ryan panted as he mouthed the Angel's neck. "No one's sexier than you. No one."

"My nature is influencing you," Vithius gasped back. "Your desperation is unlike you."

"I can handle the fugue," Ryan mumbled, burying his face against the other male's skin and inhaling the Angel's winter scent. He was exaggerating—every time he was with Anifiel Ryan proved how little resistance he had to the Angelic pheromone—but Vithius wasn't going to take advantage of his helpless, horny condition. He wouldn't force Ryan to crawl on the grass and suck his toes. This was a good fugue. This was surrender Ryan could make without regret.

"I'll show you how this feels," Ryan told him as he combed his fingers through Vithius' sleek hair. "I'll put my own fugue on you. God, hurry, Vithius. Hurry!"

Releasing a strangled moan, Vithius swooped downward suddenly and the next thing Ryan knew he was sprawled on his back, grass pricking the bare skin on the back of his neck as his Angelic lover pressed down on him.

As wonderful as that was, Ryan had something different in mind. Pushing at Vithius' shoulders, Ryan reversed their positions. He straddled the Angel's large, strong body and ground his butt over Vithius' rigid cock. The Angel gasped, his eyes widening and his hands shooting to Ryan's hips.

"Do you want to feel what it's like to have sex?" Ryan whispered against Vithius' moist lips.

He stared deeply into the velvet gaze of his lover, reading Vithius' apprehension and confused desire. "Do you want to be inside me?"

Vithius' Adam's apple bobbed up and down. The palms of his hands spread across Ryan's buttocks. "I do. If you will show me."

"You have no idea how badly I want to," Ryan replied, hiking up his tunic to bare his lower half. Vithius' cock burned like a brand against Ryan's scrotum, making him lose focus for a moment. He ground against the Angel's stiff cock. It was so hard and hot and thick and oh, god, how was it going to fit? It'd been so long since he'd last had sex.

With one arm braced beside the Angel's head, Ryan touched the fingers of his other hand to Vithius' lips. "I-I need you to help me get ready. So just—just suck on my fingers. Make them wet for me."

He blushed, feeling like a porn star for saying such a thing. *Why don't I just wish for lube?* Feeling like a perv, Ryan began to rescind the request but Vithius obediently pulled Ryan's fingers between his lips.

Once he did that Ryan's brain hopped on a bus and left town. Having Vithius suck on his fingers was truly orgasmic. Ryan closed his eyes and shuddered as Vithius' slippery tongue swirled around his fingertips. It slid wetly between his fingers, thrusting between the sensitive webbing. Ryan couldn't prevent his hips from jabbing forward in an attempt to bring his cock closer to that wet mouth and talented tongue.

Dizzy with lust, he opened his eyes. Seeing

Vithius beneath him, with his lips pursed around Ryan's fingers and his eyes closed as if he were enjoying the act as much as Ryan was, was something straight out of Ryan's wet dreams. Attacking Anifiel had been intense and heart-pounding like blindsiding the quarterback in the showers. Being with Vithius inspired a different, smoldering lust that Ryan wanted to last forever.

Fingers crept up Ryan's bare thighs and explored the curve of his ass, reminding him that he wasn't alone in his desire. Ryan slipped his fingers free of Vithius' mouth. He bent down and kissed the Angel reassuringly.

"Perfect," he breathed. "You're perfect."

As Vithius smiled against his lips and the Angel's hands caressed Ryan's hips, Ryan wished for lube. A small pot magically appeared on the grass near his knee. He used its contents to slick up his fingers and then reached back and gingerly prodded at his own puckered entrance. It really had been a while since he'd taken something into his body, but there was no way he was going to allow a little pain to prevent him from taking Vithius. He hid his wince as he slid first one and then both of his slippery fingers inside and stretched himself out.

"Will I fit inside you?" Vithius asked as his hands began to knead Ryan's ass with increasing urgency. "You were tight around my finger. When I think about how tight..." His hips jerked upwards, his leaking cock painting a streak of wetness up the underside of Ryan's. "Oh, I am sorry for my urgency."

Ryan laughed breathlessly. "Thinking about how tight I am gets you going, doesn't it?"

Vithius flushed. "I am sorry. I cannot help—"

Ryan cut him off with a kiss. "That tightness will make it good for both of us. Don't apologize for anything."

Deciding he was loose enough to avoid injury, Ryan pulled his fingers free and reached beneath him. He added the slickness to the slippery fluid that was already pearling on the tip of Vithius' cock and stroked the big shaft a little more than was necessary just because, heck, who wouldn't? Holding Vithius' large pulsing cock was enough to make him bite back a moan. Oh, how he wanted this thing inside him. Ryan only stopped stroking him when Vithius appeared to be on the verge of blowing.

"I love you," Ryan said as he lifted up enough to position Vithius' cock at his loosened entrance. "I love you so much, Vithius. I've wanted to share this with you since the moment I met you."

Vithius reached up and cupped his cheek. His dark eyes were moist. "Ryan..."

In that moment Ryan knew he had never been intended to find true love and happiness while alive—it had been waiting for him all along in Heaven. Everything that had ever caused him pain or sadness in his former existence fled from his mind as he slowly lowered himself onto Vithius' shaft. The burn was there and maybe on Earth it might have been enough to make him stop, but here in a perfect meadow on a perfect day with an Angel sliding inside him Ryan felt only a need to join them completely. When he sank down fully on Vithius and the Angel's full balls came up taut against his backside, Ryan threw back his head and let out a heartfelt moan. *This* was Heaven.

Vithius' fingers convulsed around his hips. His dark eyes went wide with amazement. "Ryan—" he choked out. "Oh, beloved..."

It was clear by Vithius' stunned, adoring expression that he thought Ryan was the most handsome, wonderful man in the Universe. It nearly made Ryan cry.

He rose up onto his knees, his spine rippling as each swollen inch of Vithius dragged out of his body until only the bulbous head throbbed inside him. Then Ryan let his weight drop, Vithius' length tunneling up through his body to stab right over his prostate. Ryan cried out helplessly, his eyes rolling up into his head. Beneath him, Vithius echoed the cry and nearly doubled up in shock and pleasure.

Ryan lifted himself again, panting at the intensity of the sensations. God, he'd never known having sex could feel this good. He'd never known being penetrated could make his entire body tingle like he'd plugged himself into an outlet.

He dropped onto Vithius' cock again and whimpered at how fully and deeply he was filled. He felt strong hands running anxiously up over his thighs and up his stomach, curving around his cock which was so swollen it nearly popped at Vithius' touch. Up and down Ryan bobbed, embarrassing sounds spilling from his lips, but he didn't care, oh, god, he didn't care. His cock was as rigid as the one plunging into his body and he knew it would be a matter of minutes before it would all be too much.

He stared up at the brilliant sky but he realized he needed to see something even more perfect. He fell forward, hips still rising and falling. He dropped his head and sloppily kissed Vithius who panted as rapidly as he did. Arms caged his body, fingers digging into his sides so that the only movement Ryan could make was to roll his hips to swallow Vithius' cock again and again. Their bodies met and withdrew in a tidal rhythm that Ryan was sure influenced the Moon.

It was too perfect, too right. Ryan waited for lightning to strike or for Anifiel to tear them apart. But no one broke the dance of his tongue with Vithius' and no one stopped his body from greedily sucking in the Angel's erection until both of them became frantic and lost their rhythm and all that mattered was grinding and grinding to get closer and closer and—

When Ryan came it was as if every atom in his body exploded and flew to every corner of Heaven. His mouth opened. He heard a cry of pure happiness fly from his lips. His inner muscles clamped down so hard that Vithius shouted beneath him before convulsing with his own release.

Ryan's body didn't glow from being filled with an Angel's cum nor did harp song fill the air with glorious melody. None of that needed to happen. He was sweaty and messy just like he'd be if he'd had sex with a human back on Earth, and that was just fine. Laughing, in love, he collapsed atop Vithius' heaving chest and planted wet kisses all over the

Angel's face in gratitude, just as he would if Vithius were human.

"That," he panted against Vithius' cheek, "was sex. The best sex in the history of sex, as a matter of fact."

"Sex," Vithius echoed dazedly.

Ryan rose up enough to study his boyfriend's expression and had to laugh again in pure joy. Vithius wore a wide smile that made his entire face light up.

"I guess I don't need to ask if you liked it," Ryan teased, stroking his fingers through the Angel's mussed hair. "You definitely look like you've been laid."

"Laid?" the Angel asked, his eyes focusing on Ryan with curiosity. Gone was the sexy lover and in his place was an innocent man whose face was full of wonder. "Is that another word for having had sex with you?"

"Yeah." Ryan swallowed. "It is. Just like..."

Losing your virginity.

Quite suddenly the reality of what he'd just done sank in. He'd had sex with Vithius. He'd shown the Angel an act which had previously been saved only for humans. Some of the afterglow began to fade. Had he just corrupted Vithius by giving him this knowledge? Had he given the Angel another gray feather?

Vithius softened and slipped from Ryan's body, an experience that made them both gasp and then share a small laugh. Vithius pulled him down and gave him a soul-searching kiss which left Ryan without doubt that the Angel loved him. It increased Ryan's sense of guilt, however. If he'd hurt Vithius by what they'd just done, Ryan would never ever forgive himself for it.

"Anifiel did not experience that with you," Vithius mused thoughtfully as he rubbed circles across Ryan's back.

Ryan tucked his face beneath the Angel's chin to hide his worried expression. "No, he's probably pretty miserable right now."

"No. I do not mean the physical, I mean the emotional bond you and I have created." Vithius sighed contentedly. "What you share with me you do not share equally with him. You and he share something different."

That piqued Ryan's interest. He curled his arms and legs around Vithius' naked body and asked, "You're not jealous of me and him, are you?"

Vithius turned his face away, but not before Ryan glimpsed the blush on his dusky cheeks. "I do not wish to be," he murmured, "but I think that I may. Forgive me."

"Vithius!" Ryan slid off of the Angel and sat up. He gently cupped his boyfriend's face and turned it back to him. "Vithius, you have nothing to be jealous of." He couldn't believe the handsome Angel would feel such a thing. "You know how much I can't stand Anifiel. I think he's a jerk. What's there to be jealous of when I hate the guy?"

"But you do not hate him," Vithius stated softly, his black gaze steady but full of understanding. "I can see that."

Ryan tried to keep a straight face, but Tofiel's

words came back to haunt him: "*Love is easy to see in Heaven, Ryan. At least it is for Angels to see.*"

Maybe that was true, but why in the world would that apply to him and Anifiel? Love was the last emotion Ryan felt towards the bullying Angel.

He shook his head incredulously. "Look, I admit that yeah, maybe there's some chemistry between us. But it's only lust! Lust means nothing. No one knows that better than I do. Lust is dumb. It comes and goes and it never ever lasts." He snorted. "And it's absolutely nothing compared to love, Vithius. A person can lust after a hundred people but he can love only one."

Vithius cocked his head. "Why is that?"

"What do you mean? Because you just can't. You love one person and that's it. That's what makes it special."

He moved back as Vithius sat up, also. The Angel paused a moment to look down at his wet, soft cock and then returned his attention to Ryan.

"Angels and humans are capable of loving many," the Angel said. "We are full of love, and to share it is simple and natural."

"But you can't share love equally," Ryan argued, growing a little annoyed. He was pretty sure he knew more about love and relationships than Vithius did. "Sure, you can love your family members or friends, but what we're talking about— soul mate stuff—you just can't divvy that up between people, Vithius. People get jealous. You can't help paying more attention to one partner than the other." He shrugged. "I know some people believe in that stuff—polyamory—but I can't see how it can be truly equal. I just don't buy it."

"Love can be equal in Heaven," Vithius stated calmly. "Fear makes you unable to open your heart. But you should not feel fear here, Ryan."

Ryan frowned. He was bothered on a deep level by this conversation and he couldn't pinpoint why. "Why are we even talking about this? I thought we were talking about you being jealous of Anifiel?"

He looked down and watched as Vithius threaded their fingers together in the grass. The Angel leaned forward and spoke against Ryan's ear in a soft puff of air: "You misunderstand my jealousy, Ryan. And I do not think you are ready to hear my truth."

Instead of replying to a comment he didn't understand, Ryan turned his head and kissed Vithius. The fugue swelled within him again and he decided it was better this way. He didn't want to argue about something he didn't care about. All he wanted was Vithius. Anifiel and the rest of Heaven could disappear for all he cared.

"Will you ever leave me for him?" Ryan whispered, hiding his face against Vithius' cheek. "Just tell me that."

Vithius tensed, and then he melted against Ryan, the Angel's weight pushing Ryan onto his back. The sky was bright and blue behind Vithius' smiling face. Ryan could stare at them both for hours.

"I will never leave you," Vithius told him, stroking Ryan's temple. "Soon you will be my equal in all things, and you will understand, Ryan. I will never leave you."

"You really believe that, don't you?" Ryan smiled crookedly. "You think I'll be an Angel someday."

Vithius' smile matched his. "We are counting on it, Ryan. I think you would be surprised by how many of us are."

~~~~~

They found a stream and spent the next hours or days—Ryan had no idea nor did he care—playing in the water and bathing each other. They didn't have intercourse again because Ryan still worried about having gone too far, but that didn't stop him from dropping to his knees in the shallow water and swallowing down the beautiful cock that had pleasured him.

Watching and listening to Vithius reach orgasm were some of Ryan's proudest moments. He felt like a god for being able to bring Vithius such pleasure. He felt attractive and sexy for the first time ever. More importantly, he began to believe that he might actually be those things and was good enough for a magnificent Angel like Vithius.

The Angel fell to his butt in the water, gasping for breath as Ryan licked his lips with a heartfelt, "Mmm, I think you taste better each time."

The Angel laughed. "Will I ever run out of this nectar you crave? What will happen then? Will you leave me?"

Ryan pounced on him, reveling in the feel of

their naked bodies rubbing together. He was comfortable being naked only in the water, where he could hide beneath the surface when he started to feel self-conscious.

"I'm addicted to you," Ryan told him before swiping his tongue across Vithius' lips to let the Angel taste himself. "You'll leave me before I leave you."

Vithius pulled Ryan onto his lap. "Then we shall never be parted," he declared happily.

Ryan kissed him again and dragged his hands through the water. He cupped the turquoise liquid and drizzled it over Vithius' shoulders and chest, admiring the rivulets as they trickled down the Angel's muscular chest and arms.

"I need to work out so I don't look like such a shrimp compared to you," Ryan observed, comparing his biceps with Vithius'. "This is shameful."

"Nothing about you is shameful," Vithius admonished.

"How am I supposed to wield my mighty shield if I'm weak and get pooped out?" Ryan challenged playfully.

Vithius' humor faded at the mention of the shield. "I had forgotten that you must learn to protect yourself." He eased Ryan off of him. "I have been distracting you from your training. The shame is mine." He stood up and extended a hand down to Ryan. "Are you ready to continue?"

Ryan pouted. "I thought we were having fun?"

"If the Demons return while you are not prepared, Ryan, this could be the last fun we enjoy together," Vithius replied ominously.

Gulping, Ryan stood up and waded to the shore for his tunic. "Okay, you may have a point there." He dragged the garment over his body and by the time he'd turned around Vithius was armed with his training stick. He handed Ryan's shield to him.

Vithius gave his stick an intimidating whirl. "Ready?"

Ryan took a deep breath and widened his stance. "Before we start, I want you to elaborate on the theory you and Anifiel won't discuss with me. You know, the one about why the Demons are attacking."

"I told you. It is because you are compelled to enter the battlefields and when you do you distract Anifiel."

"There's more to it than that. Anifiel got really mad about it. I remember. He warned you not to tell me."

He wasn't sure why he pushed this. Earlier, he hadn't wanted to know the truth. But maybe being fully intimate with Vithius had proved to Ryan that being open and vulnerable might not hurt him here as it had on Earth.

Maybe learning something he didn't want to know might not hurt him either.

He watched Vithius glance away guiltily. "There is more, but he would not be pleased with me if I spoke of it to you. You and he are alike in many ways. You both fear what you should not, but I cannot change that. You must do it yourselves."

"What does he have to fear?" Ryan asked. "I

thought he was the big, bad Commander?" He felt a little bad to be belittling Anifiel about anything associated with the battlefield since Ryan actually really enjoyed it when Anifiel was his bad self there. But he'd say whatever it took to get the truth out of Vithius, even if it was some indefensible taunting.

"Anifiel does not fear battle," Vithius confirmed, and Ryan thought he saw the other Angel's chest puff out with pride for his former battle companion. "In defense of Heaven Anifiel does not lack for courage. He inspires us all."

"Alright, then what is he afraid of? If it's not battle or the Demons, then what's left?" Ryan cleared his throat awkwardly. "It's not me is it?"

In answer, Vithius spun his stick in his hands and attacked. Ryan barely swung his shield up in time to avoid having his skull cracked open. "Vithius, what the heck?!"

"Defend yourself," Vithius stated grimly as he advanced on Ryan. "I will not see you or Anifiel hurt because of my failure to prepare you."

"But just—" Ryan threw up his shield and cringed as Vithius' stick banged against it half a dozen times. "Lighten up, will you? You're going to kill me before the Demons do!"

"If you are this weak you deserve to be turned," Vithius told him.

Ryan gasped at the remark but before he could say anything he noticed Vithius bending his knees in preparation to jump at him. Ryan reacted without thinking and dove forward into a roll. He hit his head and he landed wrong on his shoulder but he came out of the roll behind Vithius and without a second thought he swung out with his shield and knocked the Angel's legs out from under him so he couldn't attack.

Vithius crashed onto his back with a heavy thud. Ryan jumped to his feet and crouched over the fallen Angel, unsure what to do since he wasn't supposed to attack. "Yield!" he cried out, since he didn't know what else to say.

On his back, Vithius looked as though the fall had stolen his breath and then some. His eyes were round, his stick lying lax across his chest.

Ryan gradually relaxed his pseudo-fighting stance and began to feel more than a little awkward. "Er, sorry about that. Did I hurt you?"

He jumped back in alarm when Vithius flipped smoothly to his feet. The Angel grabbed him before he could dart away and the next thing Ryan knew he was being crushed to Vithius' firm chest.

"You did it!" the Angel said, hugging Ryan. "You defended yourself and stopped my attack without showing aggression toward me!"

Ryan relaxed, his heart rate slowing. "I did, didn't I?" He hugged Vithius back. "I did it! I can do this!"

"I never doubted it," the Angel breathed against Ryan's curls. "Now that I have seen your progress I am sure of it: you shall be one of the greatest Angels in Heaven."

Again, Ryan waited for lightning or Anifiel to strike them both down. When neither happened, he chuckled uneasily. "Vithius, you're going to get us both killed saying something like that." He rolled his eyes when he realized what he'd said. "You know what I mean."

"I know, and I meant what I said." Vithius hugged him tighter and Ryan sensed desperation in the embrace. "It relieves my heart that you will be able to defend yourself. I cannot lose you or Anifiel. It will destroy me."

Reminded of Vithius' condition in the days following being corrupted, Ryan closed his eyes and said with determination, "Nothing will destroy you, Vithius. I'll practice this until no Demon has a chance at me. You won't lose me. I know when I've got a good thing going. You and I are going to be together for eternity."

He felt Vithius' body soften against him. "And if you keep yourself safe, it will keep Anifiel safe, also."

Oh, joy, Ryan thought sarcastically, but his heart wasn't really in it. He didn't want to see Anifiel fall. He was Heaven's defense against the Demons and Ryan had to admit he was impressed by that responsibility and Anifiel's willingness to meet it. Not to mention a bug had flown into his ear concerning the Commander. Maybe…maybe he wasn't so bad after all?

Maybe I've been misreading him all along.

"Come, we must practice more." Vithius pushed him back and raised his stick again. "Ready?"

Before Ryan could answer, the Angel attacked. Ryan grinned and threw up his shield in time to find off a flurry of strikes.

"You'll have to do better than that," he taunted. Vithius laughed with delight.

Don't miss the conclusion of the Heaven series! Read Spoils of War.

Join the mailing list at
http://triciaowensbooks.com/list

Sin City series
Dom of Las Vegas
Limited Liability
Acceptable Sacrifices
High Roller
Most Wanted
Lessons in Obedience
Death Defying Acts
The Doms Club
Easy Money

A Pirate's Life for Me series
Book One: Captain & First Mate
Book Two: Island Paradise
Book Three: Pirate Triumvirate
Mr. Anteros

Juxtapose City series
Fearless Leader
In the Blink of an Eye
The Battle for Black
The Ultimate Team
My Lover, My Enemy
The Sound of Truth
Shattered Alliance
Exchange of Power

Realm of Juxtan series
The Sorcerer's Betrayal
The Gathering
Beneath the Greying Cliffs
The Forgotten One

A:R Earth series
Angel: Reversed
Angel: Redeemed
Angel: Released

A:R Heaven series
Territory of Angels
Spoils of War

Standalone Novels
Favorite Flavors Short Story Collection
Hunter and Hunted
Master of No One